NOT WITHOUT A CLUE

Robert Lymond came in while I was sitting at my
desk. "Roxanne — Miss Sydney, I want to keep the boy
locked up here until he is able to answer my questions.
I've put him in the stables."

I stood, full of righteous anger. "Well, you can simply
unlock him. You have no right to ride roughshod over
everyone and everything here."

He looked at me surprised. "Roughshod? Good God,
Miss Sydney, there's been a murder. If the culprit isn't
discovered, there might be another."

I sat back down. "That's ridiculous."

He sat across from me. He wasn't wearing his coat,
his cravat was untied, and there was a stubble of beard
on his face. For the first time, I noticed the circles of fatigue under his eyes.

For an instant, I thought about telling him of my suspicions about Papa's death, but I didn't want him to
laugh as everyone else had. "Who might have done
this?" I asked instead.

Lymond stood. "I don't know, but there has to be a
reason. If I could just find that, several things might unravel."

"What things?"

He smiled at me. It was infuriating. "Nothing that
should worry you," he said as he turned and left the
room.

He left the door slightly ajar, and I slammed it shut
behind him. There had to be a way to break his lease!

THE ROMANCES OF LORDS AND LADIES
IN JANIS LADEN'S REGENCIES

BEWITCHING MINX (2532, $3.95)

From her first encounter with the Marquis of Penderleigh when he had mistaken her for a common trollop, Penelope had been incensed with the darkly handsome lord. Miss Penelope Larchmont was undoubtedly the most outspoken young lady Penderleigh had ever known, and the most tempting.

A NOBLE MISTRESS (2169, $3.95)

Moriah Landon had always been a singularly practical young lady. So when her father lost the family estate over a game of picquet, she paid the winner, the notorious Viscount Roane, a visit. And when he suggested the means of payment—that she become Roane's mistress—she agreed without a blink of her eyes.

SAPPHIRE TEMPTATION (3054, $3.95)

Lady Serena was commonly held to be an unusual young girl—outspoken when she should have been reticent, lively when she should have been demure. But there was one tradition she had not been allowed to break: a Wexley must marry a Gower. Richard Gower intended to teach his wife her duties—in every way.

SCOTTISH ROSE (2750, $3.95)

The Duke of Milburne returned to Milburne Hall trusting that the new governess, Miss Rose Beacham, had instilled the fear of God into his harum-scarum brood of siblings. But she romped with the children, refused to be cowed by his stern admonitions, and was so pretty that he had the devil of a time keeping his hands off her.

The Brighton Burglar

Dawn Aldridge Poore

ZEBRA BOOKS
KENSINGTON PUBLISHING CORP.

ZEBRA BOOKS

are published by

Kensington Publishing Corp.
475 Park Avenue South
New York, NY 10016

First Printing: March, 1993

Printed in the United States of America

Chapter One

Papa was killed in late spring, and by midsummer I knew something had to be done about our situation.

One evening after our rather frugal supper, I paused, glanced around at the family, and decided it was time to act. True, there was money enough for existence, but with three younger sisters needing to make their way, I knew we needed more than just subsistence income. I had a Plan.

"A disgrace, that's what it is!" Aunt Henrietta sputtered when I informed her. "George would never allow it! Roxanne, I'm telling you, your dear father would die if he heard of this hare-brained scheme of yours!"

"Papa's dead already," I pointed out, "and Edward has everything except this house and a pittance. That's why we're in this fix."

"Don't speak ill of the dead," Aunt Hen said reprovingly. "You know George, for all his faults, was a complete gentleman."

I didn't contest this. Papa had been exemplary as a gentleman. He firmly believed it was the right and duty of every gentleman to spend his time and money on improvements. In Papa's case, however, that did not mean improving the ancestral house and property. That had long ago been given to Edward, and Papa considered it good riddance. No, Papa had other things to improve.

Papa, the third son in the family, had been a sickly child, so he had been sent abroad when he was fifteen. His mama, the redoubtable Lady Anselcey, had hoped the warm climate of Italy and Greece would cure his tendency towards tuberculosis. Actually the trip did several things: it did cure him; it showed him that he could live as he pleased and be quite happy about it away from his formidable mother; and it inculcated a lifelong fascination with antiquities. Papa was especially taken with all things Greek. He became especially interested — no, enamored is a better word — of the *Iliad*, the *Odyssey*, and the whole panoply of Greek heroes, goddesses, and rogues. He often fancied himself the spiritual successor of Agamemnon, Aeneas, Odysseus, and from some tangent which I never completely understood, Alexander the Great.

I was born, rather fortunately for me, I suppose, during one of his Alexander periods, so he named me Roxanne. It could have been worse — I could have been Clytemnestra or Electra or some such. The other girls hadn't fared too badly with their names, probably due to Mama's intervention. Next after me was Cassandra, then Olivia, and, finally, Julia. Livvy's full name was actually Olivia Cleopatra, but she dissolved in tears every time someone called her Cleopatra, so after we grew up enough to be conscious of her sensibilities, we generally ignored that name.

As it was, my half brother Edward had the terrible name and through no fault of Papa's. When Papa had returned, his mother had selected a bride for him by the name of Jane Smith. Papa didn't particularly wish to wed, but small things like that never bothered my grandmother. Papa was duly married and produced an heir which was named after Jane Smith's father. Jane obligingly passed away at this point, leaving the baby, christened with the name Edward Pompey Decimus Smith Sydney, to be brought up by Grandmother since Papa dashed back off to the Greek islands right after the funeral. He seldom saw Edward after that, nor, thank goodness, did we. Edward was ten years older than I and was as prim and proper as Grandmother and tutors could make him. We generally called him Pompous Edward, and the name fit perfectly. Edward married an equally pompous female named Matilda, and they had three quite obnoxious children. We avoided the lot of them at every opportunity.

At any rate, while he was in Greece the second time, Papa inherited a very nice legacy. He returned to England and, to everyone's surprise, married my mother almost immediately. Mother was, appropriately, named Helen. Privately I always thought that was the deciding factor for Papa, but I never said as much to Mother. She adored him, and, in his own way, he adored her as well.

Now that Papa had an income of his own, he decided to create his own Greece in England. He purchased property on the coast at Brighton so he could look out over the waters and, I suppose, pretend it was the wine-dark Aegean. He was, I own, disappointed in the lack of vegetation at Brighton and unsuccessfully tried to grow olive trees, but overall, he was content with his choice.

Papa then built himself a house *à la Grecque*. It was a large box with columns all around and friezes running across the front and back. The inside, as I recall, was to resemble a Graeco-Roman villa, but at this point Mama drew the line. To Papa's dismay, she insisted on a rather English interior, although she did allow Greek-and Roman-inspired paintings and mosaics. There were also friezes and bas-reliefs scattered from room to room. The house was built during Papa's Athenian period, which was a help. If he had been building during the Alexandrean phase, I shudder to think what he would have designed—either a Babylonian ziggurat or something resembling a Persian army tent, I'm sure.

All of this was rather much in the way of expense, but Papa took no notice. He believed a gentleman's finest contribution to culture was a giving of inspiration and thought. Unfortunately, inspired though he was, Papa never thought about pounds and shillings—his mind was off somewhere coining drachmas and talents that were easy to spend. Mama, the practical one in the family, did what she could to stem the tide while she was alive, but after she died, some six years ago, Papa consoled himself by spending lavishly on the house and on artifacts he had shipped in from Greece and various points in the Orient. I firmly believed at least eight out of ten of these to be bogus, and the figure was probably higher.

No matter, bogus or real, Papa was supremely happy except for missing Mama. He undertook a building program, constructing what began as a pyramid but changed midway into what he imagined was a reconstruction of Agamemnon's tomb, complete with a bronze door and columns all around. I went along with that until he had Mama's remains placed inside it. Only then did I discover that it was to be a mausoleum for all of us. It was a rather large, lonely thing, set out on a cliff overlooking the sea, and the wind howled there sometimes, singing through the columns. As was common in Brighton, there were no trees or bushes around, giving it a desolate air. The only times I could bring myself to go there were on sunny days—the place gave me the shivers otherwise. Papa, however, loved it and would often go sit there for hours, looking over the sea and, I suppose, communing with the spirits of ancient Greeks. And, of course, Mama.

When Papa was killed, he was well into the construction of a replica of the wooden horse of Troy. It was a huge thing because he wasn't at all sure about the size of the original model. After the funeral, I had the monstrosity towed over and put inside the mausoleum along with some other junk Papa had acquired.

As a result of all of Papa's building and spending, by the time I had paid all the funeral expenses, including the shipping bill on several crates of Egyptian artifacts that looked remarkably like dried firewood, there was very little left. Papa, as I had known he would, insisted that I be in charge of his estate and left me and my sisters the house and grounds for our own. Edward had acquired the ancestral home and legacy from Grandmother, so Papa felt no need for Edward to inherit anything.

At any rate, I now had a mausoleum that was half pyramid, half Agamemnon's tomb, a large house built in a counterfeit Graeco-Roman style, a stunning view of the wine-dark Channel, three unmarried sisters who were younger than I and not too amenable to advice, my Aunt Henrietta and the family retainers to take care of, and no money. This called for draconian measures and I was fully prepared to take them. I said as much to Aunt Hen.

Aunt Henrietta set her face in an angry scowl. "I forbid it, Roxanne. As the one closest to George and Helen, my duty is to take care of this family as they would have. I absolutely forbid it."

"Aunt Hen," I pointed out gently, "if you take care of us in the same way they did, we'll be in the poorhouse before the year's out."

She scowled. "Your father loved this house, and you should at least respect his memory." She reached for another sweetmeat.

"I assure you, Aunt Hen, I do. It's just that I also wish to eat regular meals and keep the roof over our heads in repair. Besides," here I paused for effect, "you and I do have three girls to marry off. The Marriage Mart takes money."

"The girls are pretty enough to catch someone's eye when they go to London," she retorted, mopping up mincemeat crumbs.

"That they would," I said firmly. "If they went to London right now, they'd all be traveling stark naked. It would catch every eye in town, I'm sure."

Aunt Hen glared at me. "Your humor, as usual, Roxanne, fails to impress me. You know the girls wear clothes."

I sighed. "Aunt Hen, you miss my point. The girls must look in the latest stare of fashion when they go to London. They can't go to fashionable parties dressed as they are here. And," I pursued my topic relentlessly, "I've thought this out carefully. It's either this or we'll have to sell Bellerophon."

"Sell the house!" Aunt Henrietta choked on her cake. I handed her some tea and waited until she was able to speak. "Things can't be that bad!"

I nodded grimly. "They are." I paused to let that sink in. "There's no other way. Are we agreed, Aunt Henrietta, that we don't want to sell Bellerophon?"

Aunt Hen took another gulp of tea. "We're agreed." Her voice was wavering.

"Good." I smiled at her, charmingly, I hoped. "That means there is only one course open to us—unless, of course, you wish us all governesses."

She tried to speak and couldn't. She simply shook her head.

"Then we are agreed." I was relentless—I had to be. "We let the house to boarders then."

There was a long silence, then Aunt Hen looked at me craftily. "Edward will never allow this, you know."

I tried to keep calm. Aunt Hen knew how we all felt about Pompous Edward. "Edward has no control over

10

the house or over me or my guardianship of the other girls. You know that Papa was very specific on that point, Aunt Hen. Edward tried to break the will and couldn't. He can't touch us."

"Yes, but he's titular head of the family, and we should defer to his wishes. He should be obeyed."

"*Obey? Defer?*" I paused and counted to ten. "Aunt Hen, I loathe and detest Pompous Edward. If he told me to do something, I'd probably force myself to do just the opposite even if I didn't want to, just to show him I could."

"You malign him," Aunt Hen sighed. "Edward has only the family's welfare at heart."

"Bosh." I dismissed the subject. "Don't you remember that horrible person he wanted to marry Cassie off to? No, Aunt Hen, Edward's idea of caring for the family is to have each of the women leg-shackled to one of his Friday-faced friends and spend all her time breeding and growing roses in the country."

"Roxanne!" Aunt Henrietta looked shocked but knew I was right. She dropped the idea of Edward helping and tried another tack. "If only we could discover where George hid the Treasure."

I sighed as she mentioned that for perhaps the thousandth time, and rolled my eyes upward. "Take my word for it, Aunt Henrietta, there is no treasure. None. You know yourself that Papa never had money around, and if he had, we surely would have found it. Lord knows we've torn the place apart looking for it."

My mind flew back to the terrible circumstances of our father's death and afterwards. During a period of particularly fine weather, Papa had left off wooden horse construction to oversee the repair of a leaking roof and the renovation the friezes on the south of the house. He was standing on the edge of the roof talking to a workman standing below when suddenly he plunged to the ground. Everyone called it an accident, but I knew better. I was just coming around the corner and glanced up to see Papa on the roof. I had a distinct recollection of someone standing behind him, a hand to Papa's back. I didn't even have time to yell for Papa to watch out before he fell, tumbling to the ground right in front of me. He lived only long enough to smile up at me and say, "I'm going to be with my dear Helen now, Roxanne. Take care of the girls for me and take the treasure of Agamemnon. It will see you through." Then he breathed Mother's name again and died, a smile on his lips.

I tried to revive him, but it was no use. The workmen gathered around, and I stood, looking at each one of them, wondering if someone had pushed Papa and why, or if I had dreamed it. When I tried to speak, however, I did something quite uncharacteristic — I fainted. When I came to, I tried to tell everyone from Aunt Hen to Pompous Edward to the local magistrate that I was afraid Papa had been murdered, but no one listened. To my annoyance, they dismissed my charges as the ramblings of a mind that had been disoriented by the shock of Papa's death. I was incensed.

In spite of my protests, the official verdict was accidental death. I had a difficult time accepting this, but it was the only logical explanation. Papa was the gentlest, kindest of men. After thinking about it and talking it over with my sisters, I realized it must have been an accident. The sun was behind Papa and I saw only silhouettes. Perhaps the angle of the roof and the brightness of the sun behind him distorted my vision. I wasn't sure. At any rate, nothing else happened. The workmen finished the roof repairs and the friezes, under Edward's direction, which accounted for the inordinate amount of water that dripped into the drawing room with every rain.

I had told Aunt Hen and the other girls about Papa's

last remark, but of course, we kept that information from Edward. Then, right after Edward left, Aunt Henrietta, the other girls, and I had practically ripped the house apart looking for the treasure of Agamemnon — or anybody else's treasure, for that matter. We found absolutely nothing. We even looked behind the paintings and friezes in the house, defacing several, but there was nothing. No matter where we looked, there was nothing. I finally decided that, for Papa, the treasure of Agamemnon was the house and mausoleum. After all, with a name like Bellerophon, *someone* had to think highly of the place.

However, Aunt Henrietta hadn't yet given up. She constantly talked about the Treasure as though the word was engraved in capital letters on the front of a jewel casket somewhere. She also expected to uncover the Treasure every time she picked up a sofa cushion. "We'd be able to outfit the girls properly and take care of all the bills if we could only find the Treasure," she said.

I sighed and tried to hide a grimace. "Yes, we would," I said patiently, but Aunt Hen, we aren't going to find any treasure because there is no treasure in this house. Papa didn't know what he was saying. After all, the man was dying."

Aunt Hen looked at me stubbornly. "If George said it was here, then it's here. We'll find it soon, I know. We simply need to look harder."

"We've done everything except tear out the walls," I reminded her. I saw her expression and added hastily, "We're certainly not going to do that."

Aunt Hen sighed and gave way — for the moment, at least. "Where will we go if someone else moves in here? The girls can't just live anywhere."

I smiled. "That's the beauty of my scheme. We're all going to stay right here, of course. The house falls neatly into two halves and we can move into the back half and have our own cozy apartment. Woodbury, Holmwood, Mrs. Beckford, and all the others will be able to stay as well. As for us and our privacy, we'll never see our tenants." I was at my most persuasive. "Just think, Aunt Hen, just the five of us in our own snug rooms. We won't have to be rattling around in this big house and we won't have to be bothered by whoever takes the rest of the house. And," I added slowly for emphasis, "we'll have a steady income."

Aunt Hen had been on the verge of the vapors, but the words "steady income" seemed to rally her. "Are you sure?" she asked faintly. "You know that we'll probably have to let to someone in trade who is newly rich and quite vulgar. I couldn't bear it if we were expected to . . . to *entertain*."

"Don't worry, Aunt Henrietta," I told her. "I can promise you we'll never see them except to collect the rent."

Actually I was much farther along with my project than I had revealed to Aunt Henrietta. I had dragooned the other girls, particularly Cassie and Julia, into helping me. We had spoken to an agent who handled rental properties, and he had given us particulars about what to do next. He felt it might be easy to rent the house for short terms, particularly those times when the Prince Regent was in residence at the Marine Pavilion, but I wanted to let it for a longer term. Mr. Miffle, the agent, told me that for a longer lease he would recommend letting the house to a tradesman and his family wanting to spend some time in Brighton. I had hoped for better, but Mr. Miffle said most of the *ton* owned their own homes in the country or by the seaside, or already had some long-term arrangement. After two minutes or so of deep soul-searching, I decided a tradesman's money was as good as anyone's and directed Mr. Miffle to proceed.

I had already taken it upon myself to ask the carpenters to return to redo our rooms in the back of the house and build a doghouse and run behind for the dog. Mr. Miffle had suggested I get the same carpenters who worked on the roof because they were largely reputed to be the best in Brighton. They worked together and during their busy season were extremely difficult to engage. Since the Prince was in London, all the carpenters were able to come to Bellerophon almost immediately to begin the work. All I had to do now was pave the way with Aunt Henrietta.

I had instructed Cassie to work on the paint and paper for our apartments since she always had an eye for color. Julia and Livvy were assigned the task of writing a suitable advertisement for the papers. I chose the London papers for the obvious reasons, the Brighton paper for the same, and the *Bath Chronicle* as I thought others might be looking in the advertisements there for houses to let. I felt we had an edge on Bath—except for the waters, of course, although Brighton did have the medicinal baths—as Bellerophon was situated within a short distance of Brighton and was right on the shingle so the tenants could go sea bathing. We also had a splendid, if misty, view of the Pavilion in the distance. Papa liked to say he had discovered Brighton before the Prince, but that simply wasn't true. However, Mama, Aunt Hen, and all of us girls had indulged Papa on that as we had all his other whims.

In honor of Papa's memory (and to keep Aunt Henrietta quiet), I didn't plan to do too much in the way of changes, but there was one thing that both Cassie and I agreed had to go: the name of the house. No one would want to rent a house named Bellerophon. We planned to change it to something more suitable as soon as we could get around Aunt Hen. Applegate House was our first (and only) choice; we vetoed Livvy's entry, The Tomb-By-The-Sea.

The morning following my conversation with Aunt Hen, I dispatched her to a neighbor's for a visit. She and Mrs. Bocock were good for the entire day once they started gossiping. Occasionally they would retire to the parlor of the inn and drink tea all day, commenting on everyone passing. With any luck at all, I'd have many hours at my disposal, and by the time Aunt Hen returned, the carpenters would be well into the renovation.

Shortly after nuncheon, Woodbury announced callers over the din of sawing and hammering and dog barking. "Tell whomever it is that I am *not* at home," I told him firmly, feeling my dusty cap and noting the dirt on my dress and apron.

The butler's reply was rendered inaudible by the cacophony.

"What?" I shouted. "I said tell whomever it is that I am not at home."

Woodbury, who had been privy to my project plans, although disapproving, urged me outside, away from the noise of the carpenters and handed me a rather plain card. It's a Mr. Lymond," he said, inserting his words between dog barks. "I gather he is the one who wishes to talk to you. He's accompanied by a Captain Amherst." There was a pause. Woodbury was a veteran and always felt the Army should be given consideration.

I frowned. "I don't know a Mr. Lymond, or a Captain Amherst either. Tell them to leave, Woodbury. Bue, will you be quiet!" This last was for the dog, who was unhappily tethered to one of the columns near the door.

"But —" he began.

"Quiet, I said!" I yelled to the dog, who paid no attention at all. I gave up and turned to Woodbury. "I'm in no state to receive, Woodbury. Ask Mr. Lymond to come back some other day."

"Yes, Miss Sydney," Woodbury grumbled, turning towards the door, "but he wants to rent the house for quite a while. He's out admiring the view now and he seems quite taken with it."

"Wait!" I yelped, trying to outdo the dog so Woodbury could hear me. "A prospective tenant, did you say?" I looked down at my dress, then jerked off my cap and apron. "I'll see him, Woodbury. Put them in the drawing room and tell Cassandra to entertain them until I get there."

Bucephalus, the dog, had practically chewed through his rope, so I decided to go around to the shed and leave the brute with the gardener before I met Mr. Lymond. All I needed was for Bue to get loose and run amok. The carpenters had threatened to leave if the dog wasn't tied. They took one look at him — he was roughly the size of a very small pony — and cringed. They had no idea that Bue was really quite gentle. Perhaps the gardener would help. Holmwood always had a shed or two empty.

I untied the rope with great difficulty intending to start around to the back of the house. Bue, however, immediately dashed around to the front, howling at the top of his lungs, dragging me behind him. We both crashed headfirst into a black-clad figure standing beside a cabriolet at the front. The rope slipped from my hands and I tumbled headfirst into some boxwoods. After removing myself ungracefully from the shrubs and shaking dirt and grass out of my eyes, directly in front of me on the ground I could see the poor man flat on his back with the dog standing astride him, snarling and baring his teeth.

"Bue, sit!" I commanded. Bue sat, but on the man's chest, then began lapping the hapless visitor's face. "Bue," I grunted, tugging on his rope, "get up." The inexorable Bue was not to be moved. "Get up, Bue," I ordered again.

"Please do," the man gasped. Bue had gained weight

lately and was quite heavy. The man's face was turning a rather mottled shade of deep red; I assumed, quite correctly, that he was unable to breathe. "Owen," he said in a muffled gasp, "do something."

Captain Amherst, dressed very smartly in the uniform of the Dragoons quartered in Brighton, stepped over and looked down at Mr. Lymond. "I am doing something," he said with a broad grin. "I am thoroughly enjoying this."

Mr. Lymond muttered something I thought might have been unsuitable for my ears, but I ignored it. I glared at Captain Amherst and tugged again on Bue's rope. We were saved by Woodbury, who dashed out the front door and dragged Bue away. "Mr. Robert Lymond, Capt. Owen Amherst," Woodbury announced as Bue pulled him around the corner of the house. Woodbury was from the old school, formal to the end.

Lymond sat up and looked at me. I reached out a hand to help him stand. "My apologies, Mr. Lymond." I could be as formal as Woodbury when occasion demanded.

There was a long silence as Lymond stood, dusted himself off, and looked around. I took the moment to evaluate him. He was a little taller than average — a little over six feet, I judged — and was well-built. He had broad shoulders that were suited to perfection by his black coat. His hair had a touch of a curl to it, was dark brown, and was longer than fashionable, cut in layers that fell around his face. His hair had streaks in it, as though he had been habitually without a hat. His skin was tanned, so I assumed he spent a great deal of time outdoors. His eyes were possibly his most arresting feature — they were a clear and startling blue. Altogether, I had to own that he was quite a handsome man.

A small nerve twitched at the side of his mouth and he was staring hard, seemingly enchanted by our view of the Pavilion. I started to say something, but he seemed to be struggling with himself not to say something totally unsuitable, so I didn't interrupt him while he glared into space. In the meantime, I occupied myself by evaluating Captain Amherst. The captain was busy looking at Mr. Lymond and laughing.

The captain wasn't quite as tall as Mr. Lymond and was somewhat fairer. His hair was brown, his skin a trifle pale, and his eyes were brown. Taken separately, his features were unremarkable, but when put all together, he was very nice looking, indeed. His most unusual feature, however, wasn't tangible — it was an attitude, a sort of rakish, devil-may-care proclivity that attracted one immediately.

"Enjoying yourself, Owen?" Mr. Lymond finally asked, scowling at the captain.

"Immensely. I wouldn't have missed that for the world."

Mr. Lymond glowered, and I was afraid he was going to berate the captain, so I intervened. "Would you care to go inside?" I asked. Having never been a landlady, I was rather unsure of the next step.

Lymond seemed to have made up his mind, however. "No need," he said. "I've discussed the terms with your agent and find them quite reasonable. I would like to take the house for three months, with an option for another three. Is that a problem?

"Three months? Of course, I really don't —"

He interrupted me briskly. "Wonderful. Mr. Miffle was afraid you'd demand a lease for a year, so I'm delighted that three months will be suitable with you." He looked right through me. "There will be only my, ah, wife, myself, her maid, and my man. I assume the other servants will be included with the house."

I nodded and said, "Of course," as though I knew what I was talking about.

Lymond was all business. "Your agent has my references and has, I believe, talked to some he knows, but here's a copy if you wish to read them." He handed me a large envelope. "I would like to conclude this business as soon as possible, so if everything is suitable with you and Mr. Miffle, I'd like to take possession as soon as I can."

Things were moving along too fast for me to think. "Did Mr. Miffle mention that we — that is myself and my sisters — plan to occupy the back of the house? It will be a separate apartment, of course."

Lymond nodded. "Yes. Did I mention that Captain Amherst might be staying some days with us?"

I smiled at the captain who smiled back, his engaging attitude lighting up his face. "I promise not to get in the way," he said with a smile.

"It won't matter, Owen," Lymond said before I could reply. "They'll be in their own apartments."

"Certainly," I said stiffly. Mr. Lymond was making it abundantly clear that he didn't wish company during his stay. I was beginning to think it would be better to wait and find another tenant.

"I would hate," Captain Amherst said with a slight bow, "to think that lovely ladies were about and I didn't take advantage of their company." He smiled at me. "I'm certain I would enjoy Miss Sydney's company at any time."

"Whatever." Lymond brushed this aside with an impatient wave and looked at me. "As to terms of the lease, are we in agreement, then?"

I tried to forestall him so I could think. "Wouldn't your wife like to view the house?" I asked. "She might not like it at all."

"She likes what I like. Amelia's very agreeable." He didn't look at me, but stared out at the wine-dark Channel.

"Oh." I nodded again. "Then would *you* like to see the inside and discuss any changes?"

"That won't be necessary for me, but I'm sure Amelia will want to make a few very minor changes when we move in. Nothing much — three months isn't very long." He looked again out to sea and breathed deeply. "I was looking for a place next to the sea for my, ah, for Amelia to recuperate, and this will be admirable. Because of her health, we'd like to move in immediately." He must have seen the shock on my face. "If you approve, of course."

"Of course." Mr. Lymond was going to think my vocabulary limited, but there didn't seem to be anything else to say. I took a deep breath. I was going to tell him that I simply couldn't let the house to him.

"Roxanne, whatever did you want me for? Woodbury asked me to receive some callers in the drawing room, but —" There was a pause as Cassandra came down the steps. "Oh, I'm sorry," she said as she floated up to us. Cassandra always floated. She was ethereal, in complete contrast to me. Cassie's the artistic and musical one of the family, and she always waltzed around the house, humming bars of music to herself, living in a world of her own. She favored flowing, white, Grecian-looking gowns, which added to the effect. Papa loved it because Cassie always looked as if she'd stepped right out of a frieze.

At any rate, Cassie floated up to us, and I made the introductions. Captain Amherst seemed suitably impressed, but Mr. Lymond ignored her completely. I was beginning to think he was the rudest man I'd ever seen. "Cassie," I said, "I was just talking to Mr. Lymond about renting the house to him."

Cassie smiled her usual ethereal smile. "Wonderful," she said, turning to Mr. Lymond. "Roxanne's a marvelous judge of character, so I'm sure we'll get along famously."

"Good." Lymond glanced at me and gave me an engaging smile. To tell the truth, I was surprised—it was a very nice smile. "Since we're in agreement, I'll talk to Mr. Miffle immediately. If you have further questions, I'm staying at the Castle Inn for a few days. It's been a pleasure meeting you, Miss Sydney. And you, Miss Sydney." This last was with a glance at Cassandra. "Owen, we have things to do," he said as he swung himself up in his cabriolet and lifted the ribbons.

Captain Amherst hesitated as though he had something else to say, but then shrugged slightly, gave both Cassie and me a warm smile, and joined Lymond in the cabriolet. "Good day," Lymond said shortly as they drove off.

I stood speechless for a few moments as I watched them drive away in a cloud of dust. Then the entire scene hit me. "Good heavens, Cassie, have you ever seen anything like that! What audacity!"

Now that I was free from the overpowering effects of Lymond's personality, I realized that I certainly didn't want anyone of that stripe living in my house, no matter how excellent his references. "Just what did you think of that?" I turned to Cassie and demanded.

Cassie was already floating back into the house, her Grecian sandals pattering on the steps. "Very nice. Very handsome—especially the captain. Is he married?"

"Married? Cassie, I can't believe you're asking this. How should I know? Mr. Lymond's married, but I certainly didn't pry about the captain. Why would you ask such a silly thing?"

Cassie smiled at me and went on into the house.

I was still fuming when I reached my study, where I penned a note to Mr. Miffle, saying that I certainly didn't wish Mr. Lymond to set foot in my house under any circumstances. I enclosed the references unread. I couldn't imagine having someone like Lymond around for even a short while. I felt sorry for his poor wife. With a husband like Lymond, I imagined she certainly needed a place to recuperate. The man was completely odious.

Aunt Henrietta came in that evening full of news. She was so in alt that she even approved the carpenters' work without looking at it. She and Mrs. Bocock had had a splendid day of gossip and were planning on doing the same tomorrow. Needless to say, I was overjoyed at that prospect, so much so that I was able to sit through dinner listening to a catalogue of who was currently visiting Brighton. I didn't stop smiling until she mentioned meeting a Mr. Lymond.

"Lymond! Aunt Henrietta, are you speaking of Mr. Robert Lymond? You actually met the man?"

"Oh, yes, and another gentleman with him, a most handsome man — Captain Amherst with the Dragoons." Aunt Henrietta paused and looked perplexed. "How do you know Mr. Lymond?"

I gave her a quick report of Lymond's visit and his terrible manners. Cassie inserted a few sentences about what a fine man he was, what a handsome man Captain Amherst was, and what a very nice cabriolet they were driving. I quelled her with a look and continued. "Altogether I thought the captain quite exceptional, but Mr. Lymond had no address at all — I thought him a most repulsive man," I concluded.

"We must not be discussing the same Mr. Lymond," Aunt Henrietta said, a small smile on her face. "Such a handsome man! Such wonderful manners!"

Cassie chose this time to make her contribution. "I must agree with you, Aunt Hen. He was a trifle swarthy, I thought, but altogether a perfect gentleman."

"The exact description, Cassandra — the perfect gentleman, and so devoted to his dear wife. He told me he had taken a house for the quarter here so she could recuperate.

"The nerve of the man! He has definitely *not* taken this house for a quarter or any other time. I wrote Mr. Miffle and gave him strict instructions not to rent to Lymond." I took a moment to calm myself. "Really, Aunt Hen, you should have seen him here. He came by and simply assumed he could move in here. He was quite forward and overbearing."

"And quite overset by the dog," Cassie interjected.

I waved that away. "A trifle. The point is that he is not moving in here. I wrote Mr. Miffle and was quite explicit on that point."

Aunt Henrietta looked nonplussed. "Then, dear, he must have taken another house, because I distinctly remember him sitting with Mrs. Bocock and myself late this afternoon and saying he had already signed a lease." She looked at me. "Such a fine young man, too. Whatever were you thinking, Roxanne? And his poor wife needing somewhere suitable to recuperate." She looked at me and pursed her lips in disapproval. "Oh, dear. It just doesn't seem the Christian thing to do to turn them away."

"I'm sure that's all rot, Aunt Henrietta. Mr. Lymond didn't seem at all the trustworthy sort to me. That story about his sick wife is probably nothing but twaddle."

Aunt Henrietta was shocked, but for the wrong reason. "Roxanne! I can't believe you're saying these things! 'Rot,' 'twaddle'! Just listen to yourself. You young people are much too modern!"

I glanced at the other girls and raised my eyebrows. We had all heard this before — many times, so I didn't comment. Aunt Hen had resumed her catalogue of Mr. Lymond's fine qualities. I hadn't seen any of those, but, according to Aunt Henrietta, the man had charm enough to coax birds from the trees. "You really should have let the house to him," Aunt Henrietta concluded, as I went upstairs in sheer self-defense. "He may even have unmarried brothers or cousins." I could hear Cassie, Julia, and Livvy laughing as I topped the steps.

Mr. Miffle came over the next day just as the carpenters were cleaning up. The renovations had been simple—merely adding an entrance and turning a side door into an entryway for us. Everything was ready, even the doghouse.

"Have you found a tenant yet, Mr. Miffle?" I smiled broadly at him. He was obviously full of news.

"Yes, and a most fine connection it is. He's even offered to pay extra if he can take the house immediately. I told him you would agree to that." He withdrew a packet and handed it to me. "Here you are, Miss Sydney. All signed, sealed, and delivered." He chuckled at his little joke. "As your agent I've already signed for you, and I took the liberty of accepting a deposit." He handed me a bank draft. I took one look and felt myself go pale. The draft was made to me and signed by Robert Lymond.

I shoved the draft back at him. "Impossible! I refuse to let to that odious man. What happened to my letter to you?"

Mr. Miffle looked thoroughly confused and searched through his papers. There was my letter—unopened. "Yes, that one," I snapped. "A letter telling you that under no circumstances were you to let the house to Mr. Lymond." I paced the floor. "I refuse to have that man in my house!"

Aunt Henrietta and Cassie wandered in at the commotion. "Whatever is the problem, dear?" Aunt Hen nodded to Mr. Miffle. "You seem overset."

"Look at this! Mr. Miffle has allowed Mr. Lymond to sign an agreement to take the house and has even accepted this for the rent." I waved the bank draft.

Aunt Henrietta took the draft from my fingers and

looked at it. Her eyes became the size of teacups. "Wonderful," she said, her mouth as round as her eyes. "Simply wonderful, Mr. Miffle. When may we expect them?"

"Immediately, if it can be arranged," Mr. Miffle said simultaneously with my "Never!" Aunt Hen looked from one of us to the other. "Dear Roxanne seems to have misunderstood Mr. Lymond," she said to Mr. Miffle as though I wasn't there. "I myself have met him and believe him to be an excellent tenant." She looked again at the bank draft and smiled. "Just excellent."

She pointed out the numbers on the draft to Cassie and Cassie nodded in agreement. "Yes, Aunt Hen," she said, "excellent — and so agreeable."

I glared at Cassie, but Aunt Hen was the one I had to convince. "Aunt Henrietta," I began calmly, but she stopped me.

"Now, now, dear. All of this for only a quarter's rent. It's *much* more than we planned to ask. Is this correct?"

Mr. Miffle nodded vigorously. "Yes, Mr. Lymond told me he was paying extra so he could move in immediately. The additional is to cover any inconvenience to you." He beamed at Aunt Hen. "Most advantageous, I'd say."

"Quite so." Aunt Hen beamed back and glanced significantly at the draft. "I'm sure we'll all rub along just fine."

"May I tell Mr. Lymond that all will be ready the first of the week?" he asked. "That's the date in the agreement."

"That will be excellent, Mr. Miffle," she said happily.

I watched as Mr. Miffle rode off whistling. "I protest this, Aunt Hen," I told her, reaching for the bank draft. "You were the one who was afraid to rent to just anyone, and I'm sure that Mr. Lymond will not be at all suitable."

Aunt Hen folded the bank draft and tucked it down in

her bosom. "For safekeeping," she said with a smile. "Just think, Roxanne, all this for a quarter's time! We'll be rich!" She turned to Cassie. "We'll be able to send you and Roxanne to London for a season much sooner than I had hoped." Cassie floated over to me and hugged me. It was defeat, but I had to try once more.

"The man is untrustworthy, Aunt Henrietta. I feel it in my bones. We may wake up one morning and find both Mr. Lymond and all our plate gone."

"Nonsense. Woodbury will keep a close watch on the plate."

"I'm sure the man will be a nuisance," I continued. "He looks the type to be up half the night at card parties or wild entertainments. Besides," I added darkly, "if he has friends in the Army, he'll probably have dozens of them over here every night, drinking and carousing."

"Nonsense again. He probably spends every evening reading to his poor wife. We'll never know they're on the place."

I looked at Aunt Hen and saw that avarice had her firmly in its grip. With a sigh, I gave up.

"I'm sure things will be fine," Aunt Hen said, patting the bank draft closer inside her bosom. She turned and walked away, her hand firmly over the money, and her voice floated back to me. "After all, you yourself said we wouldn't see him at all once we were in our own apartments."

Had I but known . . .

Chapter Two

Mr. and Mrs. Lymond moved in on Monday. That was the first time I saw his wife, Amelia. She was a pretty little thing, somewhat of his coloring, but with pale blue eyes. She was small, much smaller than I, and had a sweet, wistful expression on her face. She reminded me of Cassie when she was being ethereal, except ethereal seemed to be Mrs. Lymond's permanent expression. Cassie was one up on Mrs. Lymond, however: Mrs. Lymond didn't float along as Cassie did, rather Amelia seemed to wander around aimlessly.

After looking at her, she was, I decided, not at all the woman to stand up to a tyrant like Lymond, poor thing. He was, I had to own, solicitous of her, making sure she was seated as soon as she arrived and not allowing her to get up and supervise anything. He had brought along Captain Amherst to help him do that, and the captain certainly did an admirable job of it. Even Woodbury was highly impressed at the way the captain organized everything and ordered everyone around—quite nicely, but very firmly. I tried to stay out of the way and, most of all, keep the other girls out of the way, but Cassie kept floating around, offering first this one and then that one something to eat and drink. Captain Amherst was quite pleasant to her, but I imagined it was a strain on him. I know it was on me—if I had been the captain, I would have sent her to the brig—or whatever Army people have.

Aunt Hen made herself useful by talking to Mrs. Lymond. I had thought Lymond would want his wife to see to the meals and housekeeping, but he didn't. Instead, he quite won over the housekeeper, Mrs. Beckford, praising her menus and housekeeping to the skies, then coaxing her into saying she would do all the chores since poor Amelia couldn't be worried. Lymond also promised Mr. Beckford an increase in wages for this "extra" duty. I thought this was the last straw, what with strangers overrunning my house and unfamiliar possessions scattered everywhere, and I told Lymond so, in no uncertain terms. I was, like Captain Amherst, very polite, but very firm. I told Lymond I did not care for interference with the servants. "In the future," I said, with what I thought was just the right degree of iciness in my voice, "you will please not take it on yourself to raise wages in the household. This will be a complication when you leave."

"Not at all, Miss Sydney." The man was positively casual. "Mrs. Beckford is quite aware that this increase is temporary. Poor Amelia is unable to do many of the things you handle so well."

He had me there. While I searched for an answer, he continued. "I'd like to familiarize myself with the grounds, and I intend to do some riding as well. I've sent north for my own horses." He smiled, I supposed, to make his . . . his *orders* palatable. "Owen and I enjoy riding daily."

"Fine," I said faintly as he strode away, that false smile still hanging in the air. I decided the man must have a long military background, since he seemed accustomed to ordering everyone around. No wonder his

29

poor wife looked like a wraith. Since the man obviously didn't have the sensibilities that Captain Amherst did, I could see I was going to have to be firm.

I went back to our apartments to search for Aunt Henrietta and ran into a full-scale battle. It seemed that Livvy and Julia were miffed that they had to share a room while I had one of my own. I pointed out that Cassie and Aunt Hen were sharing a room, but Julia discounted that. "Aunt Hen refuses to sleep in a room by herself," Julia said scornfully. "That won't wash, Roxanne. Why can't we have separate rooms?"

"Because it isn't practical. There aren't enough rooms on this side of the house." I was wonderfully logical.

"True," Livvy said, "but there are empty rooms upstairs." She looked at Julia. "Why not those?"

"Because," I said again firmly, "we want to stay out of the Lymonds' way as much as possible. The only access to those rooms is the main hall, and I certainly don't want you two up there alone while the Lymonds and their guests are wandering along the hall."

"You've forgotten the back stairs," Julia said smugly.

True, I had, but that was a minor point. "No," I said, again firmly, "we'll stay right here, out of the way. After all, this is only for three months, and we can all endure a little hardship."

"The only ones enduring are Livvy and me," Julia said as I went out the door.

It infuriated me so that I turned back. "Julia, I can't believe you said such a thing. Do you think I *like* having to do this? Do you think I *want* someone like Lymond in Papa's house? Do you think I *enjoy* being displaced from my own room?" I paused for breath and Livvy stepped into the breach.

"We understand that we need the money, Roxanne," she said with a sigh. "It's just that's it's more of an imposition than any of us dreamed it would be."

"I agree with you both," I said with a smile and gave them a hug. "At any rate, it'll be over soon, and perhaps we'll have enough money to take Cassie to London for a season, and the two of you could go up to visit."

"Edward would give us the money," Julia said, but I turned on her before she could say more.

"Julia, how can you say that? I know Edward would give us the money, but do you want to go begging to him and that Friday-faced wife of his? I certainly don't."

"Never," Julia and Livvy answered in chorus. That decided, I left them busily arranging their room, deciding what things went where.

I met Aunt Hen in the hall of our apartments. "I've been talking to poor Amelia," she said, coming into the drawing room and plopping into a chair. "She's such a dear, so sweet. And you should hear her play the pianoforte."

"Someone touched Cassie's pianoforte?" I looked up in horror. "Cassie will die on the spot once she discovers that."

Aunt Hen shook her head. "Oh, no. Cassandra invited her to play after poor Amelia said playing cheered her so. Poor Amelia asked if you would mind, and we told her you never touched the pianoforte."

With guilt I remembered that I hadn't touched the pianoforte in ages—a year or more before Papa had died. He had thought all females should be musical and originally purchased a harp for me, no doubt because he thought it the instrument of choice for all Greek women. My playing was such a disaster that

31

the harp had been passed on to Livvy, and Papa had purchased the pianoforte for me.

At his decision, the pianoforte had been painted blue and decorated with Grecian figures so that it resembled an Attic urn. It looked very fine, but when I tried to play, that, too, was hopeless. Cassandra was given the pianoforte, and Papa purchased a violin for me. I never managed to fit the dratted thing under my chin properly, much less learn to get a note to come out of it that didn't sound like a cat yowling, so it was duly handed down to Julia. After all this, Papa rather sadly concluded that music was one womanly accomplishment quite beyond me.

"If Cassandra doesn't mind someone else playing on her pianoforte, I'm sure Mrs. Lymond will enjoy it," I said shortly. "She'll need something to occupy her time since she isn't going to be handling the household, and Mr. Lymond seems to have plans to be off gallivanting around the country every day with Captain Amherst."

"I'm afraid poor Amelia is simply too frail to do much."

I glanced at Aunt Hen as that sounded like a direct quote to me, but I let it pass and changed the subject. "I forgot to see that Mrs. Lymond's things were put into Mama's rooms. Did she like those rooms? I didn't think she would be here long enough to change anything." I hadn't mentioned it, but I was going to draw the line there—Mama's rooms would not be changed at all. It even bothered me to have someone in them. I didn't really mind Lymond being in Papa's rooms because Papa didn't care that much about his quarters— the whole house was his project. Mama's rooms, however, were her own province, and they looked like her—all flowers and brocades and soft English garden colors. I wasn't going to change a thing.

"She isn't in those rooms," Aunt Hen said. "Did you order some tea? I'm quite hungry after all the morning's activities."

"She isn't? Then where is she, Aunt Hen? Where did you put her?"

"Did you ring for tea?"

I tried to curb my exasperation. "No. Where did you put Mrs. Lymond?"

"I didn't put her anywhere—she selected her rooms all by herself. She's in your rooms," Aunt Hen said, unperturbed. "Will you ring for tea, Roxanne, or shall I? Are the other girls hungry?"

I absently rang for Meggie, the girl we had hired to help us in our apartments. "Doesn't that strike you as strange, Aunt Hen?"

"No, I would think they'd be quite hungry by now."

I bit my tongue. "I don't mean the girls—I mean the Lymonds. Isn't it strange that they wouldn't want connecting rooms? I didn't get the impression that they'd been married long, and to be occupying suites at either end of the hall . . ." I let my voice trail off suggestively.

Meggie came in and Aunt Hen sent for tea as well as an assortment of cream cakes, biscuits, a few scones and jam. As Meggie was leaving, another thought hit me. "Good Heavens, Aunt Hen! I completely forgot about eating arrangements! How are we to keep the kitchen expenses separated? We can't eat what the Lymonds have purchased, and I don't see any way to divide things. We don't have a kitchen of our own."

"Mr. Lymond probably will never think of it," Aunt Hen said complacently. "Men seldom think of kitchens, although I do admit tradesmen's bills come in for a fair share of scrutiny." Aunt Hen paused, then shook her head. "No, Roxanne, I'm sure he won't think of it. Poor Amelia tells me he's generous to a fault, anyway."

"I doubt that." I didn't try to keep the sarcasm from my voice.

Aunt Hen ignored me. "I do think perhaps you should purchase the dog's food separately. I heard Lymond ask Woodbury if the dog would be chained for the quarter. I don't believe either Mr. Lymond or Captain Amherst cares greatly for Bucephalus."

"Who does?" I asked with a sigh. "Except perhaps Holmwood. The wretch—the dog, that is—even wandered in with part of someone's coat he had unearthed somewhere. Disgusting." I returned to the topic on my mind. "Really, Aunt Hen, don't you think it's strange?"

"That Holmwood should like Bucephalus? My goodness, yes. The dog is a complete disaster. I can't imagine whatever possessed George to—"

I interrupted her. I knew it was rude, but Aunt Hen could ramble on for hours if not stopped. "No, I mean the arrangements between Mr. and Mrs. Lymond."

"What arrangements?" Cassandra asked, wafting in and settling into a chair. "Do you mean the rooms? Don't you want her in your room?"

"I don't care," I said wearily, "I merely was pointing out that most married people don't have rooms on either end of a hall."

We paused as Meggie came in with the cakes, biscuits, and tea, and Aunt Hen made herself a snack. "No, I really don't find it strange, Roxanne," she said, licking gooseberry jam from her fingers. "Poor Amelia has been quite ill, you know. They must have been married two or three years because I understand that her baby died last year."

"That's what he told me," Cassie said, reaching for

34

tea. "I wondered about it, but according to Owen —"

I interrupted. *"Owen?"*

Cassie had the grace to blush. "Captain Amherst. At any rate, he and Mr. Lymond said Amelia was unbelievably distraught and hasn't yet recovered. Mr. Lymond even asked if we would refrain from mentioning children while we were in Amelia's presence."

I thought about this while I drank my tea. It was a plausible explanation but still didn't seem just right. There was something wrong here. Just like with Papa's death, I was very good at sensing things — my *vox clamatis,* Papa called it — and I knew something was amiss. Lymond, however, seemed to have convinced Aunt Hen and Cassie, and after my feelings about Papa's death had been declared the workings of a troubled mind, I decided to keep my suspicions to myself. However, I decided I would look for something other than a feeling to offer as proof. In the meantime, Julia and Livvy, quite reconciled by this time, joined us for fruitcake and more tea.

Lymond looked me up the next morning. I was in the drawing room of our apartments, almost hidden in the corner I had appropriated as a study, working on my manuscripts. This was another of Papa's projects — a new translation of Xenophon. I never knew why Papa wasn't satisfied with the old translation, but he felt the world needed a new one, specifically his new one. So in Papa's memory and to that end, I had taken it on myself to finish his manuscript.

I was sitting at my desk surrounded by texts and dictionaries, ink on my fingers, and Bue panting quietly across my feet. Meggie ushered Lymond in, and Bue immediately leaped to his feet, almost knocking my chair over. It took a moment to get everything righted.

"That dog," Lymond said in a strangled voice, placing himself behind the sofa. Bue stood in front of the sofa, snarling. "Is he *always* like this?" Lymond asked plaintively.

I skipped wiping ink from my fingers and instead grabbed Bue's collar, a large, leather affair jangling with mock Greek coins. Bue loved to shake his head and listen to the noise. It sounded rather like a tambourine, especially in the dark. "Don't worry, Mr. Lymond," I told him. "Actually, Bucephalus is as gentle as a kitten."

"I'm not sure I can agree," he said, gingerly moving closer. Bue jerked from me and put both front paws on the sofa and began panting in Lymond's face. "Why Bucephalus?" Lymond asked, jumping backwards into the edge of a table. "I thought Bucephalus was the name of Alexander the Great's warhorse."

"Correct." I gave him a brief smile as I tugged at Bue's collar again — ineffectually. "The name means 'ox-headed.' "

Lymond regarded Bue intently. "Apt, Miss Sydney, apt." He put out a hand to Bue, who promptly snapped at him. Lymond quickly withdrew. "However, with your father's penchant for history, I would have thought your horse would be Bucephalus, and that — that animal — would be Romulus or Remus or the like." Bue was now drooling onto the back of the sofa. I managed to jerk him down. "I can't contain my curiosity, Miss Sydney. Why did you choose such an animal?"

It was a question I heard often. I sighed and tried to drag Bue along the floor. Lymond, to his credit, did come around to the front of the sofa and help me. Bue rewarded him by snarling at him and drooling on his boots. We dragged Bue to the edge of the room and I tied him to a convenient Ionic column. He started to howl but thought the better of it. After glaring at the two of us, he collapsed in a heap and went instantly to sleep.

"Tea, Mr. Lymond?" I asked as I rang for Meggie.

He nodded and we sat. "Where are your sisters and aunt today?"

I raised an eyebrow. I hadn't expected a social call. "Aunt Hen, Julia, and Livvy are visiting. Cassie has taken her watercolors and gone out to the shore to paint."

He made the appropriate murmurs, then there was an awkward pause. "Back to the dog: perhaps I could help you find a good home in the country for him," he offered, eyeing Bue warily. "I'd be glad to ask some of my acquaintances."

I smiled at him. He was so transparent in his attempt to get rid of Bue. Another reason to suspect him, I thought. "I'm so sorry, Mr. Lymond. I couldn't send Bucephalus away. Papa loved him so." That was not at all the case, but Lymond didn't know that. "Besides," I added, "Papa chose him for me and Bue and I happen to get along very well."

Lymond sipped his tea and glanced up at me, his brilliant blue eyes sparkling. "I suppose you wished for a dog to drool all over your gowns, drag you down country lanes, and keep you awake all night with his howling?"

I had to laugh. "He does all those things," I agreed.

"And does them so well," Lymond added.

I laughed again. I certainly had not suspected the man of having a sense of humor. He was even smiling. "Actually," I told him, warming, "I had originally asked for a spaniel, but Papa usually thought that bigger was better, no matter what it was, so he bought a mastiff for me. Bue was just a puppy then, and for some reason it never occurred to either of us that he would reach such a size. I have to admit that we really weren't prepared for such a large animal."

"Oh, I thought you named him after a horse because of his size. Why the name then—other than the ox-headed part, of course?" Lymond leaned back on the sofa and smiled as he finished his tea.

I poured him some more and handed him the dish. "Papa wanted me to name my horse Bucephalus, and, when I didn't, the name devolved on the dog."

"It's quite appropriate—on both counts," Lymond murmured, sipping his tea. "What, may I ask, did you name your horse: Warrior, El Cid, Caesar?"

"Buttercup," I answered primly. "I chose it myself."

Lymond threw back his head and laughed. It was a nice laugh, but it vaguely annoyed me. "What's funny about that?" I demanded.

"Nothing at all, Miss Sydney. It's just that I certainly didn't expect to discover a Buttercup in the midst of all these Helens and Cassandras and Aphrodites and . . ."

"Roxannes?" I finished for him.

He smiled at me, those blue eyes crinkling at the corners. "Exactly. But," he added, looking at me reflectively, "the name suits you—not in its historical sense, of course, but, yes, I think you do look quite like a Roxanne."

"Nonsense." I had once seen a drawing of how some artist thought the original Roxanne had looked and I certainly didn't resemble her at all. She was a little, dark, fragile-looking chit while I was, as Chaucer once so kindly put it, by no means undergrown. Besides, my hair was blond. Papa, I think, regretted my name after I was grown—he would have preferred I be called "fair Athene." Privately, I preferred even Roxanne to that.

Lymond looked at me boldly — much too boldly for a married man, I thought. "It's not nonsense at all," he said. "You look every inch a Roxanne. Quite regal, I would say."

I felt myself blush. Did the man mean I was the size of the Prince Regent? While I am a large person, I am by no means heavy. *Statuesque* was the word I preferred as it was much more accurate. "I resent your implication, Mr. Lymond," I said icily.

To my surprise, he looked contrite. "I'm sorry if I offended you, Miss Sydney. I meant that as a sincere compliment."

It was time to change the subject. "Is the house satisfactory?" I asked abruptly.

"Quite." He looked at me over the rim of his cup.

There was an interminable silence. I never knew what to say in these situations. Finally, just to have something to say, I began some idle chatter about a topic current in the newspapers. "Have you been reading about the stolen paintings?"

Lymond put his cup carefully on the saucer and set them down. "A little, but I confess I don't know much about it." He glanced casually at me. "What could you tell me about it?"

I shrugged. "Nothing except what I've read and whatever gossip Aunt Henrietta's brought home from her trips into town."

"And that is . . . ?" He seemed intent on my answer.

"Just that thieves have been breaking into houses all over the South Downs and taking valuable paintings. From what I understand, they've been very selective. I did read that the earl of Debenham has promised to use every resource of the Home Office to find the paintings. Aunt Hen's friend, Mrs. Bocock, is a notorious gossip, and she reports that Debenham's actual words were something like 'he'd see those thieves run to earth and hanged.' " I straightened up and realized suddenly that I was gossiping as much as Mrs. Bocock had ever done. "I hope your wife is feeling better," I said to change the subject.

"She's fine, thank you." Lymond leaned back, very casually. "What do you suppose has happened to all the paintings?"

"I have no idea." I realized there was a touch of asperity in my voice, and I tried to be more pleasant. "Local gossip has it that they're on the way to Germany or Italy. I suppose there are several unscrupulous German or Italian princelings who would pay for stolen goods." We had exhausted the subject. "Would you care for more tea?"

"No thank you. What about the thieves? Does your celebrated local gossip know who they might be?"

I was a little exasperated at his probing. "How should I know, Mr. Lymond? I don't dabble in local gossip. If you want to know about that, you'll have to talk to Aunt Henrietta. Besides," I added, "I doubt very much that anyone is going to be walking around Brighton with a sign on the back of his coat proclaiming him to be the celebrated painting thief."

Lymond laughed. "I'm sure the authorities wish that were true."

"It would simplify matters," I agreed. "As it is, in spite of Debenham's involvement, no one seems to be making much headway in discovering the perpetrators. I heard Debenham was planning to send someone into this area to investigate, but I think that's merely some more of Mrs. Bocock's gossip. I can't imagine Brighton being a center for thievery. There are simply too many people here. I would think thieves would want an isolated place."

"Perhaps the thieves believe it would be easier to hide their activities if there were people around. They could fade into the crowd." Lymond spoke in a bantering tone, but his eyes were serious.

"Perhaps," I said, "but why the interest, Mr. Lymond? I'm sure none of this will ever touch us. There certainly aren't any paintings of any value around here."

"True, but there are many valuable artifacts."

I stared at him. It hadn't occurred to me that anyone would dare to steal any of Papa's carefully collected things. Immediately I pictured Lymond hauling off everything I owned. "I would put Bow Street Runners onto anyone who touched Papa's things," I said quickly. "At any rate, these things have sentimental value rather than value on the market. Papa collected anything and everything."

"I thought his collections seemed a trifle, ah, chaotic," Lymond observed. "Owen and I were wondering if he'd catalogued everything."

I glanced at him sharply. What was the man asking—or implying? "Of course we've catalogued it all," I snapped. Actually, we hadn't catalogued anything, but I planned to do so immediately. Lymond could walk away with half the house, and I wouldn't know what to tell the Runners was missing.

"Excellent," he said lazily, looking at me through half-closed eyes. Those eyes weren't lazy at all. They missed nothing.

Enough was enough. "Was there something specific you wanted to discuss this morning, Mr. Lymond?" I asked pointedly.

"Not particularly." He smiled. "I wanted to tell you that my horses will be here tomorrow. If you recall, you gave me permission to ride the grounds." He paused, and I stepped into the breach.

"I recall," I said, trying to be pleasant. "However, I do have a slight problem — we're shorthanded at the stables. Papa took it on himself to rehabilitate two of the local boys and hired them to work in the stables here. Jem, the younger, disappeared without any notice whatsoever not long after Papa was — Papa died."

"I noticed there was only one — Willy, I believe — so you haven't hired anyone to replace Jem?"

I didn't want to tell him that we hadn't had the money to replace anyone. "No, Mr. Lymond," I said, smiling. "We felt we really didn't need that many people at the stables. I suppose you also noted that Willy doesn't even work on a regular basis. Since Jem disappeared, Willy is out more than he's in." I paused, trying to say exactly the right thing. "If you have several horses, I suppose we could . . ."

At least Lymond had enough address to catch my meaning. "I would prefer to hire my own men, if that's all right with you," he said with a smile. "I'm rather particular about my horseflesh." I had to concentrate on not breathing a sigh of relief. Lymond glanced at me to see if I approved, then continued. "If you don't mind the men living at the stable, I'll see to it at once. I have some friends with the Dragoons who have horses and can recommend some boys to work." He smiled at me, no doubt thinking we were on quite good terms by now. "I do appreciate you giving me permission to bring my horses and ride the grounds, but I'd like to do even more. I find the place fascinating, and I wanted to ask if you would care if I explored the grounds."

42

"*Explore* the grounds? Whatever could be here to explore?"

"Perhaps 'explore' wasn't a good word," he said with, I had to admit, another very charming smile. "One of the reasons I wanted to rent this particular house is that I, too, have an interest in ancient cultures and I wanted to look at the friezes and other decorations. If you don't mind, I'd like to look carefully at the other buildings as well. The mausoleum seems particularly interesting."

He was lying; I knew it in my bones. The only culture of interest to Robert Lymond was the *on-dits* at the local pub. I didn't think he would know ancient culture if it hit him over the head. Still, what could I say? "I don't think you'll find anything interesting, Mr. Lymond. Everything built here is either a copy or Papa's interpretation of something Greek or Roman. The only genuine antiquities are a very few Papa brought back from abroad with him."

"I still find it fascinating, Miss Sydney."

"Oh." I couldn't think of a reason in the world to refuse him access.

"Then I have your permission?" he asked, standing up. "Thank you so much, Miss Sydney. Owen—Captain Amherst—is an amateur antiquarian, and he would like to accompany me. I assure you we won't disturb a single thing."

Lymond left after the briefest of amenities and I was left sitting there, staring at his empty cup. Something was wrong here, I knew it. Lymond was simply not what he seemed. I felt that the impression he was trying to give me was entirely false—something about him didn't fit at all. At first glance, he seemed like an ordinary, indolent dullard—I had seen a thousand like that circulating through the *ton*. But then his pose would slip and there were flashes of extraordinary intelligence in those blue eyes as well as a commanding presence and an attitude of authority that reminded me of the military. Who was he really?

With a flash of inspiration, I remembered my cousin Lydia in London. Lydia was the wife of Viscount Frazee and was in the thick of everything that went on in the *ton*. She knew almost everyone and everything, and what she didn't know, her husband did. Gossip was their raison d'être. She would know about Lymond if there was anything to know. If not, she was the very person to ferret out something about his background. I went to the desk and wrote to her immediately.

"There," I said to Bue who was getting up and stretching lazily as I sanded the letter, "I have a feeling Mr. Lymond's days are numbered. Who knows, Bue, he may even be the painting thief." I stopped stock-still in the middle of sanding as soon as the words were out of my mouth. "Good Heavens, Bue! That may be it! That may be why he wanted to quiz me about what I knew. It would fit, wouldn't it?" Bue looked at me and then collapsed again, drooling on the rug. "We'll have to watch him until I hear from Lydia," I said as much to myself as to Bue. "I'll warn the other girls and we won't let him out of our sight."

I hunted up Woodbury and gave him instructions to mail my letter to Lydia immediately. Not a minute was to be lost. Then I went to get paper and drafted Woodbury into helping me to begin cataloguing everything in the house. I wanted a complete list — just in case.

Chapter Three

Late that afternoon, Woodbury discreetly knocked on the door that separated our apartments from the rest of the house. Cassandra was still off with her watercolors, while Aunt Hen, Julia, and Livvy were all settled in cozily with Amelia. I had warned them, but they completely disregarded my worries about fraternizing with the tenants. Nothing would do them except to sit and read to "poor Amelia." Already I had heard Mrs. Lymond called "poor Amelia" so often that I thought of both words as her name. Even Lymond called her that in conversation about her.

I was working on my inventory list when Woodbury knocked. "A caller for you, Miss Sydney," he announced formally. "A gentleman."

I frowned. I hadn't thought about the protocol for visitors since we seldom had any. It would not do for callers to knock on the front door, then have to be paraded through the house to the back. "Ask him to come around, Woodbury," I finally said. "Meggie will let him in."

"I thought that would be proper," Woodbury said stiffly. "I asked him to wait until I consulted with you." He turned and went towards the front, closing the door behind him. Woodbury was such a stickler for formality.

In a moment I heard the knock at our door, then an unconscionably long time elapsed before Meggie flew by me. She flung the door open and yelled at me, "Someone to see you, milady." She dashed away, leaving the caller standing outside, the door open, and me sitting there. I got up hastily and went to him. "My apologies," I said. "Meggie is quite new."

"I thought as much," the caller said charitably.

I caught myself staring at him. He was taller than I, fashionably dressed in buff and dark blue, with a cravat so white it almost glistened. His Hessians were gleaming black and the shining gold tassels on them matched the dark gold streaks in his blond hair. He was very handsome. Then he smiled, and I was dazzled.

"Won't you come in?" I stammered.

He smiled again and walked past me, holding his hat and gloves. "I'll have Meggie take those for you," I said.

"No matter, they'll be fine here." He deposited them on a table.

It occurred to me that I had no idea who he was. "You wished to see me?" I asked, sitting down.

He smiled at me again, a perfectly charming smile, and sat on a chair across from me. "Yes, Miss Sydney. My name is Justin Denver. I've been abroad for some time and have only recently returned to England." He had a touch of the foreign in his speech—only a trace, but enough to make his words distinctive. I supposed living abroad had given him an accent. He went on. "I wanted to settle here at Brighton for a few months to get acclimated before I went up to further some business interests in London. I saw a notice that your house was to let and would like to take it." He looked around appreciatively. "It's perfect."

I answered him with real regret. Now here was someone I would have preferred to have as a tenant. "I'm sorry, but the house has been taken. It has, however, been let for only a quarter if you can wait until then."

"I'm sorry to hear that." He looked crestfallen. "I wrote to your agent — a Mr. Miffle, I believe — as soon as I knew the house was available, but I never heard from him."

So this was Miffle's fault — again. "Mr. Miffle has a bad habit of not opening his mail," I said, remembering my letter to him about Lymond. No doubt Mr. Denver's letter was lying right next to it.

"When I received no word from Mr. Miffle," Justin Denver went on, "I decided to come make the arrangements myself." He looked around disappointedly. "It's such a pity the house has been taken — this is exactly what I've been looking for." He smiled again. "I deal in artifacts and paintings and, after living in Rome for several years, I'd feel right at home here."

"You can't wait until the quarter is over?"

He shook his head. "I'm afraid I'll be getting ready to move to either London or Rome then. I need something right now." He looked at me with hope. "You live in Brighton all year around, Miss Sydney. Could you suggest a place I could rent for the next three or four months?"

I frowned as I thought. "The house on the estate that matches with ours has been let for several years, although I understand it needs repairs rather badly now. The owner of Jervyne House, Jerrold, is down now, so I could ask him. I really don't know how serious the repairs are." I glanced at Denver doubtfully. He didn't look at all the kind to live in a tumbledown place. He appeared to be most fastidious.

He waved my objections away. "I would be glad to take Jervyne House as long as the roof isn't falling in," he said with his enchanting smile. "I've supervised renovations on houses in Italy and Germany, so perhaps Jerrold would allow me to do so as a condition of the rent. That's work I rather enjoy."

"I really don't know how extensive the renovation would be." I tried to convey my doubt. If I knew Jerrold, the stingiest man in southern England, he hadn't spent a farthing on the house in years.

Denver smiled again. "It wouldn't hurt to ask, and Jerrold might be delighted to accept my offer."

From what I knew of Anthony Jerrold, I was sure he would feel more than delight, but I was in no position to answer for the man. "I don't know," I told Mr. Denver, "but I'd be glad to write a short note to Jerrold about it. I could do that this afternoon if you like." The offer amazed me as soon as I realized what I had said.

"I can't thank you enough for helping me, Miss Sydney." There was that smile again. "Since your house isn't available, I'm really at a loss for a place to stay. Could I return tomorrow and find out what Mr. Jerrold has told you?"

"Of course," I found myself saying, "and could I offer you some tea while you're here?"

He accepted, and while we waited for Meggie to bring in the tea, he told me about his travels. He was really one of the most charming men I had ever met, and knew a great deal about antiquities. I wished Papa could have talked to him — they would have had so much in common.

Over tea, he told me that his family was all dead, except for a distant cousin, and that he planned to go into business with his cousin in London, buying and selling paintings and antiquities. At this point in the conversation, he asked that I call him by his given name, Justin. It was pushing propriety, but it did seem rather silly to keep calling him Mr. Denver, especially if we might be neighbors. Besides, he was so easy to talk to that I felt we were old friends.

He was telling me about the time he had salvaged a mural on a library wall in a villa in Italy when there was a commotion at the door. I glanced up and in floated Cassandra, positively glowing. She was dressed all in white and pink, and the ribbons on her bonnet had come untied and were dangling on her shoulders. Her hair had, as usual, come partially unpinned and was wafting like gossamer around her face. Right behind her, carrying her paint box, walked Captain Amherst. They were laughing and chatting like old friends. I raised an eyebrow which went unnoticed as Cassie and the captain came in and sat down. "You've had a good day?" I asked pointedly.

"Wonderful," she said, smiling. I wished to hear no more until later, so I went ahead and made the introductions. Captain Amherst nodded politely to Justin, and, as men occasionally do, they exchanged the usual types of information: Do you hunt? etc. It seemed that Justin didn't hunt, enjoyed riding, had never been in the Army, and had traveled. Captain Amherst relished hunting, delighted in riding, enjoyed the Army, and had traveled, too.

We conversed a short while longer about antiquities, but Captain Amherst was a bit out of his element on this topic, so he took his leave. I raised another eyebrow when he told Cassie that he hoped he could see her more frequently. It was, I realized, time for a session of sisterly advice.

Justin stayed only a few minutes after Captain Amherst left. As I walked him to the door, I was aware of the most pleasant, slightly spicy scent he wore. Ordinarily I do not care for scent on men, most of them perfume themselves ridiculously, but this scent seemed to fit Justin exactly. "I'm looking forward to my return visit tomorrow," he said with a smile. "I can't tell you what a pleasure it's been to meet you."

I murmured something appropriate, closed the door, and turned to talk to Cassie about Captain Amherst. As I walked back to the sofa where she was sitting, she looked up at me with wide eyes. "Roxanne! I'm amazed. Here I come back from a quiet day painting and find you sitting in here *alone* with a strange man! A very handsome strange man, at that! Whatever is going on?"

This was a strategy of Cassie's with which I was familiar. She'd used it for years. "Don't try to bring up another subject, Cassandra. I want to talk to you about Captain Amherst."

She looked miffed. "I knew you'd have something to say about Owen. He happens to be a very exceptional gentleman."

"Owen?" I paused significantly. "I'm sure he is. And I suppose you just ran into him at the door as you were coming in?"

She looked wide-eyed again. "Of course not. He and Mr. Lymond were out walking around the property—exploring, Mr. Lymond said—and they came by the beach where I was painting. It was quite proper: Ned and one of the maids was with me. Captain Amherst stayed to keep me company."

She paused, and I pinned her with a stare. "And . . . ?" I asked.

"And nothing, Roxanne. He told me about his family—they're from near Bath, it seems. He's the second son, so naturally he decided on an Army career."

"And I'd wager that he's got a lightskirt in every port."

She shook her head solemnly. "The Army doesn't bivouac in ports, Roxanne. You're confused with the Navy."

"It was a figure of speech, Cassie," I explained patiently. "What I'm telling you is not to become involved with Captain Amherst. Remember our plan: you're to take the money from Mr. and Mrs. Lymond and add it to what we have. That should give you enough for something of a season in London. If you marry well, it will virtually assure Julia and Livvy of places in society." I paused and looked at her stricken face. "It's all up to you, Cassie, and we simply can't have you throwing it all away by having a breath of scandal attach itself to you. Captain Amherst is probably as poor as a hermit, and he isn't at all suitable."

She sighed. "Why me, Roxanne? You're the eldest — you should be the one to go to London. I'd rather stay here and paint."

I glanced at the teapot and rang for more. "We've had this discussion before, Cassie. I'm frank about my looks — I could never manage to capture an eligible — much less a *rich* eligible — on the marriage mart. I'm too large, I'm too outspoken, I'm too —"

"You're too modest," Cassie interrupted. "You know you could go to London and be a success if only you would."

I shook my head as Meggie brought in more tea. "No, I'm not the type. Even Aunt Hen agrees to that. It's got to be you, Cassie, and that's why you cannot encourage Captain Amherst."

She looked stubborn, but said nothing. Actually, there was nothing to say — we had had this conversation dozens of times before and it always ended the same way. I knew Cassandra didn't particularly relish going to London — she much preferred her music or being outside with her watercolors, painting and enjoying the crisp, salt breeze. Her favorite place to paint was the mausoleum, right where she could hear the wind moaning through the columns, sounding for all the world like a wailing bunch of chained souls. Cassie said it gave her inspiration. The only thing it gave me was goosebumps.

Before I could say anything else, there was a knock on the door between our apartments and the rest of the house. I jerked the door open, ready to chastise Woodbury. "I thought we agreed that this door would not be used—" I began, but then realized I was talking to Lymond instead of Woodbury.

"A thousand apologies," he said, strolling into our rooms. He wasn't at all sorry. "Why shouldn't the door be used? Is there something wrong with it?"

"No. I simply felt we should keep to ourselves back here." I turned back to close the door, but Aunt Hen, Julia, and Livvy paraded through it. "Aunt Hen, don't you agree we shouldn't use this door and should keep ourselves to our own apartments?" I demanded, hoping to make a point with her while I convinced Lymond.

"Bosh," Aunt Hen said, sitting down in front of the teapot and pouring herself a cup. "Tea, Mr. Lymond?"

"Yes, thank you, Mrs. Vellory," he answered, sitting across from her. It had been so long since I'd heard Aunt Hen called Mrs. Vellory that it took me a moment to decide whom he was addressing. "I want to thank all of you for entertaining poor Amelia. You're so good for her."

Aunt Hen was completely taken in by all of this fustian and nodded vigorously as she handed Lymond his tea. "Thank you. The poor darling was feeling so sickly today. I recommend some chamomile tea, Mr. Lymond. It's a great restorative."

"I'll see to it." He sipped his tea and smiled at Aunt Hen, Julia, and Livvy. I looked from one to the other. What was all of this—Aunt Hen referring to Amelia as the "poor darling" and Lymond accepting suggestions for restoratives while Julia and Livvy nodded sagely. Clearly things had been happening of which I was unaware.

Lymond put his cup down and smiled again. "I came to ask if all of you would join Amelia and me for supper tonight. I know it's somewhat short notice, but it would do poor Amelia so much good to have your company."

"Impossible," I said simultaneously with Aunt Hen's "We'd be delighted."

Lymond looked from me to Aunt Hen, then decided to ignore me completely. "I'm so glad you've accepted. It'll mean so much to poor Amelia. We'll eat early, about eight." He stood and smiled all around again. He must have thought his grin mesmerizing and, unfortunately, it did have a touch of that effect. "Amelia will be delighted," he paused and looked at me mockingly, "as will I."

He strolled to the door and let himself out of our apartments. "We're going to have to get a lock for that door," I said irritably.

"Your disposition has been all at sixes and sevens lately, Roxanne," Aunt Hen said mildly. "Are you feeling not the thing?"

"I happen to be fine," I told her. "You know that I find Mr. Lymond odious, and I'm simply marking time until he leaves. I don't know why every one of you insists on extending every hospitality to them. To him, especially."

"Because we like them," Aunt Hen said, looking around at the other girls. They all nodded in agreement.

"Poor Amelia's so sweet," Livvy chimed in.

"You'd like her if you knew her," Julia said.

I frowned and started to reply, but Aunt Hen wasn't finished. "The Lymonds are wonderful renters, Roxanne, and I'm sure if you'd allow yourself to know Mr. Lymond, you'd hold him in high regard. As for poor Amelia . . ." Her voice trailed off as I gritted my teeth.

"For your information," I told them, "we could have had an excellent renter had Mr. Miffle bothered to open his mail. A Mr. Justin Denver came by today to ask about the house. He'd written Mr. Miffle and received no answer. Of course, since the Lymonds were already here, there was no way he could accept."

"Denver . . . Denver . . ." Aunt Hen mused. "Good

Heavens, Roxanne, if he's related to the Notting Denvers, then we certainly wouldn't want him around. That family is—" She glanced at the girls and then back at me. "It really can't be discussed in polite company."

"I cannot believe you're saying this about someone you haven't even met, Aunt Hen. Denver isn't an unusual name, and I happen to consider myself a very good judge of character. I found Justin, that is, Mr. Denver, to be excellent in every way."

When confronted by superior logic, Aunt Hen did what she always did. She said "Hmpf" and retreated into her room to rest. The girls all wandered away to rest and dress for supper. I tried to finish my inventory lists, but my heart wasn't in it. Finally I gave up and sat down in a chair to think about exactly what was wrong with Lymond. There was something wrong but I just couldn't put my finger on it. At the end of an hour, I still hadn't, so I went to dress for supper.

Mrs. Beckford and Cook had outdone themselves preparing food for supper. There were all sorts of tempting dishes for poor Amelia, and everyone spent most of the meal seeing that she ate them—"to keep your strength up, dear," as Aunt Hen said. Actually Amelia did look much better than she had when she first arrived. She seemed rested and she wasn't as pale and tired looking. I couldn't decide if she was really sick or given to nerves. I finally decided she had been really ill, but was on the mend.

"You're very quiet, Miss Sydney," Lymond said to me over the fish course. "I was counting on you to regale us with stories."

I glanced up in surprise. "Oh? What kinds of stories?"

"Whatever you find interesting." Those startling blue eyes assessed me. "I wondered if you had discovered anything interesting in the inventory you were taking."

I blushed as Livvy kicked me on the ankle and

smirked. She had probably let it slip. "Woodbury and I were merely updating our list," I said, refusing to look at him.

"Of course." Laughter underlay his words. "And did you discover anything you had forgotten to list?"

"We're always turning up things dear George bought and forgot," Aunt Hen said, taking time away from urging Amelia to have another bite of sole. "I keep telling Roxanne that the Treasure will turn up if we persist."

Lymond's eyebrows rose. "The Treasure?" He used a capital letter as well.

"There is no treasure, Aunt Hen," I said, ignoring the question in Lymond's voice.

"There is, I know it." Aunt Henrietta chose this time of all times to be firm. She turned to Cassie, Julia, and Livvy. "All of you believe the Treasure is around here, don't you?" A yes was given in chorus. I could have strangled them all. Aunt Hen turned back to Lymond. "George would never lie, and he said the Treasure was here someplace. If he said it, then it's true. We just haven't looked in the right place."

"A Treasure!" Amelia, for the first time, looked animated. "I do love mysteries and treasure hunts. Please tell me about it."

There was a pause while I glared at Aunt Hen. "Papa said it was the treasure of Agamemnon," Julia said.

"Tell her what Papa said, Aunt Henrietta," Livvy said, looking at Amelia. "It's really a mystery."

Aunt Hen needed no more urging and launched right into a rather embroidered version of the story, replete with innuendo and hints that the Treasure approached that of King Midas. "So you see," she finished up, "dear George died before he could say more, but I'm convinced there's a Treasure hidden here."

"It's possible," Lymond said, obviously giving the story serious thought. "Although perhaps he meant some kind of treasure other than money or jewels. That may be why you can't locate it."

"I told you, Aunt Hen," I said in triumph. I turned to Lymond. "I told Aunt Hen that Papa probably meant the house and grounds. Those things were always his treasures anyway."

Aunt Hen shook her head before Lymond could agree with me. "No, Roxanne, I'm sure your father left a chest of money or jewels around. He certainly would not have arranged for Edward to be taken care of, then leave all you girls without much in the way of funds. I know he would never have expected you to let Bellerophon."

"Aunt Hen!" I exclaimed. It would never do to let Lymond think we wanted for funds.

"Well, I for one don't think Papa would have considered leaving us without enough money," Julia said crossly. "I think there's a Treasure. We just haven't searched hard enough." She looked across the table at me. "I told you we should have dismantled the walls while the carpenters were here."

We stopped speaking long enough for the fish to be removed and the next course brought in. I decided to change the subject, and groped around for a topic. "Have you heard anything more of the stolen paintings?" I asked as the dining room door closed behind the servants.

Lymond looked at me sharply, his blue eyes narrowing. "No, why do you ask?" His tone implied I knew something he didn't.

"No reason." I shrugged and toyed with my food. "I merely thought since you had expressed an interest in the robberies, you might have heard something else while you were in Brighton."

"I heard it was a whole gang of thieves," Julia offered.

"Dangerous thieves," Livvy added.

Lymond nodded. "I'd say all thieves are dangerous."

He attacked his roast beef with something approaching frenzy, then he turned his attention to Cassandra and Aunt Hen. "Perhaps you need to employ the dog in ferreting out the Treasure. He seems to dig up everything else."

Aunt Hen nodded vigorously. "True. Today he even came in with another dreadful piece of that old coat he has buried somewhere. The smell was terrible."

"Coat?" Lymond looked at Aunt Hen sharply.

"It's nothing," I said. "The things Bue drags in are hardly a subject for table conversation."

Lymond nodded at me and then turned back to Cassie. "Have you searched the house as well as the outbuildings for the Treasure?"

Cassie nodded. "Oh, yes, we've looked everywhere. Roxanne and Woodbury searched the stables, while Holmwood went through everything in the sheds. Roxanne, Woodbury, and I went through the mausoleum inch by inch, and then all of us went over the house. There was nothing to be found."

Amelia laughed, a small, silvery sound. "Isn't this wonderful, Robert?" She turned to Aunt Hen. "Perhaps Robert and I could help you. He's very good at finding things. He tells me it's all in the organization."

"We'd love to have your help," Aunt Hen said.

I tried kicking her under the table, but she was too far away. "Aunt Hen," I said slowly and grimly, hoping she got my message, "I'm sure Mr. and Mrs. Lymond are much too busy to waste time on a futile treasure hunt."

"Oh, no!" Amelia clapped her small hands together. "What fun we can have!" She turned to Lymond. "Say you'll help, Robert. If anyone can find their treasure, you can. I know it!"

"I'm telling you, there is no treasure." My words were lost in the general hubbub of Amelia, Aunt Hen, and the girls persuading Lymond to ransack the house and

57

grounds. They finally quieted, and I opened my mouth to tell them again that there was no treasure when Lymond spoke. "You ladies have quite convinced me," he said with a chuckle, reaching over and patting Amelia's small, pale hand. "I'd be delighted to help you."

I gave up. "Good luck to all of you," I said quite calmly, I thought. "I, for one, have searched all I intend and I have better things to do. This whole hunt will be a waste of time."

Julia raised an eyebrow and gave me an arch look. "You won't say that when we've discovered the Treasure."

I looked at each of them in disgust. "If you discover the Treasure, I'll eat my new straw bonnet. I'm telling you, it doesn't exist. There is no Treasure."

"Is that a wager?" Lymond asked, laughing. I noticed his eyes not only crinkled at the corners when he laughed, but he almost had a dimple.

"A wager has to have two parts," I said. "For instance, if you don't discover the Treasure, then *you'll* have to eat my bonnet."

"I've never found either words or bonnets too digestible," he said, laughing. "Could you suggest another forfeit?"

"I know, Robert," Amelia chimed in. "If we don't discover the Treasure for them by the time we're ready to go back to London, we'll purchase a new artifact for them."

"Done!" Lymond said before I could protest. The last thing we needed around was another bogus artifact. There were boxes and boxes of them around already.

"Now," Lymond said, considering things settled, "we'll have to make several lists of likely places. It would be a great help if we knew what the Treasure was. It could be the size of a bag of jewels or the size of a large painting." He looked at me. "Are you sure you don't know what your father was talking about, Miss Sydney?"

"I haven't a clue," I told him. "The man was dying and *he* didn't know what he was talking about."

"This is going to be very difficult," Lymond said, frowning.

"I know you can do it, Robert," Amelia said.

He smiled at her. "Thank you, Amelia." It was enough to bring on nausea. I had to force myself to eat dessert, and excused myself as soon as propriety allowed it. Aunt Hen and the girls, of course, stayed late in the library with Mr. and Mrs. Lymond planning strategy. I feared Aunt Hen was regaling them as well with tales of Papa's eccentricities.

As I lay in bed waiting for sleep, I kept recalling the supper conversation. The more I thought about it, the more it seemed that Lymond had manipulated the conversation so that someone insisted that he find the Treasure. What better way to discover what was in a house than to have a treasure hunt? I still didn't trust Lymond—he wasn't what he appeared. After a while, I gave up on sleep and got up. Perhaps I needed to recheck my inventory lists and include fuller descriptions.

When Aunt Hen and the girls came in and found me working at my desk, they laughed at me. Cassie, in particular, tweaked me about what she termed "my imaginings." But this time, for better or worse, I was afraid I would have the last laugh. I didn't relish it.

Chapter Four

I awoke late with a groggy head and it took several cups of tea before I was able to speak, much less think. I had just finished the last of the strong brew when there was a knock on the door between our half and the Lymonds'. Aunt Hen didn't wait for Meggie: she opened the door and welcomed Lymond effusively. He looked positively chipper. He was every inch the country gentleman in buff breeches, a brown waistcoat, and a tan corduroy coat trimmed with brown velvet. He wore tall brown riding boots.

"Tea, Robert?" Aunt Hen asked, pouring him a cup without waiting for an answer. *Robert?* I thought. Obviously their friendship had made great strides while I was working on the inventory last night.

"Thank you," Lymond said, putting a sheaf of foolscap on the table. The top paper was covered with sketches, one that looked like a grid, another that appeared to be a rough floor plan, and a great number of closely written notes. The other girls came in, chattering, and we all ignored the papers as Lymond spent the better part of half an hour sipping tea and exchanging pleasantries. I was very cordial as well. There was no point in antagonizing the man if he was bent on mischief.

He finally picked up the papers after Julia almost

spilled her tea on them. "I made a few notes," he explained. A few? There must have been a dozen sheets of paper there. Lymond went on. "I think organization is the key to searching for the Treasure, and I've organized the entire house and grounds into a grid so we can search each one and mark it off if it proves unproductive."

"We did that already," I said, trying not to be smug. "Would you like to see our grids and lists?"

He looked at all of us in amazement. "You did all this and found nothing?"

"Nothing," Livvy and Cassie said together as I shook my head.

"There's nothing here to find," I added.

"We simply didn't look in the right place, Roxanne," Aunt Hen said. "I'm sure Robert will look at everything with a fresh eye."

Privately I had my own ideas about the kind of eye Mr. Lymond would employ in looking at everything, but I publicly agreed with Aunt Hen. "Also," I added, "I've changed my mind. I'd like to accompany you on your search." I had decided that this was the best way to keep a close watch on Lymond.

"Wonderful, Roxanne!" Julia said, grabbing my hand. "You're always so observant." She turned to Lymond. "Roxanne is the best of us at disentangling Papa's notes and words. Even Papa always said that."

"He left a note?" Lymond suddenly seemed quite interested.

"No," I said shortly. "Julia is talking about Papa's manuscripts. I helped him with those, and he was always scribbling cryptic notes in the margins. Most of them were difficult to decipher."

Lymond looked crestfallen. "I thought we might have something there, but if not . . ." He looked back at his notes and seemed to be engrossed in them. "I thought we'd begin by searching this area of the grounds." His finger on the grid indicated the far corner. "I hope you don't mind, but Owen is coming over, and I'd like to invite him to join us."

"That would be wonderful," Cassie said with a sigh. I frowned at her, then back at Lymond, but it was lost on both of them. Bue came wandering with something in his mouth. It was another scrap of someone's coat, and it was so filthy as to be almost unrecognizable. "This is three times this animal has dragged this in," I said with disapproval. "I told Holmwood to keep him from digging."

"What does he have?" Lymond asked with interest, reaching for the scrap and trying to pull it away from Bue. He was rewarded with a low, rumbling growl. He moved his hand away prudently.

"Part of an old coat," I said, trying to get Bue out the door. "Evidently someone has wrapped dead fish in this. People are always walking along the beach and throwing things down. It's amazing what will wash up on the beach." I wrinkled my nose at the stench as I shoved Bue and the scrap out the door.

"But never a Treasure," Aunt Hen said, giggling at her own joke as I shut the door on the dog. "Perhaps we should look on the beach as well as the grounds."

"We already have," I said with a tired sigh. They ignored me.

"Then it's all set," Lymond said, smiling, "and shall we begin our search in the early afternoon?"

"Fine," I said along with the others, but then I thought about something of greater interest to me than a mythical treasure. "Oh, I can't search with you. I'm sorry."

"That's quite all right." Was I hearing things, or did Lymond sound relieved?

"Why not, dear?" Aunt Hen asked. "Are you working on George's translations again? You can put that aside for a while."

"No, Aunt Hen. Have you forgotten what I told you? I

wrote to Mr. Jerrold and asked if I could bring Mr. Denver to see him this afternoon about renting Jervyne House. If Jerrold isn't engaged, that will take up my afternoon."

There was an instant flicker of interest from Lymond, but only a flicker. He sat up quickly, then adopted a negligent pose. "Mr. Denver?" he drawled, "I don't believe I've met him."

"He's been abroad for several years. He had hoped to rent Bellerophon, but . . ." I let my words trail off, then added, "All in all, he seemed most exceptional. A gentleman with very fine manners." Let Lymond make of that what he would.

"Most gentleman have exquisite manners, and little else," Lymond said, leaning back and relaxing. "I look forward to meeting this paragon. Perhaps Amelia and I could have him over for supper." He looked at me and laughed, his eyes crinkling. "Perhaps he could give all of us a lesson in etiquette."

I was speechless, and while I was trying to form a reply, he turned to Aunt Hen and the other girls and resumed conversation about the Treasure, completely ignoring me. Outrage filled me.

My mood hadn't improved greatly by afternoon. All I had heard about was the Treasure and the Search and I was already sick of it. Mr. Jerrold had answered my note, practically in alt over the prospect of a renter, so I got ready to go there as soon as Justin Denver arrived. I paid particular care to my toilette and felt I looked quite fine when he came. Lymond had managed to drift back into our apartments on the pretext of talking to everyone about the Search, so he was sitting there when Justin knocked.

As handsome as Lymond was, Justin Denver made him look pale in comparison. Justin was dressed in pearl gray and black, which set off his blond looks to perfection. He carried a gray beaver hat, pearl gray gloves, and an ebony cane with a silver head. He quite took my breath away.

Lymond stood and I made the introductions, mentioning that Lymond and his wife were the ones who had rented Bellerophon. The other girls seemed to be as taken with Justin as I had been, except Cassie. She looked rather coldly at him, then turned her attention back to Lymond. Julia, however, stared awkwardly at Justin—I hoped this was not the beginnings of a case of calf love. Aunt Hen gave Justin a cup of tea and proceeded to quiz him about his family connections. No matter how she dug up kith and kin, she was unable to place his family or discover a single connection.

As soon as she hushed, Lymond casually asked Justin about his business. This was simply too much. I stood and suggested that it was really time we left for Jervyne House since we didn't want to keep Mr. Jerrold waiting. Lymond was undaunted—he asked Justin to dinner the following night, including all of us in his invitation. Justin smiled at him and declined, giving his uncertain status as his reason. It sounded perfectly valid to me, but Lymond lifted an eyebrow quizzically, shrugged, and suggested that perhaps later Mr. Denver could join us. Justin smiled back at him and said perhaps. It was left at that.

Aunt Hen, ever the vigilant chaperon, went with us. Once we were in Justin's carriage headed towards Jervyne House, I apologized on behalf of Lymond. Justin, to his credit, just laughed, telling us that he was accustomed to such questions. I thought it very magnanimous of him. Aunt Hen proceeded to list Lymond's virtues.

At Jervyne House, Jerrold, as I had expected, was delighted with Justin's proposal to renovate in lieu of rent. Jerrold showed us the house and grounds, and even I could see that the repairs were going to be rather extensive. Some windows were broken, there were water stains on the ceilings and wallpaper, the paint was peeling, and the gardens were a ruin. I thought Justin would refuse since the cost of the work would be more than Lymond's rent for the quarter, and then there would be the bother of carpenters and such. To my surprise — and Jerrold's — Justin insisted that the repairs and inconvenience would not be excessive and that he enjoyed overseeing renovations. I thought Jerrold was going to fall to his knees in grateful joy. Justin did stipulate, however, that he would hire the workmen himself. Jerrold offered to stay in Brighton for a while and help supervise, but Justin demurred. His privacy was paramount, he said, and he had no wish to be disturbed or distracted while he concentrated on his business. I felt that supervising workmen and the enduring clatter of repairs was hardly conducive to privacy, but I said nothing.

"Thank you for suggesting Jervyne House," Justin said, once we had concluded the negotiations and were back in his carriage. "It will be ideal."

"Yes, Roxanne," Aunt Hen said, "I was surprised." She turned to Justin. "Roxanne usually doesn't bother herself with things."

"I'm always glad to help," I said stiffly, giving her a look. "However, I had no idea it was falling in, or I would never have suggested it. You can hardly conduct business and supervise all the work that needs to be done there."

He smiled. "I probably won't finish all the repairs in the short time I'll be here, but I don't mind. Mr. Robin Norwood has been recommended to me as an excellent carpenter. Do you know him?"

Aunt Hen frowned, but I recognized the name immediately. "Yes, he worked on our house. He was very good, as I recall."

Justin nodded. "Good. I plan to invite him to stay with

me at Jervyne House and supervise the repairs. You couldn't have suggested a better place for my needs." He pulled the horses up at the crossroads. "Tell me, I thought I noticed an overgrown path leading from Jervyne House towards your house. Is there a way to walk over?"

"Oh, yes. There used to be a path there that I used as a child. I was very fond of Jerrold's grandmother and used to visit her often." I smiled at the memory. "I haven't used that path in years," I added, "and I think the bridge over the stream fell in some time back."

"Then that will be the first thing repaired," Justin said, "because I intend to be a frequent visitor to Bellerophon." He paused. "That is, if you don't mind receiving me."

I felt a blush rise to my cheeks—one of the curses of being fair. "I'm sure we'd all be delighted to have you visit," I replied, avoiding his gaze.

"Yes, we would," Aunt Hen said. "You could look—" I elbowed her.

"Look?"

"What Aunt Hen means is would you like to look at the scenery?"

He looked towards Brighton. "I'd like that very much. Do the two of you have anything planned for the rest of the afternoon?"

I forestalled Aunt Hen and answered quickly. "No, certainly nothing pressing."

"Then would you be my guide for today?" He smiled at me and I felt warm all over. "I don't know very much about Brighton, but if I'm going to be staying here, I'd like to at least know who lives where. Would you mind driving with me and pointing out places of interest?" He hesitated. "I can't think of a guide who could be more charming and informed."

Aunt Hen smiled at him. "Thank you. Yes, I am rather knowledgeable about Brighton. I'd be delighted to tell you all about it."

Justin was a willing pupil as we drove along and was interested in everything and everybody. "I've been away for so long that I'm having to learn about England all over again," he explained, as we paused in front of the house occupied by Lord and Lady Downshire. "And whose house is that?" he asked, pointing to the next house.

"Lord Grenville, I believe," I told him. In truth, I was much like the rest of the Brighton natives — the London set passed and repassed so often that I was hard put to remember who stayed where. At least Aunt Hen was right — she was knowledgeable about the city.

Justin drove us down the Steine and I pointed out the sights. There were numerous soldiers about, prompting Justin to ask about them. "The 10th Light Dragoons are stationed here," I told him, "although few of us have very much to do with the enlisted men. Or most of the officers, for that matter," I added.

Thirsty, we stopped at Aunt Hen's favorite inn, one with windows on the street. Justin asked for a private parlor, but the landlord, Mr. Moore, told us all his parlors were occupied. "Mrs. Vellory, Miss Sydney?" he asked, peering nearsightedly. "Is that you?"

Aunt Hen affirmed our identities and Mr. Moore rushed off, asking us to wait just a moment. In a trice he was back, asking if we minded sharing a parlor with a friend. "Must be Mrs. Bocock," Aunt Hen said, clearly relishing the situation of being seen in the company of a handsome stranger.

Mr. Moore escorted us to a door and opened it. Without looking, I swept in, and ran right into Lymond in the small room. He and Julia and Livvy were sitting down to a tray of cakes and a pot of tea. Lymond straightened himself up and glanced past me to Justin. "Mr. Denver, we meet again. Please come in and join us."

There was nothing for us to do except enter and sit.

Worse, we hadn't been in there three minutes when Cassie and Captain Amherst came in. Cassie was glowing again.

"Did you find what you were looking for?" Lymond asked, glancing up and trying to move over. He was almost in my lap as it was.

"A perfect match," Cassie said, drawing a length of ribbon from a packet. It was a bright red, and certainly didn't match anything Cassie owned. She scrouged down between Aunt Hen and Captain Amherst. I was now between Lymond and the wall, with Justin seated across from me. I gave Lymond a shove with my elbow to move him over, but it did no good at all. I was pinned.

"Here," Lymond said, pushing the tray of cakes at me. "I imagine you're starving," he said familiarly, "since I didn't notice you eating anything for breakfast." I felt Justin look at me sharply. "Here," he picked up a slice of fruitcake, "this looks good." He poured a cup of tea and put it in front of me.

"This really isn't necessary," I said, inhaling the aroma of the tea. Suddenly I was ravenous. "If you insist," I said.

"I do insist," Lymond said, his voice filled with laughter. He looked at Justin as I ate. "Are you sightseeing? I thought you were going to Jervyne House."

"We did, and I found it most satisfactory." Justin looked straight at Lymond as he spoke and I had the distinct impression that some kind of challenge passed between them. I looked again and saw two gentlemen chatting over tea. Either something was going on that I didn't fathom, or my imagination was running rampant. "I plan to move in next week," Justin continued.

"You're lucky to find something," Captain Amherst noted.

"Yes," Julia said, finishing her cake. "The gossip is that the Prince is coming, and there's never any room when he's in town."

"I thought Jervyne House needed repairs," Cassie said, frowning. "I went over there to do a watercolor one day, and the place looked to be in rack and ruin."

"Mr. Denver is going to see to its renovation," I said. "The place is a wreck. I knew Jerrold was stingy, but the house is beyond words."

Aunt Hen shook her head. "Why would you want to take on such a project, Mr. Denver?" I glanced at her aghast, but she was only being her usual curious self.

"Perhaps Mr. Denver enjoys living in plaster dust and Holland covers," Lymond said, his smile not reaching his eyes.

"I do," Justin said, returning smile for smile.

It was time to change the subject. "What are you doing in Brighton?"

I directed my question to Cassie, but Julia answered. "We've been busy with our search," she said. "Mr. Lymond had to stop right in the middle of the grid to come into Brighton to see someone, so all of us decided to come along with him. I needed to pick up some wools and Cassie needed ribbon."

She paused and Livvy took it up. "Yes, we hated to stop our search; it was such fun."

"Search?" Justin looked puzzled. "Have you lost something?"

I groaned. Aunt Hen then launched into a rapture about the Treasure. At the end of her story, Justin offered to help. "We wouldn't think of imposing on you," Lymond said.

I wasn't about to let Lymond decide who was going to search for my treasure, even if it was nonexistent, so I looked across at Justin. "I think it would be wonderful if you could help us. I'm convinced there is no treasure, so the sooner we get everything searched, the better. I have something of a wager with Mr. Lymond."

"Yes," said Lymond lazily, his arm familiarly pressed

against mine, "I'm looking forward to seeing you eat your bonnet. Will it be the one you're wearing, or had you planned to dispose of another? I think those silk daisies would be quite tasty."

"I don't plan to eat this bonnet or any other," I said shortly. "I do, however, plan to go up to London and find an outrageously expensive artifact. You may regret your rashness."

"I usually do, but I also enjoy it immensely." Lymond looked at me and raised one eyebrow. I wanted to throw something at him. He just chuckled, then turned to Justin. "Mr. Denver, tell me about your business."

"*Really*, Mr. Lymond," I protested.

Lymond ignored me and looked expectantly at Justin, who answered like a true gentleman. "I've been abroad for several years, so I'm just getting back into things in England. While abroad, I dealt in artifacts, antiquities, and paintings. I also specialized in overseeing restorations of several palaces and villas."

"How splendid," Lymond said. "I'm glad to know someone who is a connoisseur of paintings. I'm hard-pressed to know a Rembrandt from a Rubens. I know what I like, but most of that decidedly isn't great art." He smiled ruefully. "Perhaps you could share some of your expertise with me when we have some time."

"I'd be delighted," Justin said politely, while Captain Amherst chuckled. "Good luck," the captain drawled. "Robert's eye for painting is about the same as his ear for music."

Lymond scowled at him and changed the subject. I should have anticipated his next tack, but he caught me by surprise. "What do you think about the recent burglaries?" he asked Justin. "I read that the value of the stolen paintings is so high that the authorities are hesitant to name a figure."

"I think stealing paintings is despicable. Hanging is

too good for thieves who would steal a painting from its owner." Justin leaned across the table to make his point. "A painting is valued as much for its sentimental value as for its commercial value. Some of those paintings had been in families for generations."

"You seem to have quite a feeling for bits of canvas and paint," Lymond observed. "Personally I find most paintings replaceable."

"What did I tell you?" Captain Amherst murmured with a laugh.

Justin smiled. "True, some paintings should never have been painted at all, but there are many that enrich us immeasurably."

"Possibly." Lymond sat up straight, his elbow banging my side, and asked for the reckoning. "At least the sale of all those paintings is going to enrich the thieves immeasurably." Lymond looked at me. "Would you like to ride back to Bellerophon with us, Miss Sydney, Mrs. Vellory? It would save Mr. Denver a trip out of his way. You are staying in Brighton, aren't you, Mr. Denver?"

It was not at all the way I had planned to end my day, but as usual, Lymond seemed to have his way as we crowded into the carriage like fish in a barrel. In the carriage, Lymond was unperceptive as always, chatting away with the others about the Treasure and their plans, completely ignoring me until we arrived at Bellerophon and he handed me down from the carriage.

"I regret that leaving Mr. Denver put you in high dudgeon," he murmured as he took my arm.

"I am not in high dudgeon," I snapped at him. "I merely do not care to be in the company of someone so obviously lacking in manners."

"I'm sorry," he said, "I didn't realize that Denver was beyond the pale. I thought him rather well-mannered myself."

"I wasn't speaking of Jus — Mr. Denver," I said shortly.

He laughed right out loud, causing everyone to look at him curiously. If I thought I had insulted him, I was mistaken. "You ladies go change into something suitable for searching in the shrubbery, and we'll continue our search. It's still early."

"I don't think—" I began as everyone else agreed to go.

"Wonderful," Lymond said. "Owen and I will meet you in the back." He entered the house whistling, as Captain Amherst escorted us to our door.

"Such a wonderful man," Aunt Hen sighed as the door closed.

"Yes, wonderful," Cassie sighed, floating down the hall, her hair slipping from its pins as she took off her bonnet.

Aunt Hen smiled after her. "I do believe she mistook my meaning. I was, of course, talking about dear Robert. Don't you think he's a wonderful man, Roxanne?"

I gritted my teeth. If I told Aunt Hen what I thought of dear Robert, she would be spending the next year praying for my soul. Instead I took her arm and headed for our bedrooms. "Let's go change our clothes," I said grimly.

Chapter Five

The only thing that kept me sane over the next month was the idea of having Justin Denver next door. The rest of my world was chaos. Aunt Hen spent all her time reading to poor Amelia and commiserating with her about her health. Lymond spent his days either riding with Captain Amherst or questioning me about Jem and Willy and everyone else on the place. He was gone a great deal of the time. However, he did find time to search every day, prowling around the house and grounds and checking off grids as he completed them. He had searched close to the house and was now moving farther afield. I wished him luck. I had my own problems with Cassie. I was very afraid she was developing a *tendre* for Captain Amherst, especially since the man seemed to have become almost another boarder.

I made several comments to Lymond to the effect that, although he had mentioned Amherst might stay a night or so, he hadn't indicated the man would become semipermanent. My comments were on deaf ears. I had to own the captain was dashing, handsome, charming, well-mannered, witty, and a dozen other things. However, whenever I tried to ask about his family or background, he was distinctly noncommittal. I came to believe that there was some secret in his background.

He seemed well-born, but, as I told Cassie, he probably had a dark secret and had been disowned by his family. Cassie and Aunt Hen laughed at me, but I was determined that Cassie had to go to London, the sooner the better.

I tried to probe Lymond about Amherst's background to no avail. Every question was met with either a slightly lifted eyebrow or an outright evasion. I concluded the blot on the captain's background must be enormous. I could find no reason, though, to demand that he stay away from Bellerophon — first, he was Lymond's guest, and second, the man was utterly delightful. I doted on him myself.

Lymond was another matter. All his poking around and rattling in the shrubbery searching for the Treasure seemed to give him a great deal of satisfaction. I tried to go with him most of the time. I wasn't really sure there was a Treasure, but if he found one, I wanted to be right there. The man was simply not to be trusted. I would not have put it past him to plant a bogus bag of coins or some such just to say he had found something and then watch me eat my bonnet. He even presented me with a small saltcellar to make the daisies on my hat more palatable. I smiled through my teeth.

During this time, however, Justin's presence helped me tolerate Lymond and all his machinations. As soon as he moved in, we began visiting, walking back and forth over the bridge and short path. It was difficult to talk to him at Jervyne House, what with the uproar of renovation. He was also frequently away on business. I found myself wishing him around to talk to when he was gone.

Aunt Hen, of course, didn't approve of my talking to Justin or going to Jervyne House and insisted on accompanying me whenever she could manage to leave poor Amelia alone. When she couldn't go with me, she made sure at least two of the servants went along. It was most disconcerting, although I usually managed to leave the servants outside while I went in to advise Justin on wallpaper, paint, and draperies. Mr. Robin Norwood, the master carpenter, had moved in and had brought an entire crew of men with him. He must have also recruited some others locally, as I thought I recognized some of the men Papa had hired.

One day I mentioned to Justin that it must be expensive to quarter such a crew in Brighton, and he told me they were all staying at Jervyne House. I was surprised as I had thought only Mr. Norwood was staying there, and said as much. Justin explained it was much easier to keep everyone at Jervyne House: they were able to work longer hours that way. I thought it quite logical.

Two or three times I managed to escape Aunt Hen — rapidly becoming known to Cassie and me as The Eye of Osiris — and went to Jervyne House with only Meggie in attendance. On those afternoons, Justin and I (and Meggie — I wasn't *that* brave) drove lazily around in his carriage with no real destination. He loved to look at houses and have me tell him stories about the people in them. He was interested in everything I had to tell him and was always unfailingly courteous towards me. He was a true gentleman.

The weeks passed quickly and I was faced with a quandary — I was almost sure I was falling in love with him. This should have been a cause for general rejoicing in the household, but I kept it to myself. I just wasn't sure about his feelings for me. Justin had been entertaining, interested, and polite in the extreme. He had also been flattering and deferential, but I wasn't sure that his feelings matched mine. After giving the matter much thought, I decided not to push things — the last thing I wanted to be was a forward female, and, yes, there were other ways to persuade the man.

Surprisingly, Lymond seemed to have decided to tolerate Justin's presence, even going so far as to invite him for supper frequently, a meal which all of us took with the Lymonds. When they first arrived, they had issued invitations for several nights running and finally just asked if we would consent to take all our meals with them. It was so good for poor Amelia, Lymond explained, adding that it would also be more convenient for Cook. I started to reply, but he stopped me, telling me that, of course, our scintillating table conversation was his main object. At that point, Aunt Hen, whose table conversation never varied—the Treasure and the weather—accepted on behalf of all of us.

"Aunt Hen," I said as we discussed this in our apartments later, "we can't eat meals with them. It simply isn't done."

Julia stopped her gossip with Livvy long enough to glare at me. "Since when," she demanded, "have you ever been concerned with the proprieties, except where the rest of us were concerned?"

I ignored the first part of her comment. "It's exactly because I'm worried about you girls that I say we shouldn't do this."

"Don't be silly, Roxanne," Livvy chimed in. "Think of all the eligibles Mr. Lymond will probably invite over."

"That's what I'm thinking of," I said with a significant glance at Aunt Hen, one that had no effect at all. "You—we—simply can't be consorting with strangers."

"Bosh." It was Aunt Hen, standing up and effectively ending the conversation. "It will be good for the girls—and you, too, Roxanne—to have some practice in meeting people and carrying on polite conversations."

"Really, Aunt Hen!" I exclaimed. "I, for one, know how to carry on a polite conversation, and I'm sure the girls do, too."

"Bosh," Aunt Hen said again. "Actually, our presence

will be a favor to Robert. He likes to have us around, and its so good for poor Amelia. The dear man is *so* worried about her."

I certainly didn't think much of this explanation, especially since Lymond's concern for his dear wife seemed to have dropped off as of late. He had taken to leaving her to her own devices—or to Aunt Hen's—most of the time, going off almost every afternoon on what he termed "business," usually accompanied by his man, an old Army soldier who had arrived late, a circumstance that in itself I found strange. Wyrock just appeared one day and took up. Lymond explained that the man had been home on a family emergency.

I thought Wyrock looked too old to have any family left—judging by his wrinkles, I was sure he must have been present at the Battle of Hastings. He made an effort to make himself agreeable, and I couldn't fault him for his manners, but there was something inscrutable about him. Like Lymond, he seemed to be not quite right in his role. Wyrock was a small, wiry man, and I couldn't count the times I had seen him lurking around in various doorways. After he arrived, Lymond's jaunts away from Bellerophon increased, and the two of them were always talking in low tones to each other when they thought no one else was looking. They were always up to something or going somewhere.

I had no idea where Lymond went on these jaunts, but, with Wyrock or without, he seemed to be forever in the company of one Army man or the other. As a beginning, he had brought in three men who looked like perfect ruffians to work at the stables—I knew poor Willy must have been terrified of them. Then, as if that weren't enough, there were always Army men coming and going. Part of the time, Lymond was coming or going with them to or from heaven knew where.

Once, Justin and I had seen him skulking around

Brighton with Wyrock and another man in uniform, heading for a distinctly undesirable part of town, and Julia and I had seen him at the inn, deep in conversation with three people who looked like candidates for the gallows. The man had a sinister plan, I knew it.

I tried once again. "Aunt Hen, I'm telling you—the man has you fooled. Lymond may be worried, but it isn't about Amelia."

Aunt Hen reproved me with a mild look. "Fustian, Roxanne. He dotes on her, the dear thing. Why, just yesterday he made a trip all the way into Brighton because she fancied oranges, and we had none. He spent the whole day and was crushed because he couldn't find any good enough for her."

I suppressed a snort. Instead I tried reason. "Aunt Hen, use your head. Lymond was probably looking for an excuse to pursue one of his nefarious schemes. Oranges, indeed! Think about it, Aunt Hen—as a married couple, the Lymonds seem to have less in common than any two people I've ever seen."

"But they *love* each other," Julia said, sighing over the romance of it all.

This time I couldn't repress a snort.

At any rate, also through Lymond's insistence, all of us developed the habit of using the front of the house in almost the same way as when we had lived in it. The main difference now was that our sleeping quarters were in the back. Justin, however, still called for me at the door to our apartments in the back—a touch of delicacy on his part, I thought.

One day after Lymond had asked Livvy and me to accompany him, he stopped me in the hall. "Miss Sydney, Wyrock informs me that I won't be able to go riding this afternoon since my horse has a slight pull, so would you and the other ladies like to help us search under those few sparse bushes at the base of the rise?"

"I assure you, there's nothing there, Mr. Lymond," I said with a touch of aspersion. "Mama planted those bushes and tended to them regularly, so I know Papa would never have done anything to disturb them."

His face lit up. "Then what better place. Poetic justice or something of that nature. Hiding his valuables in the spot your mother loved."

"Mama didn't love that spot. She hated it; that's why she tried to get bushes to grow there."

He brushed me aside. "No matter. It seems a likely prospect to me. Will you join us? Cassandra has a headache, but your aunt, Julia, and Olivia will be there, and Amelia says she's well enough to go with us."

I smiled right back at him. "Oh? And do you propose to enlist the aid of all the Dragoons in Brighton? Don't forget Captain Amherst and Wyrock as well." I started to apologize for sounding waspish, but thought the better of it. Instead I stared at him.

He merely laughed at me. "Oh, Owen plans to help us, but not the Dragoons. I think they have something better to do—polish their boots or some such. Wyrock won't be there either since he must help out at the stable."

As he had mentioned Wyrock working at the stables before, I took this as a gentle hint. I was one step ahead of him. "I've already made arrangements to find someone else to help so it won't be such a burden to you and Wyrock. Jus—Mr. Denver said he'd ask if Willy knew of anyone available to help. He talked to him yesterday."

Lymond lifted an eyebrow, and I could see that this was news to him, but he didn't comment. He waited, instead, for my reply to his invitation.

Cassie's feelings for Captain Amherst had forced me to go along on several of these jaunts, but since she had a headache, there was no reason for me to go. "I believe I have other things to do this afternoon," I said stiffly, "but I appreciate you asking me."

He smiled — was it relief? — and started to walk away. "If you change your mind, we'll be at the far corner of the property towards Jervyne House."

Inside, Julia, Livvy, and Aunt Hen were in a flurry of activity, making themselves ready to go watch Lymond and Amherst beat the bushes, while I ignored them. Justin came in shortly before they left, and I had planned on a quiet afternoon of conversation with him, but then Cassie wandered in on the arm of Captain Amherst. "Are you going along?" I asked her. "I thought you were indisposed with a headache." I looked meaningfully at her, a look she ignored completely. Captain Amherst looked surprised.

Cassie laughed. "Roxanne, where did you get such a notion? I feel lucky today, so I wouldn't miss this for the world."

"There's nothing there," I said flatly. "You're wasting your time."

Cassie laughed again, a silvery sound, and Amherst looked down at her. Rather possessively, I thought. "No one's searched there at all, Roxanne. Lymond might find something."

"Oh, and where are they searching today?" Justin asked. He had the same opinion of the Treasure search that I did.

I sighed. "In the grid at the far corner next to the Jervyne boundary, under Mama's shrubbery. I know they'll ruin it." I grimaced at him. "Another wasted afternoon." I looked back at Cassie and Captain Amherst standing there. There was no question that the two of them would be well-chaperoned, but I felt I needed to be there to keep a close eye on them. "Do you mind?" I asked.

To his credit, he smiled at me and stood, holding out a hand for me. "Of course not. Who knows?" He glanced at Cassie. "Your charming sister may be right — today may be lucky." I smiled gratefully back at him and we followed Cassie and the captain out the door and across the expanse of yard to where Lymond grubbed about in the bushes.

Lymond was sweating profusely in the afternoon sunshine and had removed his coat. "There you are," he said somewhat testily to Captain Amherst. "This shrubbery is damnable."

"Robert, dear," Amelia warned. She was standing demurely at the edge of the shrubs, holding a pink parasol over her head. Aunt Hen was right beside her, holding her own parasol and giving Lymond volumes of unwanted advice. "Over a trifle more. Perhaps you need to shovel more dirt." I could see Lymond was getting somewhat tense.

"What in the world are you doing with a shovel?" I exclaimed. "Holmwood will have apoplexy if we dig holes all over his yard."

Lymond leaned on the shovel handle and glared at me. "Holmwood suggested this. He's right over there with the dog."

He gestured to the left, behind a particularly large bush. Bue came bounding out to lick my hand and let us know he was aware he was being discussed. I patted him absently and he went back under the bush, sniffing the ground and scratching. Lymond looked at him, not amused. "Perhaps we should just borrow the dog to do it. God knows I've almost broken my legs a dozen times stepping in holes that damna — creature's dug."

"Robert, dear," Amelia said again, smiling at me.

Lymond went back to his shoveling as Aunt Hen resumed her advice. I went over to chide Julia and Livvy about standing in the sun — they were going to ruin their complexions.

"Tell me, Lymond," Justin began, "why are — ?"

Bue then yelped and began digging furiously, grabbed something in his jaws, and pulled. He jerked an object from the ground — it looked rather like a lump of dirt and was about five or six inches long. He ran right up to us, object in his mouth, wagging his tail so proudly that his whole body wriggled. "Good Heavens, Roxanne," Aunt Hen exclaimed, "he's dug up a bone. Do make him put it down before he gets us dirty."

I wasn't about to get dirty myself, so I called to Holmwood. He grunted at me. From long years around Holmwood, I knew that that grunt meant he'd be there when he was good and ready. I sighed — no one else but Holmwood and me could manage Bue. "Put it down, Bue," I said sternly.

Bue swiped the front of my gown with a dirty paw and, to my surprise, dropped the object right in front of me. I reached to pat him on the head as a reward when I recognized the object — it was a decaying human hand, the fingers long and splayed. "Lymond!" I shrieked, almost at the same time that Julia and Livvy screamed.

Amelia saw what the object was and keeled over in a dead faint, almost knocking Aunt Hen into Captain Amherst, who was quite occupied with propping up a rather hysterical Cassie. "Lymond!" I yelled again, putting my handkerchief to my nose. The stench was terrible. Bue nudged the hand towards me with his nose, quite put out that I didn't seem to want it. I was hard put to keep from casting up my accounts.

Holmwood sauntered into view around the bush. "What's going on here?" he asked, looking from one to the other in a rather bewildered fashion.

Lymond finally moved, putting the shovel over the hand and then placing his foot on it to keep Bue away. Taking charge, he said, "Owen, you escort those two ladies back to the house and then come back as soon as you can. Bring someone to help. Denver, will you see to

Miss Julia and . . . and Mrs. Lymond. Holmwood, you see to Miss Olivia." He paused and glared at Bue, who was nipping at his boots, trying to get him to move his foot from the shovel. "Take the dog back with you as you go." Then he looked at me, a sardonic eyebrow raised. "I imagine you plan to walk back unassisted."

"On the contrary," I snapped, "I plan to stay right here and find out just what has happened."

"It would appear that your dog has unearthed a body — or part of one, at any rate."

"I can see that, Lymond."

He put his hand on my arm as everyone else left. "Roxanne, you'd better go back. From the looks of this hand, whatever we find isn't going to be pretty."

"What — Who do you think it is?" I asked, trying not to feel faint.

He reached down and picked up a scrap of cloth. "I think it belongs to whoever was wearing this coat."

I glanced at the scrap, then looked more closely. "That's the same stuff Bue's been carrying in for ages." I looked at Lymond, right into his eyes. "Do you suspect foul play?"

"Yes." That was all he said. "You'd better go back, Roxanne. I'll come let you know what we find." I started to walk away, and he called after me. "Send Wyrock and Willy up here as soon as you get to the house. Tell Wyrock what we've found, but don't tell Willy."

I turned to stare at him. "Why not? Why do you want Willy?"

"I have my reasons," he said cryptically. He probably would have said more, but Bue suddenly took umbrage at the shovel and Lymond's foot. I was glad Lymond was wearing boots. "Dammit, do something!" Lymond howled, over Bue's snarls. There really wasn't much anyone could do with Bue when he was in such a mood, but I did my best to restrain him until Holmwood returned. Holmwood must have anticipated a problem, since he brought a chain with him. Bue was not happy.

Justin was returning to the scene as I headed for the house, and he put his hand on my arm. "Are you all right?" he asked anxiously.

"Fine," I said, although somewhat shakily. In truth, I wasn't all right, but there was nothing I could do about it at the moment. I needed to get to the house and sit down. My knees felt strange.

Justin smiled into my eyes, a smile I could have sworn could have been termed "loving." "My poor dear," he said. "Go back and rest. What you need is a cup of strong tea. I'll come let you know what we find."

He patted my arm, and I felt positively giddy, whether from his tone or from the experience, I couldn't say. I smiled rather tremulously back at him and searched for something to say, but he was looking sharply at Lymond now and suddenly dropped his hand from my arm. Without another word, he was on his way to where Lymond and Holmwood were on their hands and knees, quite obviously discovering something else. The sweet moment was gone, and I sighed and went on to the house which, as I had known it would be, was full of weeping females. I was so occupied with fetching smelling salts and the like that I almost forgot to send for Wyrock and Willy.

Captain Amherst came in after an hour or so and told us he was going for the magistrate. He also told us he thought the body was that of the other stableboy, Jem. Willy had made the identification, and, according to the captain, promptly gone into shock.

"The poor boy is probably distraught," I said. "Bring him to the house, and I will give him some brandy."

"Robert wants to question him while he's on edge," Amherst said.

"Robert?" There was sarcasm in my voice. "Shouldn't

such things be left to the magistrate? I doubt Lymond knows what he's doing."

Amherst gave me a strange look. "Robert thinks Willy knows more than he's saying and wants to find out about it now. The boy might try to run or else gain his wits and decide to keep quiet."

"Captain Amherst, I insist that Willy be brought here. He's simply a lad from the village whom Papa tried to befriend. I will not have Lymond bullying him." Amherst started to say something, but I was firm. "I will not have him frightened."

Amherst lifted an eyebrow. "Whatever you say."

They did bring Willy to the house, but it was much later, and he appeared sullen and uncommunicative. I suspected Lymond had tried to force him to talk, and Willy had become stubborn. Papa had often remarked on that trait in the boy.

Justin offered to take him to his parents' home in the village, but Wyrock refused to leave him. As it was, they met the magistrate at the stable, and, as far as I could determine, nothing new was revealed. Jem's body was almost unrecognizable, Holmwood told me, and he was identified mostly by his clothing. "Whoever did it, bashed his face clear in," Holmwood said with relish. "Must have been nothing but a raw, bloody pulp."

I was going to question him further, but Aunt Hen fainted at that point, and we had to ply her with restoratives.

I had not seen Justin since the calamity had occurred. He had helped the men, tried to console Willy, then gone back to Jervyne House. I wished I had had his assistance in dealing with Lymond, though. The dratted man had assumed complete control of my house and grounds, ordering everyone here and there. It did not matter if he had paid his rent, I didn't care for his tone. As he and the captain had had a supper tray sent to them at the stables, I didn't see him until well into the evening, but by then, I was ready.

He came in while I was sitting at my desk. "Rox-anne — Miss Sydney, I want to keep Willy locked up where Wyrock can watch him for a few days. I've put him in the stables."

I stood, full of righteous anger. "Mr. Lymond, you can simply unlock him. I will not have the people at Bellerophon bullied. You have no right to ride roughshod over everyone and everything here."

He looked at me, surprised. "Roughshod? Good God, Miss Sydney, there's been a murder here. If the culprit isn't discovered, there might be another."

I sat back down. "That's ridiculous."

He sat across from me. He wasn't wearing his coat and didn't look at all suitable for visiting so late. His cravat was untied, his boots muddy, and there was a stubble of beard on his face. For the first time I noticed the circles of fatigue under his eyes. "Would you have thought one murder could have occurred?"

"Of course not." For an instant, I thought about telling him of my suspicions about Papa's death, but I didn't want him to laugh as everyone else had. "I just don't want Willy frightened."

"He's not being frightened. He's that already. He's terribly frightened and that leads me to think he knows something he's not telling us. I want Wyrock to watch him for his own protection." He paused and smiled at me. "I assure you he's in good hands. Wyrock will take better care of him than his own mother would."

"Willy hasn't had a mother in years," I noted, then realized I was off the subject. "Poor Jem. He and Willy were always talking about doing something spectacular to make enough money so they could go to London and live there. They were always talking about the sights they would see." I looked at Lymond. "Who might have done this?"

Lymond stood and shook his head. "I don't know, but there has to be a reason. If I could just find that, several things might unravel."

"What things?"

He smiled at me in much the same way Edward had when I told him about my suspicions of Papa's death. It was infuriating. "Nothing that should worry you," Lymond said as he exited. He left the door slightly ajar, and I slammed it shut behind him. There had to be a way to break his lease.

Chapter Six

The next day, I was still railing about Lymond to anyone who would listen. Everyone was on edge, and Cassie and I got into a row about Captain Amherst. She insisted they were only good friends but I told her any fool could see that she was infatuated with him or, more probably, his uniform. After reflection, I apologized to her — she couldn't help casting eyes at that uniform. He did look splendid in it.

By the time Justin arrived, we had all retreated to our private spots — Aunt Hen off to read aloud in hopes of soothing Amelia, Cassie to paint, Julia and Livvy to sew, and myself to my desk to work on Papa's Xenophon. It was such a relief to see my neighbor. I felt someone was finally there to help shoulder my troubles, and he seemed to understand my views completely.

"I agree that Mr. Lymond seems to have taken too much on himself," Justin agreed. "It's much better to leave such things to magistrates. After all, they're trained to oversee such things." He paused. "Has Lymond said anything about the situation?"

I shook my head. "No, and I'm really afraid he may be mistreating Willy. The boy is not clever, so Lymond and Wyrock may be able to suggest all sorts of things to him." I frowned. "Jem was the smarter of the two, and sneaky as well. I'm sure he fell in with bad companions and was involved in something he shouldn't have been, then dragged Willy in with him." I smiled at the thought that I may have solved the puzzle. "That's probably it, Justin. The whole coast is working with smugglers. It wouldn't surprise me at all if Jem had been involved in contraband rum or silks or some such."

Justin nodded. "You're probably right, and you should tell the magistrates what you think." His eyes narrowed. "Do you think Willy might tell us something?"

I thought about the things Papa had let drop about Jem and Willy, and nodded. "He might. Willy usually took Jem's lead in things, so I'm sure he knows how Jem was involved. He could probably tell us."

"Has Wyrock discovered anything from him? You did say that Wyrock was keeping a close watch on him."

"A close watch?" I could finally express my frustration. "They're practically keeping him prisoner. I wish you would see if he's all right. I never cared particularly for him, but after all, he's *my* responsibility and I won't have him mistreated."

Justin smiled at me fondly and stood. "I'll go right now and see what I can do. Don't worry about a thing." He took out his watch and glanced at it. "I need to go into Brighton, so I won't be returning, but rest assured, if I discover anything, I'll take care of it. I may even go by and question the magistrates if I have time."

After he left, I indulged myself in a cup of tea and a short nap. It was so good to have someone I could depend on, someone I could trust. I felt almost pampered.

That night at supper we all tried to be conciliatory. Lymond was absent, and Amelia told us that he had been called away on urgent business for a day or two, so she hoped we would keep her company. Aunt Hen was only too glad to volunteer the entire lot of us. As a result, we spent the evening entertaining poor Amelia, who really did seem to look paler than usual. Cassie played the pianoforte while Julia and Livvy sang, then Aunt Hen read aloud to us until bedtime.

I was just getting ready to climb into bed when Aunt Hen knocked on my door.

"My sapphires," she gasped, opening the door before I reached it. "Roxanne, I've lost one of my sapphire earrings."

This was a catastrophe of the first water. Aunt Hen's sapphires were her pride and joy. They were given to her by her husband as a wedding gift, and I had never known her to take them off.

"Aunt Hen," I said soothingly, "go back and look in your room. I'm sure you've just misplaced it. Cassie and I will help you."

She shook her head vigorously. "No, I'm sure I probably lost it when we saw . . ." she looked faint, "when we were up at that . . . that awful place." To my amazement, she began to cry. "I'll probably never see it again."

I patted her shoulder absently as I thought. "Aunt Hen, I'm positive you had your earrings on at supper." I paused and frowned as I went over the evening. "You had them on in the drawing room as well. I noticed them when you were reading."

"You could be mistaken."

I shook my head. "No, it was such a boring book—

90

for all her popularity, Mrs. Radcliffe is essentially a tedious writer — that I wasn't listening. I distinctly recall seeing your earrings while you were reading. You probably dropped it in the sofa cushions." I smiled down at her reassuringly. "There, you can go to bed and get a good night's sleep. Tomorrow we'll search the drawing room and find your sapphires."

"No." Aunt Hen began to cry again. "I can't go to sleep unless I have my sapphires. We've got to find it tonight." She looked up at me with wet eyes. "Please, Roxanne."

I grimaced. "Aunt Hen, let's wait until morning. Amelia's already gone to bed, and we don't want to wake the entire household. It would be rather like breaking into someone else's house."

She looked at me, pleading. "Roxanne, I *must* have my sapphires."

"All right," I sighed. "I'll take a candle and slip into the front of the house. It shouldn't take long to search the sofa cushions or the floor around the sofa and pianoforte."

"I'm going with you."

"Aunt Hen," I began.

"After all, they're *my* sapphires." Aunt Hen began to cry again. I handed her my handkerchief and picked up the candle by my bedside. "Let's go."

"You're a good girl, Roxanne," Aunt Hen said, patting my arm.

We tiptoed towards the drawing room, shielding the candle at the windows. I tried to watch the floor where Aunt Hen had walked back to our apartments, but when she crashed into a chair, I felt it better to try to watch where she was walking presently. It seemed to take forever to reach the drawing room. Once there, Aunt Hen almost fell over a small table. I gave her the candle and strict instructions to stand still and hold it while I searched. Running my fingers under all the cushions, I said, "It's not here, Aunt Hen. You must have dropped it under the sofa." I got to my knees and peered under the couch. "Hand me the candle."

At that moment, Bue set up a howl outside, and a second later I heard a noise overhead. It sounded distinctly like someone coming down the stairs. "Quick, Aunt Hen," I whispered, grabbing her wrist and dragging her behind the sofa with me. I blew out the candle and we huddled there together in the dark. "This may be our house, but right now the Lymonds are living here. I don't want anyone to think we're prowling. That's probably Lymond returning." We stilled ourselves. "Not a sound," I warned her.

"No one could hear us anyway," Aunt Hen whispered back. It was true — Bue was working up to full voice.

Woodbury came into the hall from his quarters, awkwardly trying to put on his coat and carry a branch of candles at the same time. At the same moment, Amelia came down the stairs. She was wearing her dressing gown, and her hair was down in clouds around her face. She was still pale but looked quite lovely. She had a single candle in a holder which she placed on the newel post.

The knocker sounded, and Woodbury opened the door. A strange gentleman came in and stopped, then looked at Amelia standing at the foot of the stairs. "Amelia," he said softly. He smiled at her in the most amazing way, a very soft, gentle smile.

Amelia looked at him in much the same way. "Francis." She held out her hands for a second, then checked herself. "That will be all, Woodbury." She didn't take her eyes from the man.

"But, madam," Woodbury began, but she interrupted him in a voice I had never heard her use. "That will be all, Woodbury."

"Yes, madam." Woodbury's training has been excellent. He turned without another word and left the two of them standing there staring at each other.

Aunt Hen jabbed me in the ribs. "What—?" she whispered.

"Ssshhh," I whispered back, afraid we would be heard, although I didn't think it mattered particularly—the two in the hall were so intent on each other that they wouldn't have heard a cannonball go by. They did seem to hear the latch fall as Woodbury closed the door down the hall behind him.

Amelia held out her arms. "Francis."

"My darling," he said, embracing her. They kissed passionately.

I was aghast. "Good God, Aunt Hen, do you see what I see?" I tried to keep my voice down to a whisper.

Aunt Hen made a few inarticulate noises. It seemed to be all she could manage.

We watched as the two kissed for what seemed a very long time. "I've missed you so, my darling," Francis said as Amelia ran her fingers through his dark hair. "I've counted the moments until I could be with you again." He kissed her then, bending her over until I was afraid she was going to catch her hair in the flame from the candle on the newel.

"You're back early, my dearest," she said to him, touching his cheek. "Robert will be surprised."

"I'll wager he will," I murmured to Aunt Hen. She didn't answer, and I decided she was incapable of speech at that point.

"I hurried as much as I could because I couldn't

bear to be away from you any longer," Francis said as he smiled tenderly at her. "You're more beautiful than ever, Amelia. Robert must be treating you well."

"He has been." A pause. "He's gone up to London until tomorrow night."

Francis smiled, a strange smile. "Then I have you all to myself for a few hours?"

"Yes, and I have you all to myself as well." Amelia stepped up onto the first step, turned, and kissed him lightly on the forehead. She looked at him in the candlelight and ran her fingers across the lines on his face. "Come up to my room. We have so much to talk about, so much catching up to do." With that, Francis picked up the candle and the two of them went up the stairs, arms wrapped around each other's waist.

Aunt Hen fell back against me. "I don't believe it," she finally managed to croak. "Help me to my bed, Roxanne." She stood and grasped the back of the sofa for support, tottering a little in the square of moonlight that came in through the window.

The moonlight glittered on something else. I reached up and unsnarled her hair. "I've found your earring, Aunt Hen," I said, pulling it from her hair and handing it to her.

Once back in our apartments, neither of us was in the mood to go to bed. Aunt Hen felt the need for a restorative, so I slipped into the kitchen and made some strong tea for both of us. Aunt Hen drank a cup and a half before she felt able to speak. "I'm shattered, Roxanne," she finally said. "Shattered."

I had been giving the scene we had witnessed some thought. "Perhaps Francis could be Amelia's long-lost brother."

Aunt Hen gave me the disgusted look that remark

called for. "Do you truly think that was *brotherly?* Really, Roxanne."

"Aunt Hen, I simply can't credit Amelia with having an affair. She seems so . . ." I groped for the right word. "So sweet."

"Appearances can be deceiving," Aunt Hen said. "And to think, we have this nest of vipers right here in our own house! George would die!"

I refrained from pointing out that Papa was already dead for fear Aunt Hen would insert a choice comment or two about it being my idea to let the house. It seemed prudent to move on. "What can we do?" I asked. "They've signed a lease for the entire quarter."

"I really don't know what to do." Aunt Hen paused, then got to the heart of the matter. "We've spent part of Lymond's rent money already. If we ask them to leave, we'll have to refund."

"I know," I said with a sigh, "so that course is definitely out." I paused, wondering how to proceed. "There's something else that's been bothering me, Aunt Hen."

"You mean about Jem, you poor girl. Of course, that's been a shock for all of us."

"Yes, that." I nodded. "I've been really disturbed at Lymond's treatment of Willy. I feel Lymond and Wyrock have been trying to keep Willy away from us for some reason. Perhaps he knows something about them." I took a breath and plunged ahead. "Now, Aunt Hen, I know you felt I was fanciful when I said Papa was pushed to his death, but this is much different. There's something that's been bothering me about the Lymonds." I paused a second, saw that Aunt Hen was about to speak, then plunged ahead to stop her. "Aunt Hen, I think Lymond is somehow involved with the stolen paintings."

"Ridiculous. Robert would never do that."

"Would you have ever thought Amelia would . . . would greet another man in that fashion?"

Aunt Hen paused while she sipped more tea. "Now, Roxanne . . ."

"Please, Aunt Hen, hear me out." She nodded and I went on. "I've been wondering about Lymond since he came here. You know he's away on business many afternoons and evenings, but he never discusses it. All of us have seen him talking to various people of dubious repute in Brighton, and then there's his treatment of Willy." I took a deep breath. "Aunt Hen, I think Lymond is the head of the ring of painting thieves and that Willy knows about it. Willy and Jem might even have helped him."

Aunt Hen frowned. "I don't know, Roxanne. How do you believe that?"

"It came to me when I was talking to Justin about Willy and Jem. I was telling him that the two boys had lived here in the village, and then mentioned the smuggling that's been going on along this coast since . . . since forever. It suddenly occurred to me then that Willy could have been in league with Lymond." I paused. "After all, Aunt Hen, Lymond was very specific that he wanted a house on the coast."

"But Robert is so very *nice*," Aunt Hen said, sipping more tea and leaning back against the sofa cushions. She was very pale. "I simply can't believe he would do anything illegal." She opened her eyes wide and looked at me in horror. "If he is the master thief, then he probably had . . . he . . . poor Jem."

I nodded. "Yes, he probably did, and if that's the case, then Willy is in grave danger."

Aunt Hen thought about this, then looked at me in triumph. "That can't be, Roxanne. He would never have called in the magistrates if he had done that. Even more to the point, he would never have led us to the spot where Jem was buried."

"The murderer returning to the scene of his crime." I waved her objection away. "There's too much evidence against him, Aunt Hen," I said. "Unfortunately, none of it is concrete, so we can't go to the magistrates with anything except suspicion." I grimaced. "I speak from personal experience when I say magistrates laugh at anything except concrete evidence."

"And we don't have that." She stirred some more sugar into her tea. "Roxanne, are you *sure?*"

"About Lymond?" I shook my head. "No, not sure, but I think there's a reasonable suspicion there. Aunt Hen, if you think about Lymond's activities, it gets worse. Think about all this business of the treasure hunt—what better way to discover what we have with an eye to stealing everything we own."

"But we don't own anything of value."

That was my stumbling block. "Perhaps Lymond thinks we do. Perhaps he's looking around here while his gang is robbing everyone in Brighton blind."

Aunt Hen and I stared at each other a moment. "We can't ask them to leave," Aunt Hen said, spooning more sugar into her cup. Her tea was practically syrup.

"No, we can't, but there may be an advantage to that. Lymond is better off right here where we can monitor his activities and make sure he doesn't walk off with the plate. We can be ready to call in the magistrates as soon as we unearth some evidence."

"Don't say 'unearth,' Roxanne." I knew Aunt Hen was thinking of Jem. She paused. "But I *like* Robert," she wailed plaintively.

"I own he can be very charming when he wants to

be," I told her. "Actually, from what I've heard, most rogues are very charming. It's the way they fool people."

Aunt Hen sighed deeply. "I still think we need to find out about Francis. There must be some reasonable explanation."

"All right, Aunt Hen, here's what we'll do. Tomorrow, we'll get up early and try to discover who this Francis is and what he's doing here. Also, Lymond will be back tomorrow night and we'll take turns watching him. From now on, he doesn't get out of our sight." I frowned as I thought. "I'd like to inform Justin of our suspicions. From some hints he's let drop, he shares my thoughts on this, and he might be able to help us." I looked at Aunt Hen to forestall her. "I also don't think we should tell Cassie, Julia, and Livvy what we think. They might let something slip."

She looked at the dregs of sugar in her cup. "True, Roxanne. Cassie might feel we were being unfair to Captain Amherst if we told her we felt he was in league with someone you suspect of being a thief. Or worse." She slammed her cup down and glared at me. "I think you're wrong, Roxanne. Robert is a fine person. I like him."

"You must own that Wyrock is a suspicious character, as are some of those other Army types Lymond insists on bringing in here."

Aunt Hen looked around. "Don't let Woodbury hear you say that!" She looked at me strangely. "What are you thinking, Roxanne?"

I started at her question, then blushed. In truth, I had been thinking about Justin. He had sent word that something unexpected had come up and he had to leave suddenly for London. It would be several days before he returned, and I wasn't going to feel secure until I knew he was nearby if I needed him. "I was merely thinking about Justin," I told Aunt Hen, looking at the pattern on my teacup.

"Hmpf. Too bad Robert's married. I don't care what you think of him, Robert's worth three of your Justin. I don't like your Mr. Denver above half."

"He's not *my* Mr. Denver, Aunt Hen, and you're not being fair to him at all. You don't really know what kind of person Justin is. He's very knowledgeable about paintings and such. I asked him if someone wanted to smuggle paintings could it be done easily—not mentioning Lymond's name of course, but Justin knew who was being discussed. He said it could be done if the right network was used."

"Hmpf," Aunt Hen said again. "I tell you, Roxanne, I know when fish smells, and I think it does here. The man's *too* perfect."

When Aunt Hen was in one of those moods, there was no arguing with her. If she thought a rogue like Lymond was of more quality than Justin Denver, it was of no consequence to me. I would simply let events show her who was the better man. I let the subject drop and stood up. "We'd better get to sleep, Aunt Hen. Remember we want to get up early and see what we can discover about this Francis."

Aunt Hen involuntarily rolled her eyes toward the ceiling. "I wonder what's going on up there."

I felt myself blush. "It really doesn't bear thinking on," I said hastily. "Come on, let's go to bed."

It was after one o'clock in the morning before I managed to get her to bed. I tried to be quiet so we wouldn't wake Cassie, but we woke her anyway. I explained about the earring, but left out Francis. The less said the better, I thought.

There was still little sleep for me. Every sound

brought Aunt Hen running to my door, and I was thoroughly fagged by the time she went to sleep. Although she firmly protested Lymond's innocence, she had decided that the painting thieves were most probably in our neighborhood. Over my protests, she barricaded every door with chairs. I wound up tripping over one and sprawling all over the floor on my way to my bedroom. I fell asleep to the sounds of Bue scratching at my door and whining.

Chapter Seven

I had good intentions, but because of the late hour I went to sleep, it was after eight before I woke up. I leaped out of bed and went in to rouse Aunt Hen. "There's no getting her up this morning," Cassie said, dragging herself out of bed, "and no wonder. If she wasn't keeping you up, she was trying to talk to me. I had a terrible night."

"Is Aunt Hen ill?" Livvy asked.

"No," I said shortly. "Aunt Hen couldn't sleep last night. She'll get up after a while." I linked my arm in Livvy's and propelled her away from Aunt Hen's door. "Why don't you go visiting in town today?" I asked. "Take Julia with you. I've got some of Lymond's rent money you can use to buy some ribbons."

"The new hat I've wanted?" Livvy asked with hope.

I stared at her in amazement and moved my arm. "Good Heavens, Livvy!" I went to the desk drawer and drew out some money. "Here—have a good time."

She dashed out of the room, money in hand, before I could change my mind. I dashed myself, straight into the breakfast room, only to discover no one there. I asked if Amelia had been down and was told she had requested a tray be sent up to her chamber. Cook was particularly pleased that Amelia had wanted such a huge breakfast.

This suggested to me that Francis, whoever he was, was still in the house. For the better part of half an hour, I placed myself where I could see the stairs, but no one came down. I had halfway decided to go upstairs myself when Aunt Hen came tottering in for breakfast. I gave her some strong tea in hopes it would render her articulate, then told her that my wait had been fruitless. However, I had a plan.

Amelia came tripping down the steps shortly—alone—and I wasted no time in putting my plan into effect. I told Amelia that Aunt Hen had lost her sapphire earring and was extremely distressed. After all, it was true—I just didn't say when. I asked Amelia to help us search. She fluttered her small hands and smiled sweetly at Aunt Hen. I looked at her sharply—what was different about her this morning? She looked the same, but there was some indefinable something—she seemed more content, more settled, more *glowing*. I certainly didn't plan to ask why.

As soon as Amelia and Aunt Hen rounded the corner out of sight, I dashed up the stairs. I paused outside my old room, now Amelia's, and listened. There was no sound, and I very carefully turned the knob. The door opened; I dodged the creaky board in the floor and went in, closing the door behind me in case anyone came by. There was no one there.

Amelia's maid had already been in and cleaned because the bed was made and Amelia's toilette articles placed neatly on the dressing table. The room was immaculate—and empty. Francis, or some sign of him, had to be somewhere.

Francis proved as elusive as the Treasure. There was not a trace of him—no dirt on the floor, no coat in the clothespress, no extra water glass. If Aunt Hen hadn't seen him too, I would have begun to doubt my sanity.

"If I were Francis, where would I hide?" I asked myself as I stood in the middle of the room and looked around. I snapped my fingers as I thought of a possibility: Lymond's room. I couldn't imagine why I hadn't thought of it before. I slipped from my — Amelia's — room and dashed down the hall, looking around to make sure I wasn't seen. Then I turned the knob on Lymond's room.

I couldn't believe it — it was locked. Papa had never locked that room in all the years we had lived here. I didn't even know the door had a lock. I thought a moment, then did the only thing possible. It was time for reinforcements: I went in search of Woodbury.

I found him polishing silver in the dining room. "Woodbury, do you recall the gentleman who arrived late last night?"

Woodbury looked at me from under bushy eyebrows. "I wasn't aware you were up at that time, Miss Sydney."

I improvised. "Bue woke me." I hurried on — I've never been any good at improvising. "Woodbury, this is important. What happened to the gentleman? Francis What's-his-name?"

"I'm afraid I don't know the gentleman's name, Miss Sydney." Woodbury looked at me quizzically and I knew he wanted to ask me how I knew Francis's name. I counted on Woodbury being too particular to ask, and I was right. "Whoever the gentleman is," Woodbury finally said, frowning into the silver, "he doesn't seem to be in the house, although his horse is still in the stables. Or was, when I sent an early breakfast out to Wyrock and Willy."

"What?" I yelped. I had forgotten there would be a horse. "Does anyone at the stables know who he is?"

"I didn't ask." There was a pause. "It was very early and I sent John with breakfast. He's singularly unobservant, but I got the impression Wyrock knew the horse."

"I'll be right back," I yelled to Woodbury over my shoulder as I dashed out the door. I almost collided with Aunt Hen and Amelia who were down on hands and knees in the hall.

"We still haven't found anything," Amelia said.

"What?" I asked before I remembered their search for the earring I had in my pocket. "Oh, neither have I." I ran out the front door before I had to say anything else.

The stables were extraordinarily quiet. I lifted my skirts and walked in, the dust motes dancing in a shaft of sunlight from the doorway. I couldn't see a thing in the gloom inside. I walked down the large empty central hall. "Wyrock?" I called. There was no answer. "Wyrock? Are you here?" There was nothing. I looked around and didn't see a horse I didn't recognize. In disgust, I walked back to the house.

"There was no extra horse there," I reported irritably to Woodbury. "In fact, Wyrock wasn't even there. What do you suppose he's done with Willy?"

Woodbury turned and dropped some silver with a clang. His eyes were wide. "Not there?"

"That's what I said, Woodbury," I said with some irritation. "I looked all around, and even called out his name, but there was no one there. Not even some of those Army men of Lymond's who are always keeping Wyrock company."

Woodbury picked up the dropped silver and went

out without a word. I followed right on his heels. At the stables, he stood in the doorway, listening to the horses breathe and watching the dust motes dancing. There was nothing else. "See?" I said peevishly. I don't know why men are always doubting what women tell them.

"Well, I'll be," Woodbury said. "I didn't hear anyone leave." There was a shuffling sound in an empty stall to our left. Woodbury and I both stared at the stall door. Then there was a low moan, and both of us dashed for the door, opening the latch and running in. Wyrock was on the floor, struggling to get up. His head was bleeding on the back. He pushed himself up on his hands, then fell back down onto the floor. Woodbury and I got on either side of him and helped him to a sitting position. His head and face were covered in blood. "They hit me from behind," he gasped. "Where's the boy?"

"Boy? Do you mean Willy?" I looked around. "Willy?" I called. "Are you here?"

"Gone," Wyrock gasped. "They've got him."

"Who has someone?" I asked. "Did the magistrate come for Willy? Wyrock, whatever are you talking about?" Wyrock rolled his eyes at me and sagged. He had lapsed into unconsciousness again. "Woodbury, I'll stay with him. You go get help. We've got to get him into the house. Send someone for the doctor." This time Woodbury didn't hesitate. He ran out the door. It was the first time I'd ever seen Woodbury in a hurry.

We got Wyrock into the house, revived him, and tried to quiz him about what had happened. Other than telling us he had been hit hard from behind, he said nothing. He did ask again where Willy was. Neither Woodbury nor I had seen him. I sent men out to search the stables and grounds, but Willy was not there.

When I passed this information on to Wyrock, his reaction was much different than I had expected. I had thought he would be irritated, perhaps annoyed, but he seemed much more than that. "He'll have my head for sure," he muttered.

"Who? Mr. Lymond?" I asked, mopping again at his head. The doctor was taking his time.

Wyrock nodded groggily and winced. "He told me that whatever I did, I wasn't to let him out of my sight."

"Well," I told him, trying to be gentle as I applied a compress, "you certainly couldn't help being hit on the head. It was probably one of those ruffians Willy ran with before Papa hired him. They were nothing but a gang of gallows bait." Wyrock murmured assent, and I went on. "Tell me, Wyrock, why did Mr. Lymond want you to watch Willy so closely? Does he suspect something?"

Wyrock looked askance at me. He wasn't as groggy as I had thought. "No reason," he muttered, and that was all I got out of him even though I questioned him until the doctor arrived.

Dr. Matthews bound up his head and gave us some drops for the pain. Wyrock had a nasty cut where he'd been hit, but the doctor didn't think he'd have any damage except a crashing headache temporarily. We told Aunt Hen and Amelia that he'd fallen from the hayloft.

After Dr. Matthews left, I went to see Woodbury. He was in the butler's pantry, downing a rather stiff whiskey. He tried to hide the glass, but I told him to go ahead. "You need that, Woodbury," I said as I closed the door behind me. "Woodbury," I said, searching for just the right words. It was a time for delicacy. "I'm convinced that strange things are happening around here."

"Strange things have always happened here," Woodbury said. I frowned at him, but let that pass.

"At any rate, Woodbury, I need your help." I thought this would get him; it had always worked when I was a child. Woodbury was a soft touch. "I may as well be frank: I have reason to believe that Mr. Lymond is associated with the thieves who've been stealing paintings around the country. I think some of his accomplices are Wyrock and the others who've been coming here at all hours."

Woodbury had given me his full attention. He drew himself up to his full height. "Thieves? In this house?"

I realized I had made a slight error—he was ready to do battle immediately. "No," I said hastily, "not in the house, of course, although I do think Mrs. Lymond isn't what she appears to be. This nocturnal visit by an unknown man only confirms my suspicions."

"A den of thieves!" Woodbury exclaimed, making fists.

I tried to soothe him. "Mrs. Lymond may be perfectly innocent in this, Woodbury. She may have a perfectly reasonable explanation for her visitor." If she had, I wanted to hear it, but now was no time to quibble. I continued, "It's most important that we do nothing to alert Lymond, Wyrock, and the others. We must act normally but watch each of them carefully." I paused to gauge his reaction—he didn't seem completely convinced. "Don't you think it strange, Woodbury, that the incidents of stolen paintings around Brighton has increased since the Lymonds moved in here?"

"It could be a coincidence."

I nodded. "Yes, but what about Jem?" I waited for this to have its effect. "I think Willy probably ran from them to save himself." I didn't know that for sure, but I was worried about him. "After all, they sequestered him from us."

"He's a coward and a bad 'un. We're well rid of him," Woodbury scowled. "I'm not worried about him—sly rogues like Willy always land on their feet. He's probably home drinking." He paused and frowned in thought. "Mr. Lymond seems all right to me."

I sighed. It was time to use the ultimate call on Woodbury. "We owe it to England," I said. Woodbury was very proud of being a veteran.

He drew himself up and looked me in the eyes. "You may count on me, Miss Sydney."

"Excellent, Woodbury. Our first task is to find out something about this Francis, then we'll move on to Willy's disappearance." I tried to pace the floor as I often do when I'm thinking, but the pantry was too small. I almost knocked over Woodbury's bottle. "As for Francis: who is he and why was he here so late? Also, why were he and Mrs. Lymond acting so, um, familiar?"

Woodbury looked longingly at the bottle. I nodded and he poured himself another as I continued. "I went upstairs to search, and my room—that is, Mrs. Lymond's—room is empty. I tried to get into Mr. Lymond's room, but it was locked."

Woodbury almost dropped his glass as he looked at me in amazement. "Locked!"

"That's right, Woodbury. I didn't even know there was a lock on that door, so I need to get the key from you."

He carefully set his glass down. "I do not have a key. There is no lock on that door. Your father didn't like locks."

"Of course there's a lock, Woodbury. I tried that door myself and know it was locked." I thought of Aunt Hen and her chairs. "Woodbury, perhaps it's been barricaded from the inside." I paused. "That must be it. Let's go." I dashed from the pantry and up the stairs, Woodbury right behind me.

At the top, in front of Lymond's door, we both stood for a moment, then put our shoulders to the door. "Now," I whispered, and we both pushed at the same time. The door flew open and both of us fell in, sprawling all over the floor. Woodbury was the first to recover. He stood and dusted himself off. "It would appear, Miss Sydney, that the door was not locked."

I stood, feeling bruised all over. "I *know* it was either locked or barricaded when I tried it." I went over and looked at the door. There was a handle but no lock. I got down on my hands and knees.

"Miss Sydney, really!" Woodbury said, appalled.

"Hush, Woodbury. I'm looking for evidence, and right here it is. Look for yourself." I pointed on the floor to two long scratches in the wood that led from the door to the legs of dresser behind it. "That's what kept the door from opening. Evidently I frightened whoever was in here and now he's gone."

"But where?"

I sighed and shook my head. "Something strange is going on here, Woodbury." I sat up on my knees. "Woodbury, we need to search Lymond's room, and what better time than when he's gone. You stand watch in the hall and kick the door with your foot if someone comes by. And, Woodbury," I added, "try not to look as if you're stealing someone's sheep."

I had just gotten well into my search of Lymond's room, trying to be very careful, when there was a vigorous kick at the door, followed by a second and a third. I was opening the door when Woodbury pushed it from the other side, almost taking off my nose. "Mr. Lymond," he whispered, pulling on my arm. He rolled his eyes towards the stairs. "Now!"

I paused and listened. I could hear Lymond's voice floating up to us. He was asking Mrs. Beckford where Amelia was. I stumbled out of the room, pulling the door behind me just as Lymond came into view. He glanced from Woodbury to me and back again. "What's wrong?" he asked, a note of alarm in his voice.

"Wrong?" I laughed. "Whatever could be wrong?" I shifted to the attack. "Aren't you back early? I thought Amelia wasn't expecting you to return until tonight."

"I finished up early." Lymond paused in front of us. He looked unbelievably rumpled and tired, and had black circles under his eyes. He obviously had neither slept nor changed clothes since he'd been gone.

"Oh." I elbowed Woodbury to keep him from fidgeting and moved from the door so Lymond could enter. He gave us a strange look, brushed by us, and closed the door behind him.

Woodbury grabbed the newel post for support. "I wasn't born for a life of intrigue," he muttered as I hurried him down the steps in front of me. "After the Army, all I ever wanted was a quiet life in the country, and now look at me."

"You're doing beautifully, Woodbury." I pushed him towards the dining room and went back to our apartments so I could think about this new development. Clearly Lymond had been up all of at least one night and quite possibly more. Stealing paintings some-where? I needed to discover if a house nearby had been burgled during the past night or two. I went to my desk and wrote the facts down in a letter, just in case something happened to me. I sealed it and ad-dressed it to Justin. Surely he would avenge me if harm befell. I only wished he were here to advise me now.

Woodbury came in to ask who was going to tell Ly-mond about Wyrock's injury and Willy's disappear-ance. "He probably already knows," I muttered. "He's probably had a fine hand in it somewhere."

"He wouldn't harm Wyrock," Woodbury said. "Also, Miss Sydney, you asked about the gentleman's horse." He paused, making sure I had his undivided atten-tion.

"Yes, Woodbury," I prompted.

"The other stable hands didn't know anything about the visitor, other than the fact that his horse was a fine piece of horseflesh. It was probably quite valuable."

I sighed. It wasn't much, but now at least we knew Francis was affluent, or else stole horses from the af-fluent. Woodbury nodded agreement before he asked me again who was going to tell Lymond about Wyrock and Willy. I sighed again. "I suppose I'll have to do it. Everyone else thinks Wyrock fell from the hayloft, and Wyrock's in no condition to talk to any-one. Did he take his drops?"

Woodbury nodded. "Sleeping like a baby, he is."

I went up to Lymond's room and knocked gently. There was no answer. I knocked again, harder this time, but there was still no answer. Opening the door slightly, I looked in. Lymond was standing in the mid-dle of the room, putting on his shirt. "I'm getting there," he said wearily. "What is it?" He pulled his shirt together and ran his fingers through his hair, rumpling it.

I started to back up, but decided that this time was as bad as any other. "Would you like for me to wait for you downstairs?" I asked.

"No," he said shortly. "I assume this is important, or you wouldn't be here. Out with it."

I looked around the bedroom, trying to avoid looking at Lymond standing there half-undressed. "Right here?"

"Of course, right here," he snapped. "Or would you rather I put on evening clothes and a wig?" He reached for his coat and put it on. "There, is that better?"

"There's no need to be obnoxious, Mr. Lymond," I said loftily. "I merely came to tell you that Wyrock has been injured."

He dropped his pose and took a step towards me. "What happened? Is he all right?" he asked, truly concerned.

I took a step backwards and ran into the door. Quickly I told him what had happened in his absence, omitting, of course, any reference to Francis. I had to stop when I told him about Willy's disappearance, enduring a full minute of rather fluent profanity followed by an insincere apology.

"I'm sorry if this disturbs you," I said stiffly, looking at a point over his shoulder. It was very distracting to be talking to a man with his shirt only half on, even if he did have on his coat. "I assure you that Dr. Matthews says Wyrock won't have any ill effects other than a terrible headache for a few days."

"You've seen no trace of Willy?"

I shook my head. "He's probably joined some of his friends in the village. He could be anywhere."

Lymond let his breath out so harshly that it sounded almost like a whistle, but made no comment. "Thank you for telling me, Miss Sydney," he said, escorting me from the room. "I'm sorry this has upset your quiet life."

He had me out in the hall by then, and before I could answer, he shut the door and I heard him knocking around inside. After standing in the hall for a moment, thoroughly miffed, I went downstairs.

At the foot of the stairs, I heard excited voices in the drawing room. Amelia, Julia, Livvy, and Aunt Hen were listening raptly to Mrs. Bocock tell them all the news in Brighton. "That's twice," she was saying. "Once in London at his town house, and once here."

Amelia turned to me as I walked into the room. "Oh, Roxanne, you'll never believe the news — there's been more burglaries!"

"The earl of Debenham," Livvy said, wide-eyed.

"Debenham? Good heavens, I didn't think anyone would have the nerve. After his paintings in London were stolen, I heard he had sworn to run the thieves to the ground." I sat where I could see both Mrs. Bocock and the door. I wanted to see if Lymond left.

Mrs. Bocock was in alt. "Yes, yes, that's all true." She nodded her head vigorously. "The *on-dit* is that the thieves nicked him here in Brighton just to show him threats were meaningless."

"What effrontery!" Amelia exclaimed, fluttering her small hands.

"Yes," Aunt Hen agreed. "It would take a man out of Bedlam to enter a house alone and take paintings."

"Oh, whoever it was wasn't alone," Mrs. Bocock said, full of news. "Evidently there are several of them, and they know exactly what they're going after. That's the puzzle — how do they know what paintings are in the houses and know exactly where the paintings are located?"

"Precognition," I said with a sarcasm that was wasted on the others.

"Possibly," Mrs. Bocock said, giving it consideration. "At any rate, even when paintings are moved to other rooms or other houses, the thieves seem to know exactly where they are."

I thought about this while everyone else exclaimed about Mrs. Bocock's knowledge. "Just what is the modus operandi," I asked.

Mrs. Bocock sipped her tea and looked around at her audience. She was enjoying herself immensely. "Evidently there are several thieves and they fan out room to room, as I said, knowing exactly what they want. They take only the most valuable of the paintings, and rather than take frame and all, they cut the painting from the frame."

I raised an eyebrow. "Wouldn't that damage the paintings so they couldn't be sold again?"

"Not from what I've heard."

"And what is that?" The voice came from the hall, followed by Lymond. He looked as bad as he had before, except he was fully and carefully dressed now, in a clean shirt, cravat, and coat. He walked in, nodded at Amelia, poured himself a cup of tea, and sat down across from Mrs. Bocock. "What have you heard?"

She was only too glad to go over the story again, ending with the information that the paintings had been cut from their frames.

"I believe, Miss Sydney," Lymond looked at me, "that you had a question about this. I understand this method of removal can be done by someone who knows what he's doing. The trick is to cut the painting without damaging it since it has to be restretched and reframed. It will be slightly smaller, of course, but a thousand times easier to transport." Lymond's manner was casual—entirely too casual, I thought. He flicked his eyes at me. "And I suppose you have a good idea as to the identity of the culprit."

"I have my suspicions," I said cryptically. Let him make of it what he would.

"Don't we all," he said smoothly, putting down his teacup. "At any rate, some master thief is amassing a fortune in paintings. I wonder how he's going to manage to sell that many and to whom. He may be thinking of keeping the cream of the crop for himself."

I looked at him carefully. "It would probably be more practical to think of where he might be storing them." I was hoping for a change in Lymond's expression, but there was none. Instead Livvy spoke, and everone looked at her. "But couldn't paintings removed from their frames be stored in a small space?" She looked at Amelia. "Didn't you tell me you always did that when you moved because it was the easiest way to take them along?"

Amelia glanced quickly at Lymond and seemed to go even paler than usual. She smiled, a rather artificial smile, and poured another cup of tea for Lymond. "I really don't do anything with them. Robert takes care of all those things," she said. "He's very good with paintings and objects of art."

"Yes, he seems to know a great deal about it," I said, trying to keep my voice neutral. I glanced at Mrs. Bocock. "Do the magistrates have any idea who's doing this?"

"No, dear, but I suppose it's the same gang of rogues who've stolen paintings from every other house in the vicinity. It's strange that your house hasn't been bothered."

I gave Lymond a significant glance. "We have very few paintings in the house and nothing of value," I said hastily.

"Besides," Julia chimed in, much to my relief, "we're here all the time. It seems that most of the thievery has occurred when the houses were empty."

"True." Lymond regarded me with sharp eyes as he spoke. "It almost seems that the thieves, or some of them anyway, must live in Brighton because they seem to know when these houses are empty."

Aunt Hen gasped at the thought. "Thieves amongst us! It's enough to give one the vapors!"

She seemed to be in the throes of apoplexy, rolling her eyes at me. She wasn't at all good at subterfuge. Thankfully Mrs. Bocock didn't notice—she had other news. "Henrietta, did I tell you it's certain that the Prince Regent is planning a trip to Brighton?"

There were noises all around. Lymond stood. "I'll leave you ladies to discuss the impending visit. Thank you for the tea and conversation." He paused and, I thought, looked rather sharply at Amelia before he left. I searched for a reason to leave, but it took several minutes before I could decently excuse myself. Once outside the room, I dashed for the door, but all I saw was dust as Lymond rode away towards Brighton.

I should have expected as much.

Chapter Eight

Lymond didn't join us for supper. Amelia said he had spent the evening with Wyrock and was so exhausted that he'd gone to bed early. It sounded reasonable, and I *had* heard him go up the stairs toward his room.

The table conversation that night was desultory at best, and we soon drifted off to our own rooms. Bue was asleep by my desk, and I tried to get him out, but he was lost in dog dreams. I finally gave up and just left him there.

About midnight, I was awakened by Bue walking around whining. I got up to let him out and heard a familiar noise — the creaking of the fourth step from the top of the back stairs. Someone was either leaving or coming in, and very stealthily at that. I tried to hush Bue by shoving him into my bedroom and shutting the door. He didn't like it, but at least I could hear. Someone was leaving, very carefully. Hiding behind the door, I strained to see. There was enough moonlight through the window for me to recognize Lymond. He reached the bottom of the stairs and put on a dark cloak that hid him. Then he quietly opened the door and slipped out soundlessly.

I dashed into my room and grabbed my dress, dropping or fumbling with everything it seemed. I collided with Aunt Hen as I ran out my chamber door. "Quick, Aunt Hen," I said, trying to dodge Bue, "I've got to get my heavy shoes and my cloak so I can follow Lymond. He's gone out and this may be our chance to see what's going on."

"You can't go out there alone," Aunt Hen protested. "There are clouds coming and going tonight, and you won't be able to see." She moved aside as I grabbed my shoes. "Ladies don't go strolling out at midnight. There are all sorts of things out there!"

"I'm going, Aunt Hen. Don't try to stop me."

"Roxanne, it's dark as pitch out there." She peered through the window. "You won't be able to see anything at all."

"Yes, I will. Aunt Hen, I'd wager that after all that talk about paintings this afternoon, Lymond is going to lead me right to his hiding place." I finished putting on my heavy shoes and snatched up my dark woolen cloak. "This is the opportunity I've been waiting for."

"At least take Bucephalus with you," Aunt Hen pleaded. "I don't want you wandering around alone. What would George think?"

I glanced down at Bue, drooling noisily on the carpet. "I'd better go alone, Aunt Hen. Bue doesn't care much for Lymond, so I'm sure he'd start barking the moment he clapped eyes on the man." I glanced out the window as the moon came from behind a cloud. "He's going toward the mausoleum, so I'd better hurry." I paused at the door. "Aunt Hen, if anything happens to me, promise me you'll tell Justin about this." I closed the door quickly as she gasped.

The clouds were rolling in thicker from the Channel, and Aunt Hen had been right — when the moon was covered, it was like walking through pitch. I'm ordinarily not missish, but it was not the kind of night to be out. There were wisps of fog coming in, whirling around in

118

front of me like ghosts. The thought of going to the mausoleum in this dark gave me goose flesh. "Oh, Justin," I thought to myself, "I truly wish you were here!"

By the time I reached the tomb, the light had improved as the heavy clouds rolled inland. However, that light was fitful, coming and going as the moon was half-hidden by trailing clouds. It flickered light on the white stone of the mausoleum and made strange shadows as the wind blew the pieces of clouds across the moon's face. The steady wind blowing the clouds inland was also pushing the fog in from the Channel. I got just a glimpse of Lymond as a gust of wind came in, making a low moaning sound as it blew between the columns of the mausoleum. I had to stifle an urge to yell for Lymond to come rescue me. Bucephalus would have been more than welcome.

Looking all around, I couldn't see Lymond anywhere. The mausoleum was located on a little hill, facing out over the Channel. It was placed well back from the ocean, because Papa was afraid the sea would eventually erode the bank of the small cliff there and reach the mausoleum. The cliff wasn't very tall, twenty-five feet or so at its highest point, and was limestone. The cliff sloped on one end and was only about seven or eight feet high at that point. Right where it evened out, there was a narrow path leading down to the sea.

I started for the mausoleum, but remembered that, in my haste, I hadn't even thought of a key. It was just as well — between the white wisps of fog and the moan of the wind, I managed to conjure up every ghost story I had ever heard. I knew I needed to walk carefully around the mausoleum to try to see if Lymond was there, but I stopped. For now I would check the path along the edge of the sea. No matter that it was the farthest point away from the mausoleum and its moaning columns — it was just as dangerous.

Luckily for me the clouds parted for a few seconds as I walked towards the edge of the cliff. In that brief space, I saw Lymond walking along the strand. He didn't seem to be going anyplace. He was walking along the edge of the water, stopping every now and then to look out over the sea. He was hunched over, as though he had his hands in his pockets, and his head was bent low against the wind when he walked. As I crouched and watched him, he walked for three or four hundred feet up the strand, then retraced his steps. The only reasons I could give for such strange behavior was that he was either waiting for someone or pacing off distances. Neither boded well.

After a short while, he walked back towards the cliff and stood there for a moment. Then he moved back some more, out of my sight. I fell to my knees and crawled up to the edge of the cliff where I could peer over. I stuck my head over the edge and discovered to my horror that I was right above him, looking down on the top of his head. I was afraid to move. If I did, I would probably dislodge something and give my presence away. Also, I wondered, how was I going to escape once Lymond decided to come back up the path? There was no place to hide except for some large rocks farther back, close to the mausoleum. I scarcely dared to breathe, and there was one other problem — I was getting horribly cold and damp. What if I sneezed?

Lymond stood and stared out to sea for what seemed like an eternity to me, although it was probably only a few minutes. He said something to himself that I couldn't hear, and moved away from the highest part of the cliff, down towards the path up the low end of the cliff. I looked around wildly, wondering how and where to hide. There was no place at all. I could, I thought, brazen it out. I could simply stand up and swear by all the gods that I had been out for a stroll. Lymond would believe that for all of the thirty seconds it would take me to say it.

I peered over the edge again to find out how much time I had. Lymond had moved out of my sight again. I looked up and down the beach, but there was no sign of him. He was either right against the cliff, or there was some kind of small cave down there. I thought about it and decided I had to see what he was doing. Carefully I wiggled my way down towards the path, not making any sound. I wondered briefly what the wet grass was doing to the front of my dress, but put that thought out of my mind. I had greater things to worry about. I stopped where the cliff was about eight or nine feet high and shimmied my way farther over the edge until most of my upper body was suspended over open space. I hung on to two clumps of grass to keep from falling.

Lymond wasn't to be seen anywhere—at least not until he stood up. His head was about two feet directly below mine. He was looking out to sea again, tossing pebbles from one hand to the other, evidently just watching the waves come and go.

It occurred to me that if Lymond looked straight up, he would be staring into my face. I held onto the grass tightly and tried to edge myself back silently. A divot, however, came off in my hand, and pebbles fell, approximating to my ears the noise of the battle of Waterloo.

"What the . . ." Lymond exclaimed, whirling around and staring straight into my face as it hovered over him. Unfortunately the grass I was holding with my other hand chose that moment to give way, as did the particular piece of limestone on which I was teetering. With a crash, I fell right onto Lymond and we rolled down the shingle and into the water, a tangle of arms and legs. Lymond, I am sorry to say, was cursing fluently the whole time.

We finally stopped rolling when we hit a big rock in

the water. I was lying full-length on top of him. After I caught my breath, I looked down, halfway afraid to see his expression. I couldn't see a thing. Lymond was submerged and was fighting to get his face out of the water. I sat up and he came up sputtering and choking. "What the hell — !"

"Really, Mr. Lymond," I said, pushing my sodden hair from my eyes. "Do control yourself."

"Control myself?" he hissed. "Control myself?" I noticed he was trembling all over. "I've just been splattered into the sand, then halfway drowned, and you want me to *control myself?*"

I was hurt. "There's no need to refer to 'splattering,' Lymond. I may not be petite, but I'd never *splatter* anyone I fell on. Good heavens, my grammar!"

A moment of silence ensued, then Lymond began laughing. He laughed right out loud until I finally saw the humor in our situation and giggled along with him. "I must say, Miss Sydney," he said as he drew out his dripping handkerchief and began trying to wipe excess seawater from his face, "that life around you is never dull."

"On the contrary," I said. "Out here in the country, I lead a very boring life. Most of the excitement happens in town."

"I'd be tempted to argue that point." He shook water from his hair, reminding me rather of a shaggy dog. "I hesitate to ask, but whatever are you doing out here at this time of night?" He stood and extended a hand to pull me to my feet.

I couldn't think of a thing better than my original excuse, so I improvised. "I couldn't sleep, so I decided to come out for a stroll."

He looked at me incredulously, then chuckled softly. "I'm not even going to question that, Miss Sydney. Whatever your reason, I accept it. My system can't stand another shock tonight. I suppose we'd better return home before we both freeze."

He glanced around — looking for someone, perhaps, I wondered — then took my arm, and we started back up the shingle. "And just what were you doing out here at this time of night, Mr. Lymond?"

He stiffened and shoved me against the cliff wall. "Ssshhh." He clapped his hand over my mouth, and I couldn't breathe. Terrified, I began to struggle and try to get away. Was the man going to murder me after all? "Dammit, Roxanne, be quiet! I hear something," he hissed in my ear, pushing me farther against the cliff and keeping a firm grip on my mouth.

In just a second, I heard something as well. I stopped struggling and sagged against him. When I relaxed, he lightened his grip a trifle. "If I let you loose, will you be quiet?" he whispered. "We need to see who or what else is out here with us."

I nodded.

"No screaming? No yelling for help? No mad dash across the grass?"

Again I shook my head and made an inarticulate sound.

"All right," Lymond said, "but if you give us away, both of us may be in trouble."

"I won't," I said stiffly, my lips almost numb. "Pray give me some credit for not being stupid, Mr. Lymond."

He gave me an inscrutable look. "Stay here."

I took umbrage at his attitude. "I certainly will not," I hissed back at him in a whisper. "I'm going with you."

He gave me a disgusted look, then grimaced in defeat. "There's no stopping you, is there? Come on then, but just don't get in my way. And, Roxanne, for God's sake, *be quiet.*"

"I'm always quiet."

He mumbled something I chose not to hear and

walked away. Walking slightly in front of me, he carefully picked his way up the path at the edge of the cliff. I followed him closely, moving up beside him when we finally got to the place where we could see above the edge of the grass. The clouds were still coming and going, but in the intermittent light, I could barely see two men walking toward the mausoleum. They were dressed in dark clothes, but evidently didn't think anyone was around as they were talking aloud to each other. In front of the mausoleum they paused, looked around, and went in behind the columns. In just a second, I heard the creak of the heavy door.

"They're going in!" I gasped. "How can they do that?"

"They have a key." Lymond was snappish. "I think they unlocked the door, turned the knob, and pushed. That's the usual method of opening a door."

"There's no point in being offensive," I said icily. Then two thoughts hit me at once. "A key? Where did they get a key And, Lymond, are they stealing Papa's body?" I was shocked.

"I don't know." He looked at me, exasperated. "That is, I don't know how or where they got a key, and, no, they aren't stealing your father's body. Just be still." He turned his attention back to the dark front of the mausoleum.

"How do you know they're not?"

He turned to me, struggling to keep his temper under control. I was learning the man had a vile temper. "For the love of God, how do I know they're not *what?*"

"Stealing Papa's body."

His voice broke with the effort of keeping it low. "Roxanne, what would they want with your father's body?"

"Why else would they be in the mausoleum? Papa's body is the only thing there. Except for Mama's body and the remains of the wooden horse, of course. And maybe a few stray boxes of artifacts."

He gnashed his teeth. I have never heard anyone do that before. "Miss Sydney," he said, his voice trembling, "will you shut the hell up?"

I wanted to tell him his grammar was atrocious, but thought the better of it. Instead, we stood there in silence for the better part of half an hour, perched precariously on the crumbling limestone path, slowly freezing to death as the wind chilled us through our sodden garments. I once suggested that we leave, but he refused, again becoming quite uncomplimentary and falling into atrocious grammar. Finally I was chilled to the bone and my teeth were chattering. I resolved to wait no longer. "Lymond," I said firmly, "I'm freezing and I'm going to move. Why are we waiting here?" He didn't answer me. It was time for me to take a stand. "Lymond, if you don't move, I'm going to go up there myself and find out what those men are doing in there."

"Try it and I'll stop you."

From his tone, I really believed he would have. I tried another tack. "We really can't stand here all night or we'll both die by freezing. Why don't you go find out what they're doing?"

"Because they're small fish. I want the big one. I suspect someone else will be here to join them shortly."

As though he were a prophet, a man came riding up through the swirling fog and mist. I gasped aloud and Lymond once again clapped his hand over my mouth. I bit his thumb and he cursed softly, but moved his hand. "Dammit, Roxanne—" he began, but I interrupted him. "That was not at all necessary, Lymond." I peered over the edge of the grass. "Is that your 'big fish'?"

"I don't know yet, but possibly."

I looked closely at the mounted figure. He was riding in from the direction of the house and was dressed for the weather in a many-caped coat and a large brimmed hat. There was no way to discover his features or, under

125

his coat, even determine what size and build he was.

He reined in at the front of the mausoleum, dismounted, and tied the reins to a convenient column. With a furtive glance around, he pushed the heavy door open, its hinges creaking in the dark, and went inside. A small square of light from a candle or lantern inside silhouetted him briefly, but there was nothing to be seen except the black bulk of his coat. Then the door shut behind him, and there was only blackness and silence.

"Let's go," Lymond said, grabbing my arm. "We're going to run for those rocks. If you can't do it, stay here until I get back."

"Of course I can do it." I would have or died in the attempt.

Lymond took off in a crouch, with me close on his heels. I had to pick up the hem of my gown, and it felt as though it weighed ten stone. I made it to the rocks right behind him, quite proud of myself. Lymond, however, didn't notice. He put his hand on the top of my head and squashed me down. "Get down!" he hissed. "Do you want them to see you?"

I risked a quick look over the top of the rocks. "They're all in the mausoleum. There's no one out there, you clod."

"There will be."

To satisfy Lymond, I hunkered down behind the rocks in a very uncomfortable position. It seemed as if an eternity passed and my legs were cramping. "Lymond," I whispered, "this is ridiculous. I'm going to have to stand up."

He moved a little and ignored my distress. "I'm going over to the mausoleum and try to hear something. You stay here." I started to speak but he took my face in his hands and stared right into my eyes as though he were practicing mesmerism. "You stay right here. Do not move. Do you understand me?"

"Of course I understand you, Lymond. I'm not an imbecile."

"Good." He started to stand.

"I'm going with you."

He dropped to his knees again. "Dammit, Roxanne—"

"Lymond, I repeat, there's no need for profanity." I gathered my sodden skirts. "Shall we make a run for it?"

"Oh, hell." He moved up into a crouch. "Listen to me for just once, Roxanne. You need to stay here." He looked at me and gave up on that. "All right. If anything happens—anything at all—run for it. Is that clear?"

"Perfectly." I stood and started running for the side of the mausoleum before he could give me further instructions. I heard him running behind me and also heard him muttering under his breath. I was rather glad I couldn't understand what he was saying.

We reached the side of the mausoleum without mishap and stepped up gingerly onto the marble flagging that surrounded it. I crouched against the side of the building, Lymond in front of me. "Stay here," he ordered in a hoarse whisper and left, edging his way around towards the back.

Lymond had been gone only a moment when I heard voices. I thought I caught something—a tone, an inflection—I recognized in one of the voices, but it was muffled and I couldn't place it. I crawled along the porch as far as I dared, squirming along on my stomach, and peered around one of the columns. I heard the noise of the lock being turned. The man in the caped coat mounted his horse and looked at the other two. I tried in vain to see his features, but he wore his hat low on his head and I saw nothing. "Monday night, then," he said, and again I thought I had heard the voice before. I couldn't be sure.

The horseman turned and went off at a canter toward Bellerophon.

"I'd have to say as the Master's a sharp 'un," one of the remaining men said in what was definitely a London accent.

"He doesn't have to be too sharp to outwit these local imbeciles," the other said with a shrug. I was struck with dread—his accent was French. Horror stories of spies and Napoleon's atrocities ran through my mind. *"Allons,"* he said, tossing the key to the mausoleum up into the air, catching it, and then putting it into his pocket. The two of them went towards the sea, disappearing down the limestone path, laughing and chatting with each other as though they were at a garden party.

I lay there on my stomach for a few minutes, not sure if they were out of earshot or not, then got to my hands and knees and started crawling towards the door, hiding in the shadows of the columns. I was watching my cloak and gown, trying to keep from getting tangled in them, and I didn't see the figure crouched by the door. My head was lowered and I ran right into the back of his knees. With a muffled grunt he tumbled backwards, somersaulting over me and landing face first on the flagging behind me. I whirled and raised both fists to hit him but saw in the nick of time that it was Lymond.

"What are you doing here?" I demanded. "I thought you had gone around back."

His voice was trembling again and his nose was bleeding from bashing into one of the columns. "I did." A pause. "I thought I told you to stay in one place and not move."

"Surely you didn't expect me not to help."

He leaned up against a column, sat back wearily, and mopped at the blood running from his nose. "Help?" He closed his eyes briefly. "No, I didn't expect you to do anything I asked you to do." He opened his eyes and glared

128

MORE PASSION AND ADVENTURE AWAIT... YOUR TRIP TO A BIG ADVENTUROUS WORLD BEGINS WHEN YOU ACCEPT YOUR FIRST 4 NOVELS ABSOLUTELY *FREE*
(AN $18.00 VALUE)

Accept your Free gift and start to experience more of the passion and adventure you like in a historical romance novel. Each Zebra novel is filled with proud men, spirited women and tempestuous love that you'll remember long after you turn the last page.

Zebra Historical Romances are the finest novels of their kind. They are written by authors who really know how to weave tales of romance and adventure in the historical settings you love. You'll feel like you've actually gone back in time with the thrilling stories that each Zebra novel offers.

GET YOUR FREE GIFT WITH THE START OF YOUR HOME SUBSCRIPTION

Our readers tell us that these books sell out very fast in book stores and often they miss the newest titles. So Zebra has made arrangements for you to receive the four newest novels published each month.

You'll be guaranteed that you'll never miss a title, and home delivery is so convenient. And to show you just how easy it is to get Zebra Historical Romances, we'll send you your first 4 books absolutely FREE! Our gift to you just for trying our home subscription service.

BIG SAVINGS AND FREE HOME DELIVERY

Each month, you'll receive the four newest titles as soon as they are published. You'll probably receive them even before the bookstores do. What's more, you may preview these exciting novels free for 10 days. If you like them as much as we think you will, just pay the low preferred subscriber's price of just $3.75 each. *You'll save $3.00 each month off the publisher's price.* AND, your savings are even greater because there are never any shipping, handling or other hidden charges—FREE Home Delivery. Of course you can return any shipment within 10 days for full credit, no questions asked. There is no minimum number of books you must buy.

GET
FOUR
FREE
BOOKS
(AN $18.00 VALUE)

ZEBRA HOME SUBSCRIPTION
SERVICE, INC.
P.O. Box 5214
120 BRIGHTON ROAD
CLIFTON, NEW JERSEY 07015-5214

AFFIX
STAMP
HERE

at me. "I came around front when I heard them leave. I was too far away to hear anything at all. Did you hear them say anything?"

I crawled over and sat down beside him. "Yes. Lymond, who are those men? What on earth were they doing here in the dead of night?"

"Yes *what,* Roxanne? Will you stop talking in circles? What did you hear them say?"

"Oh, that. The man on horseback said, 'Monday night, then,' and then he rode away. One of the two others had a London accent — very plebeian, I'd say — and he said the master was a sharp 'un. The other one — Lymond, you'll never guess — sounded French, so he must be a Frenchman or even a spy. He said *'Allons'* as they left."

"Uh," Lymond grunted, dabbing at his still-bleeding nose with his handkerchief. "Was that all?"

"Only a very rude comment about the locals being imbeciles." I paused. "Lymond," I asked with misgiving, "do you think they . . . they disturbed Papa's remains?"

"I wouldn't think so," he said slowly, "unless they wanted to hide something in the coffin, and that's unlikely. Do you have your key? If you do, we'll check the inside."

"Of course, Lymond, I always carry a key to the mausoleum with me when I come out for a midnight stroll." I couldn't keep the sarcasm out of my voice. I was tired, cold, banged, and bruised, and my clothes were a dripping mess. I wanted to go home.

He shrugged. "No need to get testy. I'll take you back to Bellerophon and you can get a key for me. I want to look inside."

"Not without me, you don't." I sagged back against the side of the building. "And, please, Lymond, not until morning."

He smiled lazily at me, his face shadowed by the partial moonlight. "All right, Roxanne, morning will be fine. I'm not particularly up to another trip out here myself and I don't think anyone will be back here tonight." He got to his feet and held out a hand to help me up. "Let's go."

He pulled me to my feet and we stood there in the moonlight, close to each other. "Roxanne," he said softly, looking at my face. His voice sounded muffled and strange, but I thought it was because his nose was beginning to swell slightly. Then I looked at him again in the moonlight and realized with a start that he was going to kiss me. Worse, I *wanted* him to kiss me. With a great effort, I stepped back. "We'd better get back. Your wife will be worried about you," I stammered. The surge of emotion I felt bothered me.

"Wife?" he said as though he had never heard the word before.

"Amelia. Your wife. I know she'll be worried." I had gathered my wits by now. "Besides, we're both going to come down with the grippe if we don't get back and get out of these wet clothes."

I made a production of gathering my cloak around me and headed for the front steps of the mausoleum. Lymond followed me without a word, then caught up with me.

There were dozens of questions I wanted to ask him about the men, and why Lymond himself had known to be there, but I was also examining the feelings I had experienced during that moment in the moonlight. Lymond was a married man — that was a fact I couldn't ignore, even if Lymond chose to. I stole a glance at Lymond and he seemed preoccupied. "Why were you out here tonight?" I blurted out without thinking.

He glanced at me as if he hadn't been aware I was there. "I saw a light from my window. I thought it might be Willy."

"That's impossible. You couldn't have seen anything that far."

He shrugged. "I'm telling you why I'm here. You don't have to believe it." He said no more.

When we got back to the house, Lymond walked around back with me. At the door, I noticed he was careful to stand away from me. "I'll see you tomorrow and we'll go back to the mausoleum."

"Fine." I nodded and turned to go inside.

"I think it might be a good idea not to mention to anyone that you were out there with me tonight. I wouldn't want your reputation blemished." He grinned at me, a faintly lopsided grin. "I do believe being caught in a mausoleum after midnight with a strange man might qualify as one of the things young ladies are not to do without chaperons."

I shut my eyes. I hadn't given a thought to the effects of the night on my reputation. Much as I had wanted to tell Justin what I had seen, I couldn't. What would he think of me? Worse, now Lymond had something to hold over my head. Blackmail, as it were. I wondered if two could play at this game. "It could have been worse," I said with a smile. "I could have been with Francis."

"Francis?" The only expression on his face was puzzlement.

"No one you know," I said shortly. "Hadn't you better go on in? Amelia will be worried about you."

Lymond paused. There was something he wanted to say or ask, but didn't know exactly how. "She knows I can take care of myself."

"Can you?" I couldn't resist. "There may be times when you're unable to do that, Mr. Lymond. It happens to the best of us."

Lymond ran his fingers through his hair. "Dammit, Roxanne, I don't know how much — or what — you know."

I had no idea what he meant. I knew absolutely nothing, but I certainly wasn't going to let him know that. Instead, I smiled at him. "Again, profanity isn't necessary, Lymond. And as for what I know, you'll just have to guess." With that, I smiled at him again and opened the door. "Until tomorrow, Mr. Lymond." I shut the door behind me.

My exit was spoiled by Bue. I had forgotten he was in, and when he heard the door, he jumped straight up on me and set up a howl. Aunt Hen and Cassie dashed in in their nightgowns, all in a dither, demanding to know what I had discovered and why I was so thoroughly drenched. I told them the story, omitting several things, and they plied me with hot tea. It took some little time until we went to bed. By the time Cassie insisted I be covered with a feather comforter, I was sneezing heartily. I should have been charitable, but my last thought before sleep was that I rather hoped Lymond came down with the grippe. It would serve him right.

Chapter Nine

I planned to get up early to make sure Lymond didn't do anything nefarious, but between the late hours, the coziness of my bed, and the fact that I didn't feel at all the thing, I didn't get up until the middle of the morning.

Dragging myself to the mirror, I was appalled at my reflection. I rang for Meggie and sent her to find out about Lymond's whereabouts while I tried to repair the damage. She returned with the satisfying news that Mr. Lymond had something of a cold and had stayed in late this morning. He had just come down to eat and was requesting hot lemonade.

"*Hot* lemonade?" I shuddered.

Meggie bobbed. "Yes, mum. For his cold, you know. It's by far the best thing."

"Balderdash," I said, then took a sneezing fit. When I stopped, I sent Meggie for hot lemonade. I still didn't believe it, but anything was worth a try.

When I got to the breakfast room, everyone was there—all the girls, Amelia, Lymond, Aunt Hen, and Captain Amherst. Lymond was finishing another cup of hot lemonade and was looking more chipper than I had hoped. Amelia turned to me as I came in. "Miss Sydney, you're just the person we need to help us. We're trying to convince Robert to go to the medicinal baths with us."

"You do look a trifle peaked, Lymond," I said, peering at him.

Amelia nodded. "Yes, he's been having a terrible time sleeping. He gets up and walks about at all hours."

"A rather common complaint," I said dryly. Lymond, I'm sorry to say, smirked at me.

"You could go with us, Miss Sydney," Captain Amherst said, looking at me for a change instead of Cassie. "I've heard the medicinal baths work wonders."

I started to ask if he thought I needed wonders, but Cassie spoke first. "No point in asking Roxanne to go. She says the only thing accomplished by taking the medicinal baths is a loss in one's pocketbook."

"Such a cynic," Lymond chided. "I'm surprised, Miss Sydney."

"I question most things." I gave him an arch look, and, to my surprise, he dropped his eyes.

"Will you take us, Robert? We could go today if you like." Amelia smiled and fluttered her small hands. "It would be so good for you — just look at you today — you're hollow-eyed and catching a cold. If you'd go, you could sleep right through the night."

"She's right, Lymond," I said, giving him a smile. "Sleeping through the night would do you a world of good. I think in your condition, the medicinal baths would be just the thing."

He scowled at me, then glanced at Captain Amherst. "Owen? Do you want to play the gallant today? I have some things to do."

Captain Amherst nodded. "Nothing would please me better than to spend the day with such charming ladies."

"Good." Lymond stood up, but Amelia touched his arm. "I do have one other request, Robert. Do you have a few minutes?"

I could see Lymond growing edgy, but he smiled down at her. "I have all the time you need, Amelia. What do you want?"

"My horse needs looking at," she said. "I went out to see her early this morning, and she seems to have something wrong with her front leg."

I raised an eyebrow. I hadn't known Amelia even had a horse in the stables. If fact, I rather remembered Lymond telling me that she didn't ride. Perhaps the horse belonged to Francis. "I'll see to it," Lymond said absently and I could see that he was getting ready to see Woodbury and get the key to the mausoleum. I excused myself and went to find Woodbury first. All this talk about horses had reminded me of a duty I had entrusted to him.

I found him in the big dining room, polishing the silver. "Yes, Miss Sydney, I asked. No one saw the strange gentleman, but one of the horses is gone this morning. The gentleman's horse is here and seems to have an injury." Woodbury paused, milking every dramatic turn in his recounting. "I also must report that Mr. Lymond was out early."

I stared at him. "Are you sure, Woodbury? Meggie told me Lymond had a cold and slept in late."

"That he did." Another pause. "*After* he came in from outdoors sometime around five this morning. I suspect he knows something about the horse." Woodbury looked quite pleased with himself.

"*That* was what Amelia meant." This was a blow. "Drat, Woodbury, the ferret has slipped the cage."

Woodbury lifted his eyebrow at my use of slang, but I ignored it and he continued. "It's unfortunate that we didn't discover anything about Mr., er; Mr. Francis. I did note that the horse's right front shoe has a bad chip in it."

I immediately thought of the man on horseback at the

tomb. "I may be able to discover something about that, Woodbury. I need the key to the mausoleum."

He looked at me quizzically. "Mr. Lymond requested the same."

"Good Heavens, Woodbury, you didn't give it to him, did you?" Right now, Lymond might be beating me to whatever was out there.

"No, Miss Sydney. I told him I'd bring it shortly. I'll get it for you and tell him that you have it."

I breathed a sigh of relief and waited impatiently until Woodbury returned. I snatched the key and ran back to get Meggie to help me into my habit, tossing directions over my shoulder for Woodbury to have someone saddle Buttercup for me.

It took a while to dress because everyone was getting ready to go into Brighton to the medicinal baths, and Meggie was in a frenzy. I told Julia and Livvy to take whatever of mine they wanted and go. Tying the key to a loop in the pocket of my habit so I wouldn't lose it, I then dressed myself hurriedly, skipping a button or two in my haste. I had to get out of the house before Lymond knew I was leaving. As everyone else was chattering and heading for the front where Captain Amherst was waiting for them, I slid out the back.

I approached the stables warily, looking for Lymond but not seeing him anywhere. Bue trotted along beside me, his collar jingling. He recognized my habit and was excited at the thought of going for a run. "You'll have to stay here, Bue," I said to him crossly. He sat down, wagged his tail furiously, and grinned at me. As he had known I would, I relented. "All right, but stay out of the way. I have to hurry before Lymond gets there."

I went into the stables, pleased with myself for giving Lymond the slip. "Is Buttercup ready?" I called out.

"Yes, are you ready now?" I whirled at the voice. Lymond was standing there, ready to ride, his horse saddled and waiting beside Buttercup. "I knew you didn't want to leave without me," he said with a smile, "so I waited for you here."

"How very thoughtful of you." I led Buttercup out to the mounting block. Lymond started out the door but stopped as Bue walked towards him, tongue lolling and tail wagging. "I promised Bue he could go along. He can use the exercise, and I've rather been neglecting him of late."

Lymond put his horse between himself and the dog. He shrugged. "He'll probably enjoy himself. Perhaps we can get in a good ride after we look around the mausoleum. Did you remember the key?"

"I have it." I patted my pocket and urged Buttercup forward. Bue took off ahead of us, collar jingling and tail wagging as he zigged and zagged along the path in front of Lymond's horse, causing it to shy a little. I hid a grin as I saw Lymond trying to control both the horse and his temper. He was learning.

While he was involved, I urged Buttercup into a gallop, wanting to get to the mausoleum ahead of him, even if for only a minute or two. I wanted to check the ground in front for a chipped front hoofprint. I left Lymond behind but heard him when he thought I was out of earshot. He was yelling profanities at Bue.

At the mausoleum, I dismounted quickly and tied Buttercup to a convenient column at the side. I didn't want her trampling any evidence. Walking quickly to the front, skirting the area where the horse had been tied, I fell to my knees and looked carefully. As the grass was springy, I couldn't see a sign of any hoofprints. There looked to be one or two indentations that might have been hoofprints, but I couldn't tell. I heard Bue's collar before I heard Lymond come up behind me.

"Are you praying for inspiration?" he asked as he

reined in his horse and Bue came over to try and lap my face.

"It's a thought." I stood and brushed off my habit. "I was wondering if one of them had dropped something."

"But you didn't find a thing." Lymond dismounted and dropped the reins. In a flash, Bue was on him. In all honesty, Bue was merely trying to be friendly, wagging his tail and trying to lick Lymond's face, but he jumped squarely on Lymond and knocked him to the ground. Then he sat on Lymond's chest. "Will you get this thing off me?" Lymond gasped.

I grabbed Bue's collar and pulled hard. He bounded off and sat down beside Lymond, looking extremely pleased with himself. Lymond sat up. "He does that every time. That animal hates me."

"Nonsense. He's merely trying to be friendly."

Lymond gave me a skeptical look. "I've noticed he doesn't try that with you."

I smiled. "It's all in the training. Are you ready to go in?"

Lymond had stood and was busily dusting himself off. He had bits of grass clinging to his coat and his boots were dirty. He wiped them off with his hands while I went ahead and unlocked the door. It made the familiar creaking sound when it opened.

"I suppose you remembered tinder and candles," he said as our eyes adjusted to the pitch blackness of the inside. The only light came from the open door.

"No need. Papa always kept a metal box with candles and tinder inside. It's on the shelf above the door."

Lymond turned and reached over his head, retrieving the box and opening it. "There's only one candle stub in here." He pulled out little more than half a candle.

"Impossible. The last time I looked, there must have been close to a dozen candles in there." I thought a moment. "That was right after Papa's funeral when we brought the remains of the wooden horse in and stored them over there." I gestured to the far wall where the black bulk of the horse's body stood.

"It would seem that whoever has been using your mausoleum has failed to replace your candles," Lymond said, lighting the stub. Instead of brightening the interior, the candle flame made it seem more eerie, throwing huge, wavering shadows on the walls and ceiling.

"I'll have to bring some more," I said, propping the door to allow as much light as possible inside. I wanted to get rid of those shadows.

"No, don't do that — bring more candles for this box, I mean. If you do, they'll realize you know someone's been in the building. If you bring candles, use a separate box and we'll hide them."

I wondered what all this talk about "we" was but let it go. As Lymond held up the candle, I looked around.

"Is anything out of place?" he asked.

I shook my head. "No, but I haven't been here in months." I hesitated. "Lymond, I hate to ask you, but would you mind very much taking the first look at Papa's and Mama's coffins? If anything has been touched, I don't think I could bear it."

Without a word, he patted me on the shoulder and went over to the coffins on their shelves, holding the candle up so he could see everything. He spent several minutes looking at the tops and sides of the coffins and checking the shelves. "Nothing has been touched as far as I can see, but it does appear that whoever has been here has been eating and drinking while they waited."

"How disgusting." I shuddered.

"I suppose it's all relative," Lymond said briskly. "Has anything been moved; are there any secret panels or any kind of vault for valuables?"

Privately I thought he had been reading too many gothic novels, but I merely answered, "Nothing. I think

Papa thought about a tunnel once but did nothing about it. Otherwise, there's only the wooden horse and its parts. It wasn't completed when Papa died, so we put it in here."

"And those boxes?" Lymond gestured with the candle, throwing gigantic shadows on the wall. It was altogether an unsettling effect.

"Those contain some artifacts Papa received a day or two before he died. I have no idea what they are—I opened one box and whatever is in them looks rather like dried wood. I didn't want them cluttering up the house, so I had them moved down here."

We then heard Bue begin to bark. Lymond and I both rushed to the door. Outside, Bue was dancing around a carriage as Captain Amherst helped everyone down. "I thought you were going to the baths," Lymond said. Did I detect a note of irritation?

"We were on the way," Livvy said, "when we decided to turn off the road and stop here. Amelia's never seen the mausoleum."

Aunt Hen glanced around and walked up beside me. "Roxanne," she whispered hoarsely, "you are *not* chaperoned."

"I am now," I said grimly. "I imagine you plan to stay here until I either go home or go to the baths with you."

She nodded. "It really isn't proper, you know," she whispered under her breath. "We'll all stay with you."

"We might as well leave now," I said to everyone, hoping Lymond got my meaning. I went to the door and locked the mausoleum. "I think I'll go back home. Do have a nice day in Brighton."

"We should have a picnic here someday," Julia said, wandering over to the rocks. "It's a splendid place to see the sea."

Cassie nodded, looking up at Captain Amherst. "It's one of my favorite places to paint." She linked her arm through Amelia's. "Come see our view. You might want to bring your sketchbook and come with me one afternoon." They wandered off towards the cliff while I went to untie Buttercup. Suddenly there was a piercing scream. I whirled towards the cliff where I saw Amelia and Cassie teetering on the edge. I was closer to them than anyone, and I broke into a sprint to try to reach them. Captain Amherst ran past and grabbed Amelia as she started to fall. Cassie fell back into my arms, pointing towards the beach. She couldn't speak.

I looked in the direction she had pointed and grew weak myself. "Get Lymond," I murmured to Captain Amherst as he lay Amelia on the ground.

He looked at me quizzically, then followed my gaze to the beach. "Robert, hurry," he bellowed. The badly mangled body of what appeared to be Willy was on the beach, flies already buzzing around it.

Lymond went quickly down the path to the beach while I steered Cassie to the carriage. Captain Amherst carried Amelia and placed her against the cushions. He glanced anxiously at Cassie who appeared to be in shock. "I'll take care of them," I told him. "You go help Lymond."

With a nod, he ran back towards the beach and I herded Livvy, Julia, and Aunt Hen into the carriage. I clambered up and took the reins. I was no whip, but I could manage if I had to, and, at that moment, I had to. "What happened?" Julia asked, reluctant to leave. Briefly I told them, and we drove the rest of the way home in silence.

At the front of the house, I yelled for Woodbury and Mrs. Beckford and anyone else I could think of, and we got everyone inside. Amelia took to her bed, as did Aunt Hen, and I sat Cassie down and burned feathers for her. The feathers didn't do very much, so I gave her a glass of brandy as a restorative. I worried about calling the doctor, but she assured me she would be all right. I didn't think so — she was as pale as paper.

I had Woodbury send some men to help Lymond and Amherst. I chafed to return but felt I could do more good at Bellerophon. I don't know if I helped or not — I spent most of my time going from Amelia to Aunt Hen to Cassie and back again. Cassie seemed more affected than the others, possibly because she had known Willy — if that indeed was the identity of the corpse.

The men returned about midafternoon and confirmed it — Willy had been shot in the head, then tossed into the Channel. From the evidence, he had been weighted, but the weight had slipped. "So," Lymond said as we sat, I drinking tea, he sipping brandy, "it was only luck that we discovered the body. Whoever killed him intended for his body to sink to the bottom of the Channel and disappear."

"Who and why?" I asked. "Do you have any clues?"

Looking at him sharply, I wondered if he knew more than he said. Did he have firsthand knowledge? I dismissed the thought: I could picture Lymond as a thief but never as a murderer.

Lymond shook his head. "It could be anybody." He drained his glass and refilled it. "That's why I wanted to keep the boy under watch. I was afraid he would be killed."

I almost dropped my cup. "Why do you say that? No one here would harm Willy. Oh, he was sly and we had to watch to make sure he didn't sell the harness for drink, but no one would hurt him."

"Someone did." Lymond put his glass on the table and looked at me. We were alone in the room, and he got up and shut the door. "I need to talk seriously with you." He sat back down and leaned towards me. "Roxanne," he began, then paused. "Roxanne, I'm afraid there may be more going on here than you realize. Jem was killed for a reason—deliberately tortured and killed."

"No! That couldn't be. He was—"

"He was deliberately tortured and killed. I don't know why, but I think Willy knew why. That's the reason Willy had to be killed." He paused again. "Did your father have any *real* valuables hidden? Some jewels, some statuettes, some paintings?" This last was thrown in casually.

I gasped and involuntarily put a hand to my throat. I had been on the verge of believing Lymond didn't know anything about this—that he was the person he claimed and he was simply concerned about our welfare. But this question convinced me that he knew something about all the stolen paintings, and worse, planned to make us his next victims. There was no denying his pose: the man was a consummate actor. He sat there, broad-shouldered, sincere, handsome, his hair curling around his forehead. He looked at me with those clear, deep blue eyes and smiled. "You can tell me, Roxanne," he coaxed.

"There's nothing to tell," I said coldly, standing up. "Perhaps you should be the one to tell me exactly what you're planning."

He shrugged and looked up at me, still smiling. "My plans? Merely to try to protect everyone in the house. I feel there's something going on here."

"So do I." I turned and made a regal exit. As I closed the door behind me, I could hear him chuckling. The man was insufferable, and I was firmer in my resolve than ever to expose him for what he was. Thank God that Justin was coming back to Jervyne House.

I didn't see Lymond again that night. Everyone except Julia and me took supper on trays in their rooms, Livvy staying with Cassie. I asked about Lymond and was told he and Wyrock had gone into Brighton on business. I couldn't imagine what type of business could be conducted after dark. I didn't hear him come in.

The next morning I had Buttercup saddled, took Papa's pistol which hadn't been fired in years, and dragooned Ned, the stable boy, into going with me. Ned was Mrs. Beckford's nephew and was eager to please, so he went along when I told him I needed him. He wasn't ideal, but perhaps he'd fulfill Aunt Hen's chaperon requirement.

That done, I rode back to the mausoleum. Ned was not happy to be there, so I set him to walking Buttercup while I explored inside. Neither of us wanted to look at the beach.

I had set my candle on a box and was prowling around the wooden horse when Lymond came in. "Having fun?" he asked, walking up beside me. He pulled some candles from his coat pocket and put them beside mine. He didn't wait for me to answer. "This is quite something," he remarked, running his hand along the side of the wooden horse. "A good hiding place."

"There's no treasure here, if that's what you mean," I said shortly. "It was one of the first places we looked."

Lymond stood back, his shadow looming over me. "How many people could get into that thing?"

I shrugged. "Three, I suppose, four or five if they didn't mind being packed in like herrings." I ran my hand along the painted head. "Papa wasn't really sure about the scale."

Lymond inspected the teeth, which were ivory, and looked at the enameled eyes. "Quite a labor of love."

"Yes." It seemed to be darker than when I first came in. I glanced back at the door. Lymond followed my gaze, amused. "Ned's still there if that's what's worrying you. Believe me, I'm a gentleman through and through." I suppressed a snort of derision and sat down on a bench along the wall. Lymond stuck his head up into the horse's body. "Nothing here that I can see." He sat beside me. "That's the logical place to hide something. Roxanne, are you *sure* there's not some kind of false compartment in that horse?"

"I'm positive. I helped Papa with the plans for it."

Lymond shook his head. "That dashes that idea, then." We sat in silence for a few minutes, Lymond thinking about heaven knew what and I watching the candle flame make patterns on the walls. I was just thanking my stars that I had brought Ned along when Lymond reached over and touched my fingers. "We'd better leave," he said, his voice strangely thick.

I jerked my hand away and stood, almost knocking over the candle. Lymond grabbed at it, steadied the flame, and held it aloft. "What's this?" he asked, going over to one of the walls to look at a painting.

"Oh, that." I smiled at the memory. "At the end, Papa was in something of an Egyptian phase and wanted to put wall frescoes all over everything. He originally planned a pyramid here, but when Mama scotched that plan, he decided the inside of his mausoleum would have frescoes like the pyramids and Egyptian tombs. If you look closely, you'll note that those Egyptians are really Papa, Mama, Pom — Edward, the other girls, and me."

Lymond peered at one of the frescoes, then turned and grinned at me. "I trust none of you posed in those transparent linen dresses."

"Of course not." I was indignant. "We didn't pose at all."

To my surprise, Lymond began feeling the walls, running his fingers over every joint in the rock. He finally climbed onto the bench and ran his hands over the frieze at the top. "Nothing there," he reported.

"I could have told you that."

He turned to me. "There's got to be some reason for

those men to meet here." He thought for a moment, running his fingers through his hair, the curls falling around his ears. "Perhaps," he said slowly, "this is only a meeting place since it's close to the sea and not exactly a place frequented by a crowd. They may be hiding the booty somewhere else."

"Hiding what booty? Lymond, are you trying to tell me that we're harboring pirates and freebooters in our mausoleum?" I was incensed at the implication.

Instead of answering, he smiled at me again. "Are you ready to leave now?"

"I have no intention of going anywhere until I get some answers from you," I said. "Lymond, I insist—" I stopped. Lymond had snuffed the candle and we were in pitch darkness. The flame from the candle had been feeble enough, and there was very little light from the door. I was completely disoriented but hesitant to yell for Ned. "You might have waited until we were outside to blow out the candle," I told him as I tried to blink my eyes to adjust to the darkness.

I felt his fingers on mine. "Roxanne," he murmured.

I paused and felt the pressure of his fingers tighten. Why did I feel this way whenever I was around Lymond, a man bound to another woman? I took a deep breath and moved my hand, trying to steady myself. "We need to leave." To my credit, my voice was firm.

He hesitated, then took my hand again, but he was all business this time. "Let me help you. The door's over here."

By this time, my eyes had adjusted, and I made my way towards the square of light that marked the door. Both of us blinked once we got outside, to adjust to the sunlight.

Without another word, Lymond shut the door behind us and I locked it. Ned brought Buttercup and Lymond's horse up. "I don't see Bucephalus." Lymond said, and I had to laugh at the relief in his voice.

He grinned back at me, then put his hands on my waist and lifted me onto Buttercup. He paused, as though he wanted to say something, but he checked himself and took the reins of his horse.

Once I was mounted, I whistled for Bue and he came bounding up the limestone path from the sea. He looked thoroughly disreputable, all wet and covered with mud and sand. He stopped and shook himself, sending filth all over Lymond.

"Regrettably I spoke too soon," Lymond said as he mounted. "Where to now? I'd planned to ride, but if you'd rather, I'll be glad to escort you back to Bellerophon."

"That isn't necessary." The key was tucked safely in my pocket, and I decided I could leave Lymond to his own devices. I pulled Buttercup around and motioned to Ned. "Ned and I have other things to do." Ned looked rather amazed but followed me. "Good day, Mr. Lymond." I didn't look back as we rode off.

Chapter Ten

I should have looked behind me. Lymond caught up with us and maneuvered his horse between Ned's and mine. "A friendly wager on a gallop?" he asked.

I glanced at the horse he was riding — if he'd purchased that, he didn't know much more about horseflesh than Cassie did. I nodded at him and we were off.

Lymond's horse was certainly deceiving. Just when I thought I had him beaten, his horse stretched out into the most ungainly gallop I had ever seen and passed by Buttercup. Lymond reined up at the top of the rise and waited for me, laughing. As I rode up, he patted the horse's neck. "It happens every time. People take a look at The Bruce and think he's a broken-down heap of bones. They don't realize he's a prime racer."

"He looks rather more like a prime candidate for glue." I sighed. "How much do I owe you, Lymond? A wager is a wager."

He laughed and appeared to be thinking. "The pleasure of your company for a ride."

I raised an eyebrow. "That's all? You'll never make a living as a betting man."

"I have my moments. Shall we go?" He cantered off towards the inland. Before we had ridden very far, I recognized our direction. "Lymond, there's no need for us to

148

go to Jervyne House. Justin isn't home and there's no one about except some carpenters. Justin's gone to London and won't be back until tomorrow or Monday." I paused, realizing I had been using Justin's first name rather freely. What of it? I thought, let Lymond make of it what he would.

Lymond reined in The Bruce, almost bumping into Ned, and gave me an amused glance. "I noted his absence from Bellerophon and thought a look at Jervyne House might put you in a better mood." Lymond smiled at Ned and he dropped back shyly. "Ned, you can go back if you wish. I'll be glad to chaperon Miss Sydney."

"Stay where you are, Ned," I snapped. I lifted an eyebrow in disbelief. "Really, Lymond, I hardly think my moods are any of your concern. Besides," I added, "I happen to be in an excellent humor."

"It isn't any of my business," he agreed promptly, "and I do admit you've been caustic only half a dozen times this morning. However, you do owe me a ride, and I want to pay a neighborly visit and see how the repairs are coming on. Jerrold certainly got the best of that bargain, didn't he?"

I resolved to be pleasant. I didn't know why Lymond always brought out the worst in me. I smiled brightly and nodded in agreement. "Jerrold is the stingiest man alive, and I was appalled at the condition of the house. Justin is going to have a fortune tied up in repairs. He could have stayed at the Castle Inn cheaper."

"I doubt the Castle Inn would have met his particular requirements. It is rather public, you know."

I glanced at Lymond and wondered what he was trying to say, but he went right on. "What do you know about Justin Denver?"

"What do you mean? I know Justin Denver is a true gentleman, which is more than I can say for some people in this vicinity. He has exquisite manners."

Rather than getting angry, Lymond threw back his head and laughed. "Quite a requirement for romance, those exquisite manners. I'm most impressed with your taste, my dear Miss Sydney." He stopped laughing and gave me a suddenly somber look, glancing behind to make sure Ned was out of earshot. "Often things and people aren't what they seem."

"I said the very same thing to Aunt Hen the other day," I answered, remembering my suspicions of Lymond. "Furthermore, I resent you casting aspersions on Justin Denver when you really don't know him."

"I'm hardly casting aspersions." He slowed his horse to a sedate walk. "I'm simply curious. Mr. Denver seems to be spending a great deal of money on a house that isn't even his. I can't imagine anyone doing that unless there was a reason behind it."

I refused to look at him. "He enjoys paintings and beautiful things. He also enjoys restoring old houses to their former beauty as well. Have you considered that facet of his personality?"

"No." He thought a moment. "I don't think that will do — if he wanted to restore an old house, he'd buy one so he could live in it and enjoy it forever." He paused and looked at me. "I wonder about his business trips. What kind of business does he have?"

Lymond's question grated, but I smiled. I was determined to be pleasant. "He advises many others on paintings and art objects, as well as buying and selling those things himself. There's a great deal of travel as well as expertise involved."

"True." There was another pause. "Where do you suppose he gets his money?"

"Good Heavens, Lymond! This is beyond the pale. Gentlemen do not go around wondering how someone else gets money. I can't believe you asked such a crass thing."

He grinned at me. "I did, and I'll ask it again — where do you suppose he gets his money? You see, I can ask such a question since I don't believe you account me a gentleman."

"You're quite right on that head." I minced no words as being pleasant was eluding me. "As for Justin's income, let me set your mind at ease: he told me he inherited it. Does that satisfy you?"

"Not really. I'd like to know for sure. Denver could tell you anything."

I had forgotten about being pleasant and was rapidly getting angry. "And you think I'm gullible enough to believe whatever he chooses to tell me?"

Lymond didn't reply; he merely looked at me and grinned.

I was infuriated. "You're wrong, Lymond. I happen to be an excellent judge of character. At any rate, the source of Justin's income and what he chooses to do with it really isn't any of our business, is it?"

He shrugged. "Perhaps. Perhaps not." We had come into sight of Jervyne House. "Is Denver's friend in charge when Denver's away? What's his name?"

"Mr. Robin Norwood," I answered shortly. "He's a master carpenter, as anyone around can tell you. Papa was quite taken with his talents. As for Jervyne, it's amazing what Mr. Norwood and his men have done to that house."

"Amazing may not be the word," Lymond said cryptically.

We were close to the house, so I didn't ask him what he meant. Instead I cantered Buttercup right up to the front where one of the men held her while I dismounted. Ned came straggling in and I handed him the reins while Lymond dismounted. Mr. Norwood played host in Justin's absence and was extremely cordial, showing us around the still-unfinished rooms on the lower floor. The work was progressing rather slowly and probably wouldn't be finished by the time Justin was ready to give up the house and move to London. I wondered if Jerrold would finish it. I rather doubted it.

I stopped in the dining room. "Mr. Norwood, what happened here? I distinctly remember that Ju—Mr. Denver asked me to advise him on wallpaper for this room, and I recommended the Chinese scenes." I walked over to the wall and ran my fingers over the rough paper on the walls. "I can't believe Mr. Denver would want this paper here."

I didn't say it, but I was also appalled at the workmanship. The paper was lumpy in spots as though the glue hadn't been applied correctly.

"This isn't finished yet," Mr. Norwood said. "I'm sure we'll have what you and Mr. Denver selected when we're through."

"I certainly hope so," I said, giving a last look at the room. The wallpaper didn't fit at all.

"I was not aware that decorations were part of your repertoire," Lymond murmured behind me. "You have many talents." I ignored him and went on into the drawing room, Lymond on my heels.

The dining-room ceiling was a well-done piece of plasterwork. To give credit where credit was due, I said as much to Mr. Norwood. "Nothing but the best for Mr. Denver," he said, while I refrained from mentioning the dining-room wallpaper. "The ceiling was done by a man who once lived in France. He's done plasterwork on many of the ceilings of Paris chateaux."

"It's excellent, Mr. Norwood. My compliments on a job well done."

"It's far from done," he said with a smile.

Lymond had been exceptionally quiet, poking around in odd corners, stopping to converse with the workmen. I chatted with one of two whom I recognized. They did not seem to be exceptionally busy; in fact, some of them seemed to be lounging around. Lymond mentioned this and Mr. Norwood told him the men were waiting on materials. I felt sympathy for Justin, having to bear the cost while his men frittered away their time.

We went outside to get our horses, and Ned was helping me mount when Justin walked around the corner of the house. He seemed as surprised to see us as we were to see him. He recovered quickly, however, and smiled broadly at the two of us. "Mr. Lymond, Rox — Miss Sydney, what a pleasant surprise."

He strolled over to us as I motioned Ned to wait. Again I was struck by his appearance. He was dressed in a dark blue coat, a cravat tied just so, pale blue breeches, a cream waistcoat embroidered with bluebells, and gleaming black boots. Lymond looked absolutely provincial in comparison.

"Good to see you, Denver," Lymond said, not too warmly. "When did you get back from London?"

I was aware of an undercurrent of tension between them and looked questioningly from one to the other. Justin, however, just smiled. "I just rode in, as a matter of fact." He looked at me fondly. "I finished my business early and hurried back." Giving me a significant glance, he said, "I found I quite missed the charms and attractions of Brighton."

I felt myself blush. Lymond, however, paid no attention to this piece of business. "You rode back this morning?" Lymond appeared surprised. "You had to have stopped over."

"I did," Justin answered easily. "I had hoped to get back late last night, but with one thing and then the other, darkness fell when I was still too far to ride in. I stopped at an inn, left early this morning, and just got off my horse. I haven't even been inside the house yet."

"I'm delighted you're back," I said, meaning it, "and you'll be delighted at what's been done on the house in your absence."

"Has Robin shown you around?" He reached for my hand and his fingers felt warm and firm. Very nice, I thought.

"Yes," Lymond answered for both of us, "and I agree with Miss Sydney that you and he have done a splendid job. Miss Sydney, I believe it's time for us to get back to Bellerophon."

I wondered if this was part of our wager. I thought about staying but didn't want to make a scene in front of everyone. Besides, if Justin had ridden all that way, he was tired. I nodded at Lymond, and Justin dropped his fingers from mine. He didn't wait for Ned—he put his hands around my waist and lifted me up onto Buttercup. "Perhaps you could visit tomorrow, or are you planning to spend another day searching for that famous treasure?"

I looked down at him, right into his eyes. They made me feel slightly giddy. I forced myself to look at Buttercup's mane. Lymond answered for us again. "We can continue our search tomorrow if you'd like to come help," Lymond told him. "We've made no progress at all."

I didn't want to be forward, but Lymond had extended something of an invitation. "Will we see you tomorrow, then?"

"Without fail," he said with a smile. I didn't get an opportunity to say anything else. Lymond said his goodbyes and struck out for home. There was nothing for me to do except bid my neighbor adieu and follow. Bue was already bounding after Lymond, and he might need my help.

Lymond and The Bruce kept well ahead until we came to the rise overlooking Bellerophon. There he reined in and I pulled up beside him. Ned looked at the two of us quizzically, and when I nodded, he cantered on towards the stables.

I glanced at Lymond before I urged Buttercup on home. I thought he was looking at the scenery — the house sitting in the midst of green grass and Holmwood's flowers, the mausoleum over to the side, alone on its little rise, and the sea beyond, sparkling in the sunlight. "It is beautiful, isn't it?" I said, drinking it all in. I loved this place.

"What? I'm sorry, I was thinking about something else."

"Obviously." I moved to leave. "Lymond, you're impossible."

He reached out to stop me. "Wait. I have to say something to you." He took a deep breath. "Roxanne, don't get involved with Justin Denver."

I was stunned at both his bluntness and his lack of manners. "Lymond, what are you saying? I don't know what you mean."

"I mean don't get involved with Justin Denver." He looked at me steadily. "There's something not right there. I neither like nor trust the man."

I was furious. I might have to listen to this faradiddle from Aunt Hen, but I certainly wasn't going to listen to it from Lymond, a man I neither liked nor trusted. "How dare you? How could you?" I began, but again he paid me no mind.

"Did you notice his clothes and boots?"

I turned in my saddle and glared at him. "What are you attempting to imply, Lymond? Of course I noticed his clothes and boots. Do you want me to describe them to you in the manner of a fashion plate? If you do, I'll begin with his coat and work down to his boots. Would that satisfy you?" I stopped for breath. My voice was shaking with anger.

"His boots weren't dusty."

I closed my eyes and tried to control myself. "No, his boots weren't dusty. They were, as usual, gleaming and were decorated with gold tassels."

"They weren't riding boots, and they weren't dusty," Lymond said again. "Look at yours and look at mine."

I glanced down and saw that my black boots and Lymond's brown ones were coated with dust. There had been fog and drizzle, but it hadn't rained a good soaking rain in days, and all the inland roads were dusty. Lymond pressed his point. "Did you also notice that his clothes weren't dusty or even wrinkled?"

I couldn't help it. I looked at the hem of my habit. It was dirty around the bottom where it had hit the ground. There were bits of dry grass all along the edge. I looked at Lymond's clothes—he had little bits of horsehair, dog hair, grass, and dust plastered all over him. He didn't wait for me to answer him; he kept on relentlessly. "Have you ever ridden a horse hard without getting dusty and dirty?"

"He said he'd stopped over for the night, Lymond. I don't imagine he'd have ridden far this morning." I was grasping at straws. Lymond was calling Justin a liar and on the surface the evidence appeared irrefutable. I was sure there was a reasonable explanation if I could just find it.

"I don't think that's true." Lymond appeared to be looking at the scenery again. "If Denver had been that close, he would have ridden in last night. He said he was too far away to come in." There was a pause, but I couldn't think of anything to say. "He hadn't been riding at all, Roxanne."

I closed my eyes and pictured Justin, dressed all in blue. He had looked immaculate, and I could even remember how he smelled. Not at all like a horse, rather he smelled of that scent he wore that had just a small touch of spice in it. I remembered it distinctly. "Perhaps he had been home long enough to change."

"He said he had just ridden in. He made a point of that." Lymond's voice was flat.

"I'm sure there's a good explanation, and I resent your implication," I snapped. "That such suspicions should come from you, of all people, is beyond belief."

He turned and stared at me. "What do you mean by that?" His voice was hard and his eyes had turned a flat blue.

"Make of it what you will," I said angrily and wheeled my horse.

I kicked Buttercup harder than I should have and she broke into a gallop. We didn't stop until I reined up in front of the stables. I called to Ned, but he wasn't around, so I dismounted by myself and walked Buttercup around to cool her. Lymond rode up as I was beginning to unsaddle her.

"I'll do that for you," he said, dismounting.

"Take care of your own horse. I'll do this."

There was a small silence, then he unsaddled The Bruce and led him to a stall. He paused in front of the stall door. "I'll be glad to rub her down for you," he offered.

"I'd rather do it."

Lymond tied The Bruce to a post by his stall, then came over and stood in front of me. He leaned back against the stable door and folded his arms across his chest. "You're acting rather like a spoiled brat, you know."

I whirled on him, currying brush in my hand. "A spoiled brat! You, of all people, saying that! You're the rudest, most unmannerly, most overbearing person I've ever seen."

"You forgot to add that you don't consider me a gentleman," he said mildly. The man was laughing at me.

"I didn't have to add that. Anyone who knows you

knows you're no gentleman." I turned my back to him and began brushing Buttercup furiously. Lymond walked over and put his hand on my arm. "Keep that up and you're going to take the hide from that poor horse," he said. "Let me."

"I don't seem to have any choice in the matter," I answered acidly as he took the brush and began brushing her down in long, firm strokes. I stood there awkwardly for a moment, then Ned ran towards us, carrying a chunk of buttered bread. "So sorry, Miss Sydney, Mr. Lymond." He was all out of breath.

"It's quite all right, Ned." Lymond gave him a smile as he spoke. "Do you want to finish with this horse? The Bruce could use rubbing down as well, and perhaps some oats."

Was I mistaken or was that hero worship in Ned's eyes when he looked at Lymond? How could the boy be so misled? I hoped Lymond hadn't adversely influenced the boy. Because of the connection with Mrs. Beckford, Ned had always been at Bellerophon and was almost like family. As I walked towards the house, I heard Ned and Lymond talking and joking.

Lymond caught up with me as I went around the corner to our quarters. "Rox — Miss Sydney, I don't believe we've finished our conversation."

"Yes, we have. We have nothing more to say to each other."

Lymond started to speak when we almost ran into Holmwood, kneeling beside the walk, working on the flowers. "Good morning, Holmwood," Lymond said cheerfully, as though there had been no words spoken between us at all. "Everything's looking wonderful this morning as usual."

To my amazement, Holmwood preened, he smiled, he blushed. "Look at this," he said proudly, showing Lymond a rather large, striped dahlia.

"Superb," Lymond said reverently as though he knew what he was discussing. He didn't have the opportunity to say anything else, however, as Bucephalus bounded around the corner and right on to Lymond's back, flattening him. Lymond landed face first on the dahlia.

Holmwood grabbed Bue's collar and pulled him to one side. Lymond rolled over and looked right up into Bue's eyes as Bue shook his head and set his collar jingling. Lymond sat up quickly. I wasn't sure whether it was to avoid being drooled on or if it was to appear in command of the situation. In either case, it didn't work.

"That animal is determined to do me in," Lymond said, standing and brushing dahlia petals from his chin.

"You know what they say about little children and dogs being able to determine a person's character," I said sweetly, sweeping around him and going in the door. Only then did I allow myself to laugh.

Chapter Eleven

I had just settled in to work on Papa's translation of Xenophon, a chore I had neglected of late, when Woodbury brought me a letter from Lydia. "At last," I exclaimed. She hadn't been overly hasty in her reply.

I left Woodbury dying of curiosity, took my letter and myself to my bedroom, and sent for something cool to drink. Only then did I allow myself to tear into my letter and — finally — discover something about the Lymonds.

I had to wade through a great deal of gossip about Lydia's friends, which were legion, and then a rather long section trying to make me feel guilty about not visiting her. I had tried staying with Lydia once, and that was enough. Lydia, with Edward's urging, of course, was determined to marry me off to any eligible man in London who would have me. She must have paraded half a hundred men of various descriptions and ages through her drawing room. I fled to Brighton as soon as I could.

Finally I reached the part I wanted, right at the end of the letter. It was a disappointment: Lydia knew nothing; no one knew of them; no one of her wide acquaintance had ever heard of Mr. and Mrs. Robert Lymond. This was indeed curious. The Lymonds were obviously well-bred and just as obviously had London connections.

Why, then, did no one know of them? Lydia wrote that I shouldn't despair, she had one more avenue to explore. One of her friends, a Miss Sarah Ann McDuff, had married a man who had had to change his name to an uncle's in order to inherit. Lydia thought his name originally might have been Lymond or something similar. He was now Charles Sebastian, earl of Rywicke. I grimaced as I read. This tenuous thread didn't sound at all promising.

I ignored the last few sentences — merely an invitation for me to visit and another list of eligible men who, Lydia insisted, would be perfect as husbands. I shuddered at the thought.

The letter was a disappointment. All in all, I knew nothing more about the Lymonds. I dashed off another missive to Lydia restating what meager information I had and telling her to let me know immediately if she discovered anything. I omitted any reference to Francis. What Lydia knew, all of London knew.

Also, feeling something like a traitor, I asked her if she knew anything of Justin Denver. The suspicions Lymond had planted made me wish to know more about him. When I examined what I did know, it was very little. True, Justin answered all questions I put to him, but when I looked at the answers, I found I knew very little more than when I had asked. Besides, there were certain things one simply could not ask politely. I gave the letter to Woodbury to post and went to find the girls and Aunt Hen.

Everyone, including the Lymonds, was in the front drawing room, all in a twitter. It was true, they told me: the Prince Regent was to arrive on Monday afternoon. All of Brighton was coming awake. Aunt Hen reported that the shops on North Street had already reopened and that everyone was returning. Many of the houses were occupied, and every room available was taken. Aunt Hen reported that Mrs. Bocock had said there was not a place to be had in all of Brighton, for either love or money.

The girls immediately began begging me to take them to watch when the Prince came riding into town. I, as usual, said no, but Amelia offered Lymond's services. He was as horrified at the thought as I was amused, but there was no going back. Amelia had firmly committed him to taking all of them to stand on the Steine so they could watch the stately progress of the Prince from Race Hill down to the Marine Pavilion.

"Will you be going with us?" he asked me. He was none too happy, and I suspected he foresaw the need for some help in restraining the girls.

"No need to ask Roxanne," Aunt Hen sniffed. "She thinks going to view the Prince is a waste of time."

"Yes, it ranks right up there with going to the medicinal baths," I said. "I fail to see why anyone would stand around for hours in that crush just to see an overweight man burdening some poor horse."

"What blasphemy!" Lymond said, looking shocked, an expression I knew was a pose. He was merely jealous because he couldn't stay at home. "I would have thought," Lymond said with a smirk, "that you and Mr. Denver would be standing on the Steine together, watching the Prince's progress. Is that the plan?"

"There is no plan," I said shortly.

"There's no arguing with her," Cassie said, patting my hand. "Roxie did go once and swore she'd never go again."

"True. I was almost trampled in the crush, besides almost being blown away by the wind from the sea. I prefer to stay here and work on Papa's manuscripts. I've neglected them of late."

Since I had made such an issue of it, I felt constrained to muddle about in Papa's manuscripts for the rest of the day while everyone else was twittering about their wardrobes, sewing on new ribbons, and so on. Frankly I had a dull time of it, and, as had been the case lately, didn't accomplish anything of value.

I was better off than Lymond, however. He had decided to spend the afternoon making friends with Bucephalus and had taken a basket of buttered bread, Bue's favorite snack, with him. Being prudent, he had also taken Holmwood. I looked out my window several times and noticed Lymond wasn't making much headway on his project. Bue was eating bread from the hand that fed him, but he was also racing Lymond all over the yard. It seemed Bue was the one in control.

Early that night I went to talk to Cassie. She had seemed animated enough during the afternoon, chattering about the Prince's visit, helping Julia with her dress, and so on, but I was still worried. Underneath the veneer, she seemed worried and withdrawn. She was propped up in her bed when I opened her door quietly and slipped in. She was against her pillows and seemed as pale as her bedclothes, hair neatly braided for the moment and her fingers nervously tracing the embroidery on the coverlet. She looked unhappy.

I sat down on the bed and held her hand. "Cassandra Helen," I said sternly, "remember you're a Sydney and we're strong stock. I know seeing Willy was a shock to you, but you can overcome it. Get up and come have some chocolate with me. You'll feel better."

Cassie looked at me and tried not to cry. "You're right, Roxie." She took a deep breath and sat up on the edge of the bed. "I'm being foolish." She gave me a watery smile. "Roxie, I think I should go to London as soon as possible."

I tried not to raise an eyebrow in surprise. "Has Captain Amherst been reposted to London?" I asked lightly. "Or have you decided to forsake Brighton just when the Prince threatens to bring some excitement to the place? I daresay London will be quieter than Brighton for a few weeks."

Cassie managed a laugh, albeit rather shaky. "It probably will be," she agreed, then looked at me seriously. "Roxie, I think you know that I care very much for Captain Amherst." There was no point in my denying this, so I simply nodded and she went on. "I've thought about the things you've said—that we really don't know anything about his background, that I owe it to Julia and Livvy to make an advantageous marriage—and I know they're all true. I'm going to London."

"Perhaps the change will do you good." We sat for a moment, then I pinned her with a look. "Cassie, has he—Captain Amherst—said anything to you? Has he offered for you?"

She shook her head and a tendril of hair escaped her braid. "No, he's said nothing. He's been polite, and often I think he wants to say something to me, but he never has." She paused. "Roxie, I don't want to encourage you in your fancies, but this time I think you may be right. I believe Owen and Mr. Lymond are posing. I've seen them talking and suddenly stop when others walk up. My window faces the side entrance, and I've seen all sorts of people coming and going during the night. Owen himself came in—stealthily, I might add—about two o'clock last night. Wyrock came in right after him, along with two others I've seen around but don't know. I think one of them is working in the stables now in Willy's place."

"Why didn't you tell me about this, Cassie? You knew I was suspicious."

She made a face and leaned back against the pillows. "I suppose it was because you were suspicious, Roxanne. I desperately wanted those nocturnal visits to be innocent, but after seeing Willy's body and Jem's hand, I . . ." She stopped.

I took a deep breath. "I know, Cassie. I've been hesi-

164

tant to admit the full extent of my worries. The magistrates haven't been helpful, and after they laughed at me over Papa's death, I won't go to them until I have some real proof. If we suspect Lymond—and Amherst—we've got to find something to tie them to these murders."

"Do you really think they're murderers?" Cassie's eyes were wide. "That's impossible, Roxanne. You've accused them of dabbling in smuggling or something of that ilk, but murder—no. Couldn't Willy and Jem have met with accidents?"

"Willy was shot in the head, and I think it would have been very difficult for Jem to bury himself after he had had his brains bashed." My voice was dry.

Cassie laughed shakily. "I know, Roxanne, I know. I simply can't believe that Owen and Mr. Lymond are connected to murder in any way. I can't believe they're connected to *anything* nefarious." She looked at me, her eyes almost pleading. "Owen's one of the kindest, gentlest people I've ever met."

"Cassie," I said ruthlessly, "Mad Jim Barnwell was kind to animals and little children, and he slit the throats of eight men. There's no way to know." I paused. "Still, I agree with you—I dislike Lymond, but a murderer . . ." I shook my head. "I can't believe he'd do it."

"We could just ask them if they're involved."

"I'm sure they'd laugh at us, just as the magistrates did at Papa's death." I looked at her. "I know you want to get away, Cassie, but you can't go, at least not yet. It's up to us, my dear—we've got to get proof about what's going on here. I agree—I can't see either Lymond or Captain Amherst committing murder, but stranger things have happened. Assuming they didn't actually do anything, I think the two of them know who might have done it." I looked at her fixedly. "Cassie, I think Wyrock might be capable of murder."

We stared at each other and Cassie's eyes widened. By

now, her braid was almost undone. "Wyrock! Yes, Roxie, I think he could! Do you think there's any danger to us? After all, he's here all the time." She frowned as she thought. "He was watching Willy and had the opportunity, but who hit him on the head?"

I frowned. "That could have been a ruse to make it appear that he had been overpowered. After all, the doctor said all he would have was a serious headache. A small price to pay to remove suspicion." I patted her hand. "You've got to see if you can discover something from Captain Amherst, but you've got to be strong as well. Cassie, you simply can't let yourself develop a *tendre* for someone who might be a criminal."

"I should just go to London."

"No." I shook my head and frowned as I thought. "No, you're the logical one to pry into Captain Amherst's secrets. He does seem to be quite partial to you, and he'd talk to you. I think this might be the weak link in their chain." I stood and held out a hand to her. "It's up to you, Cassie. You're the one who's going to have to come up with our proof. I'll do what I can, but I think Captain Amherst is the logical point of attack."

"He isn't." She looked at me stubbornly. "A criminal, I mean. I know he's evasive about his background, but he's a good person. He could never . . . never do anything to hurt anyone else."

"Good heavens, Cassie. Of course he could hurt someone else; the man's in the Army. After all, aren't they trained to kill people?" I regretted the words as soon as they were out of my mouth.

"You're wrong about him, Roxanne."

Cassie was livid. I had never seen her like this before. "Now, Cass — " I began, but she interrupted me and continued.

"Don't try to soothe me, Roxie. Do you know what I'm going to do?" It was obviously a rhetorical question because she didn't even pause an instant for a reply. "I'm going to stay here and prove to you that Owen and Mr. Lymond can't be involved in this." She stopped for breath.

"All right, Cassie," I said before she could begin again. "I think that's a good idea. The only thing I'm asking is that you keep a clear head about Captain Amherst. If you discover anything, it's your duty to tell me or the magistrates."

"Of course." Her voice was ice.

"Cassie, we're sisters, and probably the closest of the four. Don't let this come between us."

"*I'm* not." She glared at me. "Don't worry, Roxanne. I don't intend to conceal anything, but I think *you* need to keep a clear head as well."

I sighed. This was as close as we had been to quarrelling since we were children. I reached over and took her hand. "Agreed. Do you want some chocolate?" She crawled back into her bed and didn't smile at me as she said no. I left with a heavy heart.

The next morning was Sunday and we all went to church together. Wyrock went with the Lymonds, and we all sat together. I always got the impression that Lymond wasn't much of a churchgoer. He usually seemed to forget which part of the ceremony came next. On this day, no one noticed since the whole place was buzzing with *on-dits* about the Prince's pending arrival.

Justin had come and quite took my breath away. He was wearing a black coat, a perfectly tied cravat, a gray brocaded waistcoat embroidered with black and red thistles, cream breeches, and, as usual, magnificently polished boots. Lymond looked quite rumpled in comparison, his cravat slightly askew and his hair curling casually around his face. He made a point of asking Justin to join us for nuncheon, a move which surprised me greatly.

Things went well, considering Aunt Hen brought

Mrs. Bocock along and she monopolized the conversation. The only topic seemed to be the Prince. Lymond did manage to mention paintings once or twice during the conversation, but no one seemed to notice. Captain Amherst came in while we were eating and joined us. He was forced to sit a distance from Cassie and had little to say. Livvy kept him occupied with stories about some of the Prince's previous visits.

Afterwards Justin asked if I would like to drive around Brighton with him in his carriage. He included Aunt Hen and Mrs. Bocock, much to their joy. As he handed the ladies into the carriage, he explained that he hadn't really had the time to explore the center of town, and, since all this talk of the Prince's visit had piqued his interest, he wanted the two of them to tell him all about it. As I knew it would, his charm melted Mrs. Bocock immediately, and, by the time we reached Brighton, she was chattering about who lived where and who owned or let.

Justin managed to get a word or two in to question her about some of the houses, especially the ones built of buff and blue brick, the Prince's colors, while Aunt Hen pointed out some things Mrs. Bocock missed. I was surprised at the extent of their knowledge. I had little idea what was in the houses, but both of them had an encyclopedic listing of almost everything and everybody in Brighton.

Justin stopped before one particularly fine house. "And whose is this one?" he asked.

"That," Aunt Hen said importantly, "belongs to Lord Debenham. Of the Home Office, you know."

"Debenham?" Justin looked puzzled. "I've heard the name, I believe. I've been away for so long that many things have changed. The Home Office, you said?"

"Yes." She and Mrs. Bocock bobbed their heads in unison.

Aunt Hen said, "Young Debenham's new in politics, but he picked up right where his father left off."

When she paused for breath, Mrs. Bocock continued without missing a beat. "He's fabulously wealthy, you know, so he's able to give all his time to his governmental duties."

"England's fortunate to have such men," Justin said, stemming the torrent and signaling for the carriage to move on.

"Yes," Aunt Hen agreed. "It's too bad that he's been the victim of crime and hasn't been able to locate the thieves." She lowered her voice an octave. "I heard it said reliably that the Prince has questioned Debenham's abilities since he hasn't been able to apprehend the culprits."

"Culprits?" Justin smiled at her. "Mrs. Vellory, that should be easy; the government is full of culprits."

Mrs. Bocock shook her head vigorously. "The thieves, we mean. He hasn't been able to apprehend the thieves."

"It's said that perhaps his career will be ruined," Aunt Hen noted, "although I think he's suffered enough by having his paintings taken." She and Mrs. Bocock looked at each other and nodded in agreement.

Justin looked puzzled, and I decided it was time for me to take a hand. "Debenham, in case you didn't know, had both his country seat and his house in London burgled. According to the *on-dit*, a great many valuable paintings were stolen. I'm surprised with your interest in paintings that you hadn't heard of it."

Justin smiled at me. "The people with whom I deal usually know nothing about stolen paintings." He frowned slightly. "The name, however, does seem familiar. Does he have paintings here?"

Aunt Hen was not to be stopped. "Yes, he does, and some very fine ones from what I hear. Such a shame about the others, though. Some had been in his family for generations, and when they were taken, Debenham

169

swore revenge. He said he'd track the culprits to ground if it took every cent he had."

Justin lifted an eyebrow. "I certainly wish him success. I—"

He was interrupted by the passing of a closed carriage and gasps from Aunt Hen and Mrs. Bocock. *"That woman!"* Mrs. Bocock said as she and Aunt Hen stared after the carriage. "Mrs. Fitzherbert." They looked at each other and nodded, their day complete.

The chatter back to Bellerophon concerned the Prince, Princess Caroline, Mrs. Fitzherbert, and Lady Hertford, all topics that did not concern me at all. We were almost home before I could manage to ask Justin about something that had occurred to me while we were looking at houses. I took him to task about the wallpaper in the dining room at Jervyne House. He looked rather surprised when I mentioned it, and I thought perhaps he hadn't realized the paper didn't suit. Often men didn't see those things. He smiled at me and promised to look at it as soon as he returned to Jervyne House.

As he drove away, Aunt Hen looked after him through the window. "A strange man, Roxanne. When I'm talking to him, I think he's a very fine gentleman indeed, but when I have time to think about him, I don't care for him at all. I wonder which is the real Mr. Denver?"

I grimaced. "You sound very much like Lymond."

I didn't wish to discuss this further in front of Mrs. Bocock. Instead I went to find Cassie. I needed to mend my fences and also discover if she and Captain Amherst had managed to speak. She was in the back garden, painting a picture of Holmwood's dahlias. Bue was panting in the shade of the house.

Cassie glanced up at me and went on painting. "There's no one home except me," she said. "And, no, I had little opportunity to speak with the captain. We exchanged pleasantries, he talked to Mr. Lymond for a few minutes, and then they and Wyrock left together."

I relaxed. Cassie seemed her usual self. "This may be a clue, Cassie. Do you know where they went? Were they in a hurry?"

"No to both questions." She leaned back and sighted her work critically. "Do you think this dahlia has more of a stripe than I've painted?"

I threw up my hands. "Good heavens, Cassie! Murders are happening all around us, and you're worried about the stripe on a dahlia! Don't you want to do anything?"

"No." She looked at me, the hint of a smile in her eyes. "You always get so up in the boughs, Roxanne. It isn't good for your health, you know."

"The next thing I know, you'll be suggesting I take the waters," I said, walking off. Cassie could be maddening at times.

I wondered if either Livvy or Julia knew where Amherst, Wyrock, and Lymond had gone, but the two of them had gone visiting. Woodbury knew nothing either, but I had him check the plate, just in case. He reported that everything seemed to be where it was supposed to be.

Lymond and Wyrock didn't return until very close to midnight. I was propped up in bed, attempting to read a rather vile novel. When I heard them come in, I reached over to the table beside my bed, flipped open Papa's watch, checked the time, and then blew out my candle. Curiosity was certainly hard on one's sleep.

Chapter Twelve

My curiosity certainly wasn't appeased the next morning. I was groggy at breakfast, Lymond was exceptionally chipper, Cassie picked at her food and didn't eat, and everyone else chatted about the Prince's visit. It was a relief when they all left to work on their wardrobes. I stayed in hopes of a few minutes with Cassie.

It was not to be. Lymond returned in a moment, sat down, and produced a key from his pocket. He tossed it down in front of me. "Don't you recognize it?" he asked.

I picked it up and frowned. "I don't recall seeing it before."

Lymond plucked it from my fingers and repocketed it. "Really, Miss Sydney, I'm disappointed. What we have here is the key to the mausoleum. I stole it this morning, just to see if I could."

"What? You did what?"

"I stole it. Rather, I wandered into the butler's pantry where Woodbury was working and lifted it off the hook while his back was turned. Quite a simple operation, if I do say so myself."

"But why would you want it?" Cassie asked, looking at him in a puzzled way as she pushed food absently around her plate.

Lymond looked at me. "You haven't told her?"

I shook my head and Cassie frowned. "Told me what?"

I started to give her a brief recounting of the events at the mausoleum, but Lymond interrupted me and told her about it, leaving me entirely out of the story. I was quite surprised at his delicacy. I hadn't thought him capable of it. He told the whole thing as something that had happened to him, but that he had discussed with me. For the first time, I had to own him something of a gentleman. "So," he concluded, "Ned and I escorted Miss Sydney"—he glanced at me—"back there the next day, but she didn't find anything missing. It was a puzzle, however, as to how the intruders had a key."

"What you're saying is that anyone could have taken it." Cassie's eyes were wide.

Lymond shook his head. "No, what I'm saying is that someone took it who's familiar with this house. Whoever took it probably had a duplicate made, then returned this one. That would take some doing, even if Woodbury is rather vague about his keys. Also, there was the risk that someone would need the key and search for it while it was being duplicated." There was a commotion at the door and Captain Amherst came in.

"Good morning, Owen," Lymond said. "You're early. Have some breakfast with us and we'll discuss the problem of the mausoleum."

Captain Amherst sat across from Cassie and smiled at her. She didn't return his smile. She didn't even look at him. I sighed—Cassie certainly would never get any information that way. Lymond held up the key to the mausoleum like a trophy. "We're discussing how this might have been taken."

"He knows as well?" I asked rather bitterly. "I suppose the rest of your cronies also know. Have you put a notice in the *Times*, Lymond? You could hire some urchins to pass out broadsides."

Lymond threw back his head and laughed. It was infectious—in just a moment we were all laughing. After the hilarity passed, he returned to the topic of the key, putting it on the table and telling Captain Amherst what we had discussed.

"That gives us," Amherst said, between bites of breakfast, "the probability that the person made an impression in soap or something similar."

Lymond nodded. "I thought of that. It would have taken only a few minutes." He picked up the key, tossed it in the air, and caught it as it fell back down. "In either event, Miss Sydney, someone who shouldn't have access has been into your keys. Has there been any kind of disturbance that would have upset the household routine?"

"You were in London," Cassie said to me.

I nodded. "But that was when Papa was alive. We used the key after that."

"Yes, at Papa's funeral." Cassie's voice was shaky. "I know it was here then."

Lymond leaned towards me. "Then whoever has a copy must have acquired it after that time. That means recently. Are you sure nothing untoward has happened since then? Think hard, Miss Sydney. It may have been only a brief thing."

I was getting exasperated. "I told you, no. Edward came down, of course, and spent some time, but he certainly wouldn't have taken it."

"Edward?" Lymond's voice was sharp and probing. I got the impression that he had done this type of questioning before.

"Our brother," Cassie said, coming to my defense. "He doesn't—"

"There was no one," I said flatly. There was no reason for Lymond to know the family history.

"Nobody else at all?"

This was too much. "Let it go, Lymond!" I said, exas-

174

perated. "I said there was no one. The only people who have been here since the funeral have been Edward, the servants, Mr. Miffle, Justin, the family, and then you and your guests." I put a slight emphasis on the word "guests," then paused. "And, of course, the carpenters."

It hit all four of us at once and we turned and looked at one another. "The carpenters," I said slowly.

Lymond looked shocked for an instant, then his face shuttered. He looked at Captain Amherst. "Perfect," he muttered, "and so simple. What a perfect scheme."

I couldn't believe I hadn't seen the connection. "I wonder which one it was? They were all over the place and it could have been any one of them."

Captain Amherst nodded. "People are always calling in carpenters and plasterers. There'd be no better way to examine a house and see the contents."

"Papa," I said, looking at Cassie. She must have been thinking the same thing I was because she was staring at me with wide eyes.

"What do you mean?" Lymond asked, leaning towards me intently.

I hesitated. I wasn't going to have him laughing at me about my suspicions. Having one of the local magistrates, Lord Franklynne, pat me on the shoulder and tell me I was only having girlish imaginings, then having Edward chime in and say that I must have inherited Papa's vivid imagination had been too much to bear, and I certainly didn't trust Lymond enough to tell him anything. "Nothing," I muttered. "I was only thinking of the carpenters."

Lymond looked at me strangely but let it drop. "When you did your renovations recently, were all your carpenters local people?"

"Most of them were local. We'd had some of them before when . . . before when Papa did some of his work. I engaged several because we wanted to get the work done

175

quickly. If you recall, I even saw a few of them working over at Jervyne Hall."

Lymond jerked as if he had been stuck with a pin, and a quick glance passed between him and Captain Amherst. It was over in an instant, and his face shuttered again. His voice was light when he spoke. "Would you like to ride over there on a visit this morning and see if you recognize any of them?"

"I can't go over there and ask to have all the carpenters line up for inspection," I said with a tinge of disgust. "Are you out of your mind?"

He laughed, although it wasn't particularly mirthful. "Perhaps my mind *is* going. Since I've been in this house, that seems to be a definite possibility."

"We could all go." We stared at Cassie and she repeated herself. "We could all go." She fluttered her hands. "After all, Mr. Denver *has* asked us over to visit several times and we've always said we'd wait until he finished the house. We could all be out riding and just happen to stop by." She blushed and dropped her eyes. "I suppose not. That would be dissembling, wouldn't it?"

"Yes," Captain Amherst agreed, "but it's a perfect solution. I think we should always be neighborly, shouldn't we?"

"All right, we'll all go," I said. I needed to talk to Justin about this. Lymond reached out and held my wrist. "I don't think you should go, after all," he said, staring hard at me.

I felt my eyes widen. "And why not?" I pulled my wrist away and glared at him. "I need to—"

"You think you need to speak to Justin Denver and warn him about the carpenters. This is exactly what we don't need." He paused, searching for words. "Miss Sydney—Roxanne—I may as well be blunt. I don't want him warned."

"*You* don't?" I demanded. "Since when have you given

me orders, Lymond? You of all people." I stopped, catching myself before I let him know my suspicions of him. I glanced at Cassie, expecting support.

"I think Mr. Lymond may be right, Roxanne," she said. "Perhaps we should simply go see which of our carpenters are there. We don't want to say anything to Mr. Denver until we're sure. I'd hate to slander an innocent person."

Lymond looked at her gratefully and I knew that wasn't the reason he didn't wish Justin warned. Still, it was true — we had seen some of those carpenters around since we were children and I didn't wish to malign anyone unjustly. "All right," I said grudgingly. "I promise I won't say anything to Jus — Mr. Denver. At least, not now, not until we have proof of some sort." I looked significantly at Lymond, but he ignored my message.

We set out for Jervyne Hall in record time, waiting only long enough for Cassie and me to put on our habits. The morning was fine, and our excuse about being out for a ride would be plausible. It really was a wonderful morning for a ride.

When Jervyne Hall came into view, I was struck by the quiet. Before, it had seemed there were dozens of carpenters about, but today, everything seemed still. We reined in at the top of the rise and looked at the house, peaceful in its setting. "Perhaps they're all working inside," Cassie suggested. "After all, the outside does look complete."

"Probably replacing that terrible wallpaper in the dining room," I told her. "Cassie, I want to get your opinion on that. I told Mr. Denver that the paper was all wrong. It's too heavy for that room, and the paperhangers did a bad job on it. I could see lines and wrinkles."

Cassie nodded as we rode down to the house. As we dismounted, Robin Norwood came out the door and greeted us. "Mr. Denver isn't at home this morning," he told us.

We stood around awkwardly for a moment, then I decided to take matters into my own hands. "We didn't really come to visit him," I said. "He had invited us over to see the renovations, so that's why we stopped by. Cassandra hasn't seen the house yet and is looking forward to it. Could you show us around? I'm sure it would be all right."

He hesitated, but we held our ground. "Certainly, I'd be delighted," he said, but he didn't sound delighted at all.

To our surprise, there were no carpenters working. Lymond hinted around, but I finally came right out and asked Mr. Norwood why no one was there. "Mr. Denver gave them some time off to go into Brighton to view the Prince's entrance into town," he said. "They'll be back at work tomorrow morning."

Since there was now no point to our visit, I took Cassie to the dining room to see the paper, and she agreed with me that it was atrocious. Mr. Norwood reassured us that it would be replaced, probably within the week. The paper had already been ordered. With that, we went back outside and mounted up, thanking Mr. Norwood and promising to return. I waited until we were back up on the rise where we could see Bellerophon before I said anything to Lymond. "Are you satisfied now?" I asked.

"We still don't know anything," Cassie said with a frown. "We'll have to come back."

Lymond nodded. "Owen, will you escort the ladies back home? I want to go take another look at that mausoleum." He looked at me. "I'll let you know if I discover anything interesting."

"Oh, no, you won't," I said, pulling Buttercup around. "I'm going along." I paused, remembering the last time we went to the mausoleum. "Cassie, would you like to come?"

Lymond looked surprised, then looked at me and laughed. He knew exactly what I was thinking. I felt my face flame and knew he could read my expression. "Let's all make a morning of it, then." He put The Bruce to a gallop and we all followed him. The man was completely exasperating.

To my surprise, Lymond rode past the mausoleum and on down the coast, the rest of us right behind him. He finally stopped on a rise where we could look back and see both the mausoleum and Bellerophon glistening white against the green grass like opals and emeralds. Tears almost sprang to my eyes as I looked at it. I think right then I loved it as much as Papa had.

We cantered back down the edge of the sea until we came to the mausoleum. Lymond and Captain Amherst helped us down and walked the horses a few minutes before tying them. Lymond took a small metal box from his saddlebag. "Candles," he said briefly, handing me the box. "I thought we'd better have our own, unlike our last foray."

"What do you mean?" Cassie demanded. "I think I should know."

Lymond and I glanced at each other, and I shrugged. I was sure Cassie would understand why I was out unchaperoned with Lymond and would never tell anyone. Briefly, and with a great deal of delicacy, Lymond re-edited his story, putting me into the nocturnal visit to the mausoleum. Cassie's eyes were wide. "You're sworn to secrecy on this, Owen," Lymond said, glancing at the captain. "I never want to hear a word against Miss Sydney."

Captain Amherst looked offended. "Good lord, Robert, do you really think I'd say anything?"

Lymond grinned at him. "No, but I just wanted you to know where I stood."

Amherst gave him an odd smile. "I know just where you stand, Robert." To my surprise, Lymond averted his eyes. I wondered just what that exchange had been about.

"You were really brave, Roxanne," Cassie said, clasping my hand.

It was my turn to avert my eyes. "Let's go inside," I said to cover my embarrassment.

Lymond inserted the key and it turned noiselessly in the lock. "They've even oiled the lock for us," he said, making a face.

We all went inside, stopping first to take a candle from the box and light it. "We need to find a place to hide these," Lymond said, turning around and holding up the candle as he looked for a place.

"Here, in the horse," I replied, walking in front of him toward the far wall. I stepped in something and almost slipped. When I looked down, I was standing at the sticky edge of a puddle of something. "What's this?" I stepped back, my boots adhering slightly to the floor.

To my surprise, Lymond shoved the box towards Captain Amherst and Cassie. "Stay back, the both of you," he ordered as he knelt and touched the puddle. "Unless I'm greatly mistaken, it's blood."

I looked down at the puddle and felt my knees get slightly weak. The same thing must have been happening to Cassie as I noticed she sagged noticeably. Captain Amherst put his arm around her waist for support. I forced myself to stand straight, but it was an effort. "Very well, Lymond," I made myself say calmly, "if it is blood, where did it come from and whose is it?"

Lymond shook his head. "I have no idea." He touched his finger to the puddle, sniffed it, then wiped his finger on his handkerchief. He stood and held the candle so that

180

more of the interior was illuminated. "I don't see anything here or even a trail of blood. This is fairly fresh," he glanced at Captain Amherst, "I'd say during the early hours of the morning." He looked back at me. "Is there any other way out of here?"

"No. Not that I know of anyway." I looked around.

"With Papa, one never knows," Cassie said.

I walked around the edge of the puddle. It was in the middle of the floor and seemed to start and stop there. There wasn't even a trail of blood drops out the door. "Cassie, look around at the door," I said. "There may be something there."

"All right," she said faintly.

I looked up sharply at her. She was very pale and her eyes were enormous. "Owen," Lymond suggested delicately, "perhaps you should take Miss Sydney out for some fresh air before you look around. Check the flagstones out front while you're there."

Captain Amherst nodded and guided Cassie back out the door. He did not seem reluctant to do this and kept his arm firmly around her shoulders. I glanced at Lymond, but he was busy, down on hands and knees examining the floor around the puddle.

"Lymond, look here." I pointed to a large smear on the side of the wooden horse. He stood and brought the candle over. "They've evidently had a fight in here," he said, looking at the boxes of artifacts that had been stacked against the wall. One of them had been knocked down and the contents scattered. We bent to put them back in the box. "What are these things, anyway?" Lymond asked.

"I have no idea. This shipment arrived the day of Papa's funeral and I really didn't take the time to look at it. We opened a box—this one, I think—and stacked them in here until we had time to examine them. To tell the truth, I never went through them."

He held one up in the candlelight and his eyes widened. The flickering light on his tanned skin highlighted his cheekbones. I shuddered. He looked almost like an Egyptian tomb robber. I put the thought out of my mind and averted my eyes. Lymond hadn't noticed my reaction.

"These look like some kind of papyri. Didn't you say your father was in some kind of Egyptian phase when he passed away?"

"Yes," I said with a sigh. "We'd talked him out of making this a pyramid, so he was planning to build a pyramid on the front lawn. Just a small replica." I tossed the artifacts back in the box. "More junk, I suppose." I replaced the lid. "I told you Papa collected anything and everything."

"You should take these to an antiquarian I know," Lymond said, standing and holding out a hand for me. The candle was a column of light in the dark mausoleum, Lymond and I inside it. Face-to-face, we looked at each other for a long moment, and time stopped. "Roxanne," he said, an odd note in his voice.

I stepped back quickly into the darkness. "We'd better go outside and see about Cassie," I said, a husky tinge to my own voice. For some reason, I was breathless.

Lymond nodded and the moment was broken. We went to the door, Lymond turning and closing the door behind us. Captain Amherst and Cassie were out front, perched on the edge of the porch. "Are you all right, Cassie?" I asked, sitting beside her.

She nodded as Lymond walked down to stand in front of us. "I'm fine but if you have time, I think I'll walk out to the cliff edge."

I smiled at her. "Wobbly knees?" She nodded and Captain Amherst helped her to her feet. "I'll be back in a moment. I just think the walk will do me good."

I nodded and watched them walk towards the cliff.

"They make a handsome couple," Lymond observed.

"Cassie's going to London for a season," I commented. I wanted to let Lymond know how things were.

He shrugged. "Just as well. Owen will probably never marry."

"Why do you say that?"

Lymond looked at me, started to speak, then changed his mind. "Just a feeling I have." He paused. "Enough about Owen. Miss Sydney, while we have a quiet moment, I'd like to discuss something with you."

I leaned back against a column. "All right." There was a long pause. I was getting ready to prompt him when he began talking. "I know, Miss Sydney, that you don't hold me in very high regard—"

"That's not true, Mr. Lymond." I surprised myself. Once the words were out, I realized I really meant them.

He shrugged again; he obviously didn't believe me. "I also know that you think I'm involved in some kind of clandestine dealings." There was a pause, but I said nothing this time. Lymond glanced at me, out to Captain Amherst and Cassie, then went on. "In actuality, I *am* involved in something, but I want to assure you that I'm doing nothing illegal. On the contrary, I'm working to try to stop, um, certain activities. I wish I could tell you more, but I can't. Perhaps there will be a time later when I can explain fully."

"Why not now? Do you think I'll tell someone?"

He hesitated. "I don't know. There are certain things and people involved that I can't disclose right now." He looked at me. "I'm also afraid there might be some danger to you. We're dealing with a very unscrupulous person."

"Dealing with?"

"An unfortunate choice of words," Lymond said. "I personally have no dealings with this person."

I started to add two and two. "Are we talking about the

person referred to as 'the Master' by those two rogues?"

Lymond nodded. "He's known as the Master of Criminals on —" He paused as Cassie and Captain Amherst walked up, then turned briefly to the captain. "I judged it was time to tell Miss Sydney about our adversary."

Captain Amherst raised a well-shaped eyebrow. I knew he didn't approve. "Whatever you think best," he said, helping Cassie sit beside me.

Lymond looked at Cassie, and I knew what he was thinking. "Whatever I know, Cassie knows, and vice versa," I told him. "I assure you that whatever you tell us will be confidential." I paused. "Unless, of course, we feel you're doing something illegal. Then, of course, we'd be forced to alert the magistrates."

"We're doing nothing illegal, I assure you. We're trying to catch the painting thieves. We have reason to believe they're operating out of Brighton and that the man I told you about — the Master of Criminals — is the spider behind this web."

"Here? In Brighton? Do you mean *here*?" I demanded as Cassie gasped. "Do you mean here at Bellerophon?"

Lymond glanced at Captain Amherst, but he wasn't talking. He was letting Lymond be in charge. "Yes."

There was a pause while he let us think about this. "Are you sure?" Cassie asked quietly.

"Not positive, of course, but as sure as we can be." Lymond must have guessed our thoughts. "I know you think this is a dull place except when the Prince is here, but it's ideally situated for some things. There are many wealthy members of the *ton* here, many rich houses, and it's close to the sea. Also, it's cosmopolitan enough so that a foreigner wouldn't be overly remarked."

"A foreigner? The Master of Criminals is a foreigner? That's impossible, Lymond."

He looked at Captain Amherst and they laughed.

"Why impossible? Do you think the English have a monopoly on thievery?"

I was stung. "No," I answered, "but I think this person must have a very good idea of who's who in the *ton*. From what I hear, he's very selective, so he must have some very good acquaintances in society." I thought about it for a moment. "Lymond, are you —"

He grimaced. "No, I told you that I'm involved in trying to catch them." He looked at Cassie and at me, then at Amherst. "Please remember that this is confidential. Do not repeat this to *anyone*. Not to your sisters, not to Mrs. Vellory," he gave me a curious look, "not to Mr. Denver." He hesitated. "Do I have your word on that?"

Cassie nodded immediately, but I paused. I had planned to tell Justin about this curious conversation. He might be able to help. "Roxanne?" Lymond asked.

"I pledge her word," Cassie said. "Roxanne won't say anything."

"I'm perfectly capable of pledging myself," I said. "I won't talk to anyone — except a magistrate if I have to. Although," I added, thinking about my previous experience with them, "I'd probably be better off going to London and trying to see Lord Debenham. I'm not sure the locals would believe me."

Lymond laughed and looked at Amherst again. "Wonderful. If you need to, or if anything happens to me, go straight to Debenham. You see, I'm here working under orders from him."

I hated to be skeptical, but I was. Cassie on the other hand, swallowed it all. Her eyes widened. "And you're here to catch the criminals?"

Lymond nodded. I still wasn't sure but said nothing. Lymond continued, "I decided to tell you because I'm afraid the thief or thieves are involved in the things that have been going on at Bellerophon. I think both Jem and

185

Willy were involved and were killed because they were weak links — they would have talked under the right circumstances."

"And the carpenters?" I sat and tried to think this through.

"It's a perfect scheme," Cassie said. "Carpenters, plasterers, painters. People think nothing of having all those workmen wandering all over the house. The houses here are always having to be painted and refurbished because of the wind and salt, so these people would be called in constantly."

"Also," Captain Amherst added, breaking his silence, "the Prince seems to have started something of an explosion in building, so it's happening all over the country. There have been paintings stolen from Scotland to all the way south."

"We think they're all being funneled to the Continent through an outlet here at Brighton," Lymond said, looking out to sea.

"I see," I said slowly. "So whoever organized all these thefts has a wide network. He must be something of a criminal genius."

Lymond glanced at Amherst. "Yes, the man is acknowledged as brilliant. He's stolen things all over Europe for years and eluded every trap ever set for him. We knew it was only a question of time before he started operations here."

"Do you know his name?" Cassie asked.

"Or rather," I added with a grimace, "the name he's using now in England?"

"No, we don't know his real name, and he uses many aliases. In fact, no one knows who he is. His minions simply refer to him as 'the Master,' and no one is really sure what he looks like. He's reputed to be not only a master at organizing and conceiving crime, but he's also a master of disguise. From what we've gleaned from agencies on the Continent, the only sure thing known about him is that he's of English origin. As far as his person, he appears in a different incarnation and with a different name every time."

Captain Amherst gave a short, bitter laugh. "One of the reasons he's never been caught."

"Carpenters," Cassie said in amazement. "What a simple idea. No wonder it worked so well."

I frowned at this. "I know I promised you, Lymond, but I feel we should warn Jus — Mr. Denver. He's in grave danger."

"You gave me your promise, Roxanne. Denver knows, I'm sure of it." He touched my arm lightly. "Do I have your word?"

I hesitated, looking into those startlingly blue eyes. I could have sworn that, at that moment, I saw the truth in them. "You have my word. I won't say anything to anybody unless we discuss it."

"Thank you." He glanced at both of us. "I shouldn't have told you as much as I have but," he paused, "I have my reasons."

Cassie smiled at him warmly. "We understand perfectly, Mr. Lymond, and you can be sure we plan to cooperate in every way possible."

She was interrupted by the sound of hooves as Wyrock rode at a gallop over the field. He was coming from the direction of Brighton. After he reined up sharply and dismounted, I saw that he quite obviously had a message and was just as obviously reluctant to say anything in front of us. Lymond took him by the arm and they walked towards the sea, out of earshot. Captain Amherst got our horses, and Cassie and I prepared to go back to Bellerophon.

Lymond walked quickly back to us. "They've hit again. Bowater's house this time. He had two prized Holbeins and a great deal of junk. The Holbeins are missing." He hesitated and looked directly at me. "It evidently happened this morning."

"Has he had carpenters in the house recently?" Cassie asked before I could.

Lymond nodded. "Last week. He wanted to refurbish before the Prince's visit and had the whole house repainted." He looked troubled. "I need to go into Brighton immediately. Owen will escort you back home." Before we could ask anything else, he was mounted and off with Wyrock.

I questioned Captain Amherst all the way home to no avail; he was as expert as Lymond when it came to dodging questions.

Chapter Thirteen

Captain Amherst left us safely at home and went immediately to join Lymond in Brighton. I thought he was probably dodging more questions, but it didn't matter since he gave no answers. Cassie and I closeted ourselves in my room to talk, an easy thing to do since everyone else was gathered in the front, sewing and chattering about the Prince's visit.

"Do you know anything I don't?" I pounced on her as soon as I closed the door.

She floated across the floor and climbed up on my bed, leaning back against the pillows, making herself quite comfortable. "No," she finally said, a slight frown on her face. "From what I gleaned today, however, I suppose you know a great deal that I don't."

I sat down gloomily. "I can't figure out Lymond." I almost bit my nails but remembered Aunt Hen's exhortations in time. I put my hands in my lap. "I think he's telling the truth, but something still seems not quite right."

"Perhaps he's telling only part of the truth."

I grimaced. "I've decided that as well. The question is, which part of his tale is the truth and which isn't?" I looked at Cassie. "Did you get anything at all from Captain Amherst?"

She shook her head. "Only that he didn't think it a good idea for Lymond to tell us anything. He seems to feel that if we know anything at all, we could be in danger."

"I doubt anyone would bother us. After all, there's nothing really valuable here. I know Papa collected all sorts of things, but most of it's junk and the rest is of minimal value."

"Think about Jem and Willy." Cassie's voice was low.

I frowned. "I don't think their deaths had anything to do with us. They simply got mixed up with the wrong people. You know that both of them, Willy especially, were always wild." I paused while I thought. "Cassie, there's got to be something else — some other piece of the puzzle that will make all the rest clear."

She grinned at me. "All we have to do is find it."

We talked for a while longer but reached no conclusions, finally giving up and joining the others in the front. The chatter about the Prince and clothes and furbelows annoyed me, but at least it took my mind away from the puzzle I couldn't solve. I kept looking at Amelia, wondering if Lymond ever confided in her, wondering about Francis, wondering about everything. Lymond and Amelia seemed mismatched if ever a couple were. They often seemed more like strangers than husband and wife. However, I reminded myself, from what I had seen of Edward and Matilda, they were much the same. I gave up my imaginings and tried to concentrate on my stitches after both Livvy and Aunt Hen complained my rows were crooked. They were, but then my sewing was always crooked.

That night after supper, Amelia entertained us with her playing and singing. The other girls took turns as well. I sat back out of the way, an extra chair beside me, hoping Lymond would come sit beside me and tell me what had happened in Brighton. He had come in right before supper and had said only a few words during the meal. I looked several times in his direction but he ignored me. Actually, he ignored everyone, seemingly lost in thought. No matter that I was dying of curiosity. Cassie did come sit beside me after a while.

"Cassie, I'm going to explode if I don't discover something. I'm even thinking of asking Lymond to meet me down here after everyone's gone to bed. You could chaperon."

"Roxanne!"

I knew the idea was a poor one when Cassie gasped. "Oh, all right," I said. "I just know I won't sleep a wink tonight. I think he's ignoring me deliberately."

"He probably is," Cassie agreed, laughing.

I did get up and prowl around my room during the night, did consider trying to see Lymond, but even I didn't have that much nerve. I finally went to sleep vowing to see Lymond in the morning and drag some information out of him, one way or another.

Amelia was at breakfast when I went in, and she was looking quite pretty. She had certainly bloomed of late—since Francis's visit. We ate and chatted, the usual things. She did mention that Lymond was out talking to Holmwood. I left the rest of my tea and dashed back to our apartments to go out the door there. I didn't want to appear overly eager.

Lymond and Holmwood were discussing the vegetation in Brighton or rather the lack thereof. I stood there, trying to smile, while they droned on and on. "Do come look at this," I finally said, almost dragging Lymond over to a flower bed. Holmwood started to follow us, but Bue bounded over, Lymond dodged behind me, and Holmwood became involved in dragging Bue back to his doghouse.

"What did you want to show me?" Lymond asked, stepping from behind me.

"Nothing, and you know it. I want to know what you discovered in Brighton. Why on earth didn't you tell me last night?"

Lymond rolled his eyes. "Always a dozen questions at once. I didn't tell you anything because there isn't anything to tell. Bowater's paintings are gone. That's all. No clues, no witnesses."

"But you suspect the Master." He nodded, and I went on, not waiting for him to speak. "Lymond, why don't you just have someone draw a picture of this man and circulate it? That way, everyone could be on the lookout for him."

"No one knows what he looks like." Lymond grimaced. "I told you he's a master of disguise and as far as what his person is like, no one knows. He appears in a different incarnation and with a different name every time. From what we know, he could look like Holmwood today and like me tomorrow. That's one of the reasons he's never been caught."

I gave him a sharp look. Was he trying to tell me something? Was he really trying to catch this criminal, or was this all fustian? Was he telling me everything or just enough to allay my fears? Could Francis, whoever he was, have anything to do with this? Could Francis be the Master? Could Lymond have been disguised as Francis? It was too much. "Lymond," I asked as lightly as I could, "does Amelia know all these things you've told me? She could be in danger."

He looked at me sharply. "I don't think Amelia's in danger, but the answer is no. She's much too ill to be disturbed with this.

"She seems to be feeling better."

"Physically, I think." He hesitated. "I suppose you and Amelia have talked."

I shook my head, but Lymond was looking into the distance and didn't see me. "No," I said.

He took my elbow and we started to walk the grounds, ostensibly admiring Holmwood's work, but really seeing nothing. "There was a child," he said, "a daughter. A beautiful little thing, all blue eyes and curling wisps of hair. She lived for four months and then died. We — I thought Amelia was going to die from grief and she's just now regaining her health. You and your family have done wonders for her, and for that, I thank you."

"You're welcome." I didn't know what else to say and thankfully was spared having to say anything else because Cassie and Captain Amherst came across the lawn towards us. "Look who's come to visit," Cassie called out.

I looked at them, then looked again. They made a lovely couple, walking across the grass together, the sun shining on them. They complemented each other.

"Talking about yesterday?" Captain Amherst asked, flicking a glance at Lymond. Lymond nodded, and Amherst continued. "Have you decided whose blood was on the floor?"

Lymond shook his head. "No idea. Whoever he was, he was probably killed and his body thrown out to sea. It might be days or weeks or never before we find it." He looked at me and his mouth twisted into a cynical smile. "I told you Brighton had its advantages." He and Amherst looked at each other again, a strange, passing look. Then Lymond turned to me. "Miss Sydney — Roxanne, Cassandra — I don't want to cause either of you any distress, but I need to know the answer to a question, and only one of you can give me that answer."

He hesitated and I prompted him. "Go on."

"Is there any possibility that your father's death could not have been an accident?"

I felt as though the wind had been knocked out of me and almost doubled over. Lymond led me to a nearby bench and I sat down gratefully. Feeling myself go pale, I didn't say anything. "You'd better tell them, Roxanne,"

Cassie said gently, sitting down beside me. "Tell them everything that happened. They'll believe you."

I sat there paralyzed as images flashed through my mind of the moment Papa's accident had occurred. I was inside, working on Papa's manuscript, transcribing some notes he had made, then went outside to see if he had a moment to answer a question. The day was bright. Papa, always loving to be in the thick of things, had climbed up on the roof to give directions to the workmen. He was standing near the edge, and suddenly there was a black silhouette beside him. Then there was Papa's body crashing down right in front of me, making a heavy thud as it hit the ground. I glanced up quickly as a black silhouette, the sun behind him, wheeled around and moved from my sight. It had all happened in an instant. I fell to the ground beside Papa, but there was nothing I could do except listen to whispered words about the Treasure. He died in my arms and I fainted.

When I finally came back to myself, I was inside on my own bed. Everyone assured me it had been an accident, no matter what I said. I tried to talk to the magistrate, but he noted that I had been hysterical and dismissed my story as the ravings of a grief-crazed female. He was patronizing, as were all the men around, especially Edward. I had vowed never to mention it again.

"Are you all right?" Lymond asked me, touching my elbow. "I'm sorry to overset you so, but I'm trying to eliminate every possibility. Was it an accident?"

Cassie put her arm around my shoulder. "Tell them what you told me, Roxanne," she whispered. "They won't laugh."

I shut my eyes to keep back tears, then took a deep breath. I wasn't going to break down in front of Lymond. I tried to look at him, but those startlingly blue eyes were staring at me, full of worry. I averted my eyes and looked at the ground. "I don't know," I whispered. "There was no

194

reason for anyone to kill Papa. He was the mildest, sweetest man alive." It was the same argument I had used on myself for months. It still wasn't working.

"Look at me." Lymond's voice had an edge and it angered me. "I'm asking you again, and I want a truthful answer: was your father's death an accident?"

"No!" I flung the words at him, not caring if he believed me or not. "No, it wasn't! Someone pushed him off the roof. I don't know who or why, but I know I saw someone up there." I took a big gulp of air now that the words were out and sat there, waiting for him to laugh at me.

Instead, he smiled gently at me, his expression full of sympathy. "I thought so. Do you have any idea who pushed him?" He hesitated. "I'm sorry to be asking you these painful questions, but I —" he glanced at Captain Amherst — "we need to know. I think all these events are related."

I was amazed. Someone actually believed in me. He wasn't going to laugh, he wasn't going to tell me I was merely a hysterical female. "I understand," I said, trying to keep control of myself. "If you can help us find out who . . . who killed Papa, then everything will be worth it. I'll tell you."

I proceeded to describe that day in detail and how I had been disparaged by Edward and when I finished, there was a moment of silence. "So," Lymond said slowly, giving Captain Amherst a significant look, "I think you might have been the only one who was right."

Amherst looked sympathetically at me as well. "Robert, we should thank Miss Sydney for helping us. This must be very difficult for her."

Cassie came around in front of me and looked at me anxiously. "Yes, it is. Are you all right, Roxanne?" She sat down on the facing bench as Lymond sat beside me. Captain Amherst placed himself next to Cassie. We must have looked as if we were having a comfortable chat on a sunny afternoon in the garden instead of talking about murder. "That's what it was," I said, "murder. I know it was."

Lymond started to put his hand on mine but thought the better of it. When he spoke, his voice was warm and persuasive. "Miss Sydney, I don't want to overset you, but can you think of any reason someone might want your father out of the way—any reason at all, no matter how trivial it may seem."

"The Treasure?" Cassie asked. "Papa was always making jokes about finding the treasure of Priam or some such."

I shook my head. "No. At first I thought it might have had something to do with that, but the first time Papa ever said anything in front of the workmen about the Treasure was when he died. Besides, I'm convinced it doesn't exist."

Amherst added a question. "Has anyone tried to purchase the house or buy his artifacts?"

Cassie looked at me and I shook my head. "Over the years there have been several offers for the house, most of them from members of the *ton* who'd like a place in Brighton, although we're rather far from the center of town. Papa didn't intend to sell, so he ignored the offers. Edward's received several offers, but Papa left the house to us because Edward would have sold it right out from under us. I've ignored the offers just as Papa did. As for his other possessions, Papa was always buying, selling, and trading artifacts with others who had similar interests. I can't imagine any of them doing murder for antiquities."

"Murder has often been done for very little, Miss Sydney." Lymond glanced up at the sun. "I think, Owen, that we have some things to do in Brighton." He stood and helped me to my feet. Did he hold my hand slightly longer than was necessary? I wondered.

196

Things went on normally for a few days. Justin came to visit, and although I was tempted to confide in him, I remembered my promise to Lymond. I always keep my promises, although I could think of little else while Justin was talking. He was full of news about the Prince's visit and the latest *on-dits* from London. He seemed to have assimilated the local gossip quite well. He even impressed Aunt Hen by knowing an item about Mrs. Fitzherbert that neither Aunt Hen nor Mrs. Bocock had heard. Justin invited me to go with him to watch the Prince arrive. I probably would have gone if he had asked me before I had declared in front of Cassie, Captain Amherst, Amelia, and Lymond that I wouldn't go see the Prince if he were wearing horns, a red devil suit, and a tail. Lymond, in all gravity, assured me that, considering the Prince, this costume might be a real possibility.

At any rate, Justin seemed quite disappointed by my decision to stay at home while the rest of Brighton and south England was watching the Prince. I was quite pleased at his disappointment. A very good sign if I was any judge of character at all, and I did pride myself on being a good judge of character.

It was midafternoon of a glorious, sunny day when the Lymonds, Captain Amherst, and all my family left for Brighton to see the spectacle. The Prince did know how to choose his times.

Thoroughly bored and secretly regretting my decision, I paced the floor for a while, then took a novel and propped up on the bed to read. Bue collapsed on the rug beside my bed but began to snore loudly. I yelled at him several times, but all he ever did was get up, flop back down, then begin snoring again. Finally I left my bedchamber, determined to put him outside and do something constructive — such as go look around Lymond's room. I had to drag Bue to the outside door and bend down to hold his collar with one hand while I turned the knob with the other.

I opened the door and Ned fell right in on top of me. We made a flailing pile in the floor — Ned, Bucephalus, and me. Finally we got untangled, and I took Ned to task. "What are you doing here, Ned? Has something happened down at the stables?"

He stared at his feet for a moment, then looked me right in the eyes. His face was full of boyish determination. "Mr. Lymond and Captain Amherst told me to stay here and watch after you. Mr. Wyrock's watching you as well. We're not to leave for anything." With that, he backed out the door, almost falling over Bucephalus in the process, and sat down with his back against the door frame and his legs stretched out across the opening. I thanked him very much and shut the door. I didn't know what else to do.

I prowled around the apartment restlessly, went into the front to the drawing room, and ran right into Wyrock. I started to ask him bitterly if he was enjoying keeping a watch on me, but remembered about flies and honey and smiled at him instead, asking if I could get him anything to drink. He declined but actually smiled back at me. That old adage, I reflected as I went back to our apartments, must be true, at least in Wyrock's case. I did notice that Wyrock, for all his casual demeanor, watched my every move.

I paced the floor for a while, thinking. Why had Lymond felt I needed protecting? What did he know that he wasn't telling me? Just how did he know that Papa's death might not have been an accident? They were questions with no answers.

After walking several miles back and forth across the floor and picking up, then putting down, every movable object in the room, I checked the door again, only to find both Ned and Bucephalus there, blocking both entrance and egress. A quick look in the front found Wyrock lounging against the front door. Finally I dragged out Papa's manuscripts and tried immersing myself in Xenophon. At least it passed the time.

It was almost dark when the family, Amelia, and Captain Amherst returned. Lymond wasn't with them. "You'll never believe it, Roxanne," Livvy and Julia chorused together, running into the room. "Never. Thefts in broad daylight while everyone was all along the Steine watching the Prince. Can you believe it?"

"Thefts? Pickpockets?" They were common in crowds.

"Roxanne!" Cassie came in, her eyes huge. "Did Livvy and Julia tell you?"

It took a moment for the general noise to abate, then Cassie was elected to tell me. "Not pickpockets, Roxanne. Paintings. While everyone was watching the Prince, several houses in Brighton were robbed. There was a terrible hue and cry when the thefts were first discovered. Everyone ran home to check, so I don't know how many were robbed."

Aunt Hen came in during the recitation and collapsed in a chair. "My vinaigrette, Livvy." Livvy waved the vinaigrette under her nose until she sneezed as Captain Amherst wandered through. Our apartments were looking rather like a crush. I addressed Amherst. "Does Lymond know anything we don't?"

He shook his head. "No, he stayed to try to discover something. I think Debenham has called a meeting to discuss the situation and try to catch the thieves before the trail gets cold." He bowed slightly towards Aunt Hen and me, then gave Cassie a speaking look. "I'm going back to Brighton. I don't know when I'll be able to return."

"Fine," I said shortly. Cassie was shocked at my lack of sensibility, but I had other things on my mind. "When will Lymond be back? Do you know?"

Captain Amherst regarded me oddly. "I don't really know. My best guess would be that he'd return before midnight."

Cassie and I exchanged glances. "I'll sit with Amelia until then," Cassie said. "Aunt Hen, could you see about making her one of your famous possets? I think we all could use something restorative."

Aunt Hen, ever noble in the face of adversity, got up and took charge. To tell the truth, Amelia did need a restorative; she was pale and exhausted. She went to sleep early, and Cassie and I pretended to go to bed so we could get Aunt Hen to sleep. We met about eleven in the front drawing room. I lit some candles and had Woodbury build up a very small fire to make sure the chill was out of the room. It had started to drizzle outside.

Cassie and I sat down to wait for Lymond.

Chapter Fourteen

Lymond did not come home at all that night. Cassie and I sat up for the duration, one or the other of us dozing off every now and then. I should have taken the opportunity to talk to her about Owen Amherst, but I had other things on my mind. I did tell her all about Lymond setting Ned and Wyrock to watch over me. Cassie reported that Wyrock was still outside and that Lymond had dispatched some men to join him. There were, she guessed, seven or eight men on the grounds watching.

Around six in the morning, we decided Lymond wasn't coming back until later. I felt reasonably good, having slept off and on all night, but Cassie decided to go to bed for a short while. I went to my room, rang for Meggie, bathed, and dressed in clean clothes. Then I went outside to reconnoiter. No one was about.

"Woodbury," I asked, finding him in the kitchen, "have there been any strange people around here?"

He gave me a look and chuckled. "You know what I mean, Woodbury," I said irritably. "I'm talking about strangers. Cassie told me that Lymond had sent some men to stand watch."

Woodbury nodded. "They all left as far as I know. About an hour ago when Mr. Lymond returned."

"Lymond's back? And you haven't told me? Where?"

"I just took him his breakfast in the breakfast room," Woodbury said formally, nodding in the general direction. "I've seen Mr. Lymond looking better."

This last was an observation made in the general direction of Cook, who nodded vigorously. "Worn to a frazzle, he is," Cook said. "I put a dollop of brandy in his tea."

I waited for no more but sped to the breakfast room, slowing down and sauntering in the door as though I had all the time in the world. "Ah, good morning, Lymond," I said cheerily.

He *did* look wretched. His clothes were dusty and wrinkled, his hair uncombed, his cravat untied. His beard-stubbled face was streaked, as though he had perspired.

I sat across from him. "Lovely day, isn't it? I thought we were in for rain last night, but it was only a short drizzle. I think today will be quite lovely."

Lymond stared down into his teacup, then drank it at one gulp, dollop of brandy and all. "Quit chattering, Roxanne, and ask me what's on your mind. You don't give a damn about the weather."

I lifted an eyebrow. "What ill manners, Mr. Lymond."

I poured myself some tea and offered more to Lymond. He nodded, but as I was pouring, he disappeared. He returned in a moment with the brandy bottle and finished filling his cup. "More ill manners," he said, downing the contents.

He looked at me. "You want to know what's going on, I suppose."

"Of course. However, you do seem a little rag-mannered this morning. A trifle thwarted, perhaps. Dare I draw my own conclusions that you know nothing more?"

"Draw what you please." Lymond poured more brandy.

I leaned across the table. "Lymond, please do not take your shortcomings out on me. If the earl of Debenham chooses to rake you over the coals because you're inept, pray do not do the same to me."

To my surprise, he broke out laughing. Also to my surprise, Woodbury ushered Owen Amherst in. A complete contrast to Lymond, he was immaculate and his uniform was perfectly pressed and arranged. "I thought you'd be ready. We need to get there as early as possible," he said, glancing at me.

For a moment I wavered between demanding to know what was going on or trying to be charming enough for them to tell me. It had worked with Wyrock, so I decided to try charm. "Sit down, Captain Amherst," I said with my best smile, "and I'll see to your breakfast. It'll be a few minutes until Mr. Lymond's ready to leave."

Amherst's look of surprise turned wary. "Thank you, but no," he said, ignoring my kind offer. "Let's go, Robert, or the bird will fly."

"All right," I said, standing up, my hands clenched into fists. Charm obviously wasn't working. "Exactly what are you up to, Lymond? Where are you going that's so important? What bird?"

"It never stops, does it?" Lymond said with a grin, giving Amherst an amused glance as he stood and finished his tea.

Cassie came floating in. "I thought I heard someone up and about," she said with a smile. "Captain Amherst, are you joining us for breakfast? What a pleasant thing to do."

Amherst looked at her and smiled, a *very* warm smile. "I wish I could, Miss Sydney, but Robert and I have urgent business this morning."

Cassie smiled prettily at him, and it struck me that the two of them were completely ignoring Lymond and me. I looked sharply at Cassie—was she doing more than merely playing a part to get information? She certainly looked involved. Moving inside the room, she came to

203

stand beside me rather than Amherst. I sighed with relief; my imagination was certainly overactive.

Lymond put his teacup down. "Ready," he said, nodding towards Amherst. "Ladies." This with a nod towards us.

"Lymond, you haven't answered my questions," I said as he and Amherst went out the door. "What are you doing? Where are you going?"

"I'll tell you later," he said over his shoulder, drawing the door shut behind him. Cassie and I were left staring at the paneled door and nothing else. "Well!" I said, sitting down with a thump. "What an ill-bred man! What rudeness!"

Cassie got her breakfast while I told her what little I knew. That consisted mainly of my conclusions from Lymond's vague hints. "The stables!" I jumped to my feet. "Cassie, we can see which way they're going and follow them."

"Roxanne, have you lost all reason?"

"Yes," I yelled back at her. "I'm going to the stables."

The stables were quiet, even Wyrock seemed to have disappeared. Ned came around a corner and I proceeded to interrogate him on the spot. "I don't know nothing," he protested. "I swear I don't!"

"I don't expect you to know anything, Ned," I said in exasperation. "You must, however, have some inkling of which way they went. It's very important that I know." I hesitated. "I have a very important message for Mr. Lymond." It wasn't exactly a prevarication. It was more or less true, and I kept my fingers crossed.

Ned shook his head. "I don't know. Some of the men came here with Captain Amherst, Mr. Lymond joined them, and they rode off towards Jervyne House."

I caught my breath audibly. So that was it. "Is that all you know, Ned?" I smiled at him.

"I don't know nothing."

He didn't even realize he had told me anything. "Thank you, Ned. I'll be sure to tell Mr. Lymond that his confidence in you was well-placed."

Ned beamed and I left, almost running back to the house. I had thought briefly about having Ned saddle Buttercup but decided to walk towards Jervyne House instead. I could cut through the back field that marched with Jerrold's and be there just as quickly. I ran inside and told Cassie what I planned. She tried to stop me, then gave up, grabbed her shawl, and went along with me, protesting vigorously with every step.

We had crossed the property line but hadn't reached Jervyne House when we ran into Justin. He was walking along quickly and when he caught sight of us, changed his course and came over to us. "Good morning," he said with a smile that quite took my breath away. "How charming you two look this morning. Isn't it a fine day for a walk?"

Cassie looked puzzled. "Good morning, Mr. Denver. What are you doing out this morning?" She looked in the direction from which he had come. "Have you been down to the sea?"

"As a matter of fact, I have." He smiled again and looked right into my eyes. I felt slightly dizzy. "Things were in such an uproar at Jervyne House that I wanted to get away for a while."

"Oh, then everyone's already there." She turned to me, a frown on her face. "Roxanne, I thought you said all those men had just left a few minutes ago."

Did I sense a sudden tenseness in Justin? Although his stance remained the same, there seemed to be a wariness there. He didn't say anything; he merely looked at us, smiling.

I was trying to decide the best way to answer Cassie when she looked at Justin, smiled, and went on. "I should have known you'd absent yourself while the men

205

searched Jervyne House, Mr. Denver. It must have been quite a shock to you."

"It certainly was," Justin said. "I don't believe that you two ladies are walking that way. Do let me escort you back to Bellerophon." Without quite knowing how he did it, I found myself turned around and walking back to the house. "Please excuse my behavior; I wasn't aware that the two of you knew about the situation at Jervyne House," he said, walking along. I had to walk rapidly to keep up and noticed that Cassie seemed to be doing the same.

"Oh, I didn't know about it," Cassie said, catching her breath. Justin glanced at her and slowed his pace. I supposed it was the excitement that had made him hurry so. "Roxanne just told me about the men going to Jervyne House, and I supposed from what Owen — Captain Amherst had told me, that Lord Debenham was with them. Tell me, did you see him?"

"Not this morning," Justin said, giving her a smile. "Actually, we've never met."

I was feeling quite left out of the conversation. "Justin, if you knew all this was going on and the carpenters were involved, why didn't you say something? It would have saved all of us a great deal of worry and fretting."

He looked at me, right into my eyes again, and seemed so contrite that I was sorry I had spoken. "I know it would have, but believe me, I was unable to say anything. Am I forgiven?"

"Of course you are." I was suddenly feeling quite giddy and averted my eyes. We were nearing the house and Bue came bounding across the grass to greet us. He wagged his tail, woofed a time or two, then passed right by us and bounded on towards Jervyne House. "He probably senses Lymond somewhere in the vicinity," I remarked. "I only hope Bue lets him get down from his horse so we can find out what's happened." I glanced at Justin and smiled. "Lymond and Bucephalus just don't seem to get along. Perhaps we'd better wait outside and restrain the dog when Lymond rides up. I don't want to wait a moment longer than necessary to hear what they've found."

Justin glanced behind him. "I wish I could, but I promised Lymond I'd go into Brighton for him. He'll be upset if he discovers me here. I left in a hurry and he told me to stop and get a horse from his stock. I don't mean to be rude, but . . ."

"We understand," Cassie said with a smile. "As you know, Wyrock's gone with Mr. Lymond, but just tell Ned what you need."

"Thank you for understanding," Justin said, smiling at both of us. His glance lingered longer on me. "Perhaps this evening we could have a talk," he said. "I think it's time." Then he turned and went to the stables.

Cassie lifted an eyebrow. "You may have to answer an important question, Roxanne." We watched Justin striding around the corner of the house towards the stables. "Yes," I sighed. "I'm not really sure. I was a short time ago and don't know why I hesitate now." I looked at Cassie, worried. "I simply don't know what's the matter with me. I usually know exactly what I want to do."

She laughed and hugged me. "Roxanne, why do you always try to dissect everything? Come on, let's go talk to Amelia. Aunt Hen tells me that she's been feeling better, but I know she must miss Mr. Lymond. He's been away as much as he's been here." I had to agree with that. After we went inside, though, were careful not to mention anything except the latest in fashions or embroidery.

An hour later we heard Lymond and Amherst before we saw them. "Dammit," Lymond was bellowing, "how could he slip the net again? I knew we had him — I just knew it!" There was the sound of a blow, as if he had hit the wall with his fist. Then the door was thrown open and Lymond stood there, glaring at us. "Sorry, ladies," he said with great control and slammed the door. We all looked at the closed door. "Please don't mind Robert," Amelia said, frowning at her tiny, even stitches. "He really hasn't been himself."

Cassie and I glanced at each other and nodded. It took us a few minutes to come up with an excuse, but we managed to escape on the pretext of going to hunt up some pattern cards. Out in the hall we congratulated each other on being so clever. "What will they say when we don't return?" Cassie whispered.

"We'll be back," I whispered back as we went down the hall searching for Lymond and Amherst. "It will take us a very long time to locate our pattern cards."

It took a while to locate Lymond. We finally heard him, still ranting and raving, behind the closed doors of the breakfast room. I opened the door and peeped inside—I certainly didn't want to interrupt him if he was conferring with several men. However, he and Amherst were sitting at the table, Lymond's back to the door. Lymond was in full voice, drinking a glass of an amber liquid, banging on the table with his fist for emphasis. Cassie and I slipped inside the room and closed the door behind us. "What did you discover?" I asked.

Lymond jumped straight up, spilling some of the contents of his glass. "Dammit!"

Amherst laughed aloud. "Robert, calm down before you die from apoplexy." He looked at us. "I apologize for Robert's language, ladies. Do come in and have a cup of tea with us."

"Your apology is accepted, Captain Amherst," I said with great dignity. "I'm delighted that *someone* around here has some manners." Lymond was mopping up the spill which I now recognized as whiskey. "Isn't it a little early for spirits, Lymond?" I asked, ringing for tea for all of us.

"If you'd had the morning I've had, you'd be doing worse than this," he said, gulping down the last remaining swallow. "Did you warn Denver?"

"What are you talking about?" I demanded.

"Did you warn him?" Lymond pinned me with those startlingly blue eyes. They were like blue ice.

"No, I didn't warn him. I didn't warn anyone," I answered with heat. I had to stop because Mrs. Beckford came in with the tea and bustled around for several minutes. I knew she was hoping for a choice bit of gossip to take back to the kitchen. She was disappointed, but it took her long enough to leave. "I didn't warn anyone," I said more calmly after we were alone again. How could I? I didn't see anyone until Justin — Mr. Denver ran into us while we were walking."

"What?" Lymond and Amherst said it together. "You met him?" Amherst said, looking directly at me. "Where?"

I glanced at Cassie. "Roxanne and I were out walking this morning and met Mr. Denver," Cassie said with her charming smile. It didn't seem to have any effect on the gentlemen, however. She went on, "He was only doing as you had instructed him, Mr. Lymond."

"As *I* had instructed him?" Lymond stirred extra sugar into his tea. "What do you mean?"

"She means," I said, moving the sugar bowl, "that he was on his way here to borrow a horse so he could run your errand for you. He was in a hurry, worried about your displeasure."

"He'll have more than my displeasure," Lymond muttered. "Did you say he was running an errand for me?"

Cassie nodded. "He was going into Brighton as you had asked him to. We told him to borrow one of your horses."

Lymond and Amherst looked at each other and Amherst broke into laughter. "By God," he said, wiping his eyes, "this is rich, Robert. We're beating the bushes for him while he takes one of your horses and slips the knot."

I looked at Cassie and she was as puzzled as I. "Just what is so funny?" I demanded. "Justin was just helping you." I glanced at Cassie. "They must be hysterical from disappointment."

"That I am," Lymond said, grim again. "I may as well be blunt about this, although I would prefer not to hurt you." He hesitated. "Miss Sydney — Roxanne — I, that is, we believe Justin Denver is the criminal we know as the Master. He's the one who's been the spider behind the web of thieves who've been stealing paintings." He took a deep breath and touched my hand as it lay lifeless on the table. "I'm sorry to have to tell you this. As we thought, the carpenters were working with him and that's why he wanted everyone at Jervyne House with him. It was a perfect scheme."

"No." It was all I could say at the moment. Cassie came over and put her arm around my shoulders. I shrugged her away. "No," I said again, staring at the wall, seeing nothing. "Papa?" I whispered.

"I think Denver was responsible for that as well," Lymond said gently. "I don't have proof, and at this point I don't know why, but I think his hand was in it. I agree with you that it wasn't an accident."

For a moment I wanted to run away and cry, but then I took a deep breath and rubbed my eyes with my fists, hard. I looked right into Lymond's eyes. "Are you sure? Are you really sure?"

"We can't be completely sure about your father, but about the other, yes. Enough of the 'carpenters' have confessed, that we've been able to piece together most of the puzzle. The man posing as Justin Denver — we don't know his real name — is the man known as the Master, and he's been responsible for the thefts."

"And for the deaths of Jem and Willy," Amherst added quietly.

Cassie gasped. "Those poor boys."

"Yes," Amherst agreed. "He evidently convinced them that they could fall in with him and be on the road to riches. Their greed brought about their deaths."

"Did he—" I stopped and got my breath so I could speak steadily. "Did he kill Jem and Willy himself?"

Lymond looked at me for a moment, then concentrated on the pattern in the table. "Evidently he killed Jem right outside your window, then dragged him to the hiding place. We think he got Willy to help bury Jem. Willy was probably killed by Robin Norwood on orders from Denver. They were afraid he'd implicate them in Jem's death."

"Willy just knew too much," Cassie said softly.

Captain Amherst nodded. "He was dangerous because they couldn't trust him not to break and confess. Wyrock was working on him."

"Did Denver say where he was going?" Lymond asked.

"On your horse," Captain Amherst added with a wry smile.

Cassie looked at him and gave him a fleeting smile in return. "He said he was going to Brighton to do an errand for Mr. Lymond. That was all he said."

Lymond stood. "He could be anywhere. Let's go to the stables and see if Ned knows anything." He looked down at me. "Again, I'm sorry to have to tell you all these things. I wish it could be good news, but . . ." He paused and shrugged. "I have no choice."

I stood up to face him. "I understand." I hesitated. "Lymond, just who are you and what are you? I've known from the beginning there was something wrong, but I was never able to place it. You don't fit what you say you are, Amelia doesn't fit, nothing fits."

Lymond glanced over my head to look at Captain

Amherst. "Not now," he said, taking my hand. I was surprised at his touch. "I promise that later I'll tell you everything, but not right now."

Captain Amherst stood up. "Right now, we need to get the men together and try to find Denver. He could be anywhere."

Lymond dropped my hand and turned towards the door. "He's probably on his way to France, unless he's got something else to do. He doesn't have the paintings with him, and he'll probably try to get them before he leaves this area. I can't see him leaving empty-handed."

"Better empty-handed and free than to have the paintings and a noose around his neck," Captain Amherst said, going out into the hall. Lymond shook his head. "You and I would think so, but I believe Denver thinks he's more intelligent than we are. He'll stay around to get his paintings."

"Where are they?" I asked, following them out into the hall.

"Who knows?" Lymond said with a sigh. He looked incredibly tired. "They could be anywhere—just like Denver." He paused by the door. "I'll have men posted all around even though you won't be able to see them. You'll be safe."

"And you'll catch Justin if he tries to come back here?"

Lymond and Amherst nodded. "It's a possibility we can't overlook. Don't go away from the house. If you must go somewhere, take one or two of the men with you. Please make sure the other girls, your aunt, and Amelia stay inside," Lymond said.

The mention of Amelia's name jolted me. "Is Amelia in danger?" I asked.

Cassie came to stand beside me. "Would he try to harm Amelia as a way to harm you?" she asked.

"He'd try anything," Captain Amherst said. "Please stay in. You'll be safe here."

Lymond started out the door, then turned back to look at me, a slight grin on his face. "I need a promise," he said to me. "Do you promise to stay here?"

I hesitated. "All right, I promise. Why do you ask?"

He laughed and touched the tip of my nose with his finger. "Because I know you. If you thought you could, you'd be out on your horse scouring the country, trying to save the world. Am I right?"

"You certainly are not!" I was indignant.

Cassie put her hand on my arm, laughing. "You most certainly are, Mr. Lymond. We'll stay here, so don't worry."

"Thank you." This time he smiled at Cassie, then he looked at me. "I know your next question and yes, as soon as we return, I'll let you know what we've found, if anything."

With that, the two of them left and Cassie and I went back to sit with the others. Cassie told them we couldn't find the pattern cards, which was true as far as it went, and we sat there interminably, sewing.

My stitches were abominable and I stuck my finger three times. It was the longest day I ever spent.

Chapter Fifteen

Lymond and Captain Amherst didn't return until almost time for supper, and the first time Cassie and I saw them again was at the table. Naturally we couldn't ask them anything then, and I was quite surprised when Lymond introduced the topic of the stolen paintings into the conversation. Aunt Hen pounced right onto it, but Lymond was unable to add anything to her knowledge, and so she returned to her favorite topic, the Treasure. We finished the meal by going over possible hiding places for the Treasure for perhaps the thousandth time.

After supper, we all adjourned to the drawing room so Amelia could entertain us with her singing. I sidled up to Lymond when he came in to join us. He smelled of whiskey and cigars. I had always thought I would find such smells repellant, but to my surprise, they seemed quite pleasant. "Were you able to find him?" I asked under my breath as Amelia sang.

He shook his head. "Not a trace. I think he's somewhere in the vicinity. I feel it in my heart. He's not going to leave without those paintings and perhaps a quick strike at either Debenham or me."

I glanced up at him quickly. "Are you in danger?"

He shrugged. "No more than I've ever been. Has anything unusual happened here today?"

I shook my head and tried to concentrate on Amelia's singing. "Nothing."

"Keep a sharp eye out," he murmured, "and be sure to tell me if anything at all happens. Even something that doesn't seem to apply might be important."

"All right," I murmured back as Aunt Hen frowned at me. I smiled back at her, but refrained from saying anything else until Amelia had finished. She did have a rather pretty voice.

That night Cassie came to my room after the others were asleep, and we talked about what had happened, discussing it first one way and then that, but we could reach no conclusion. Finally, exhausted, we both snuggled down in my bed and went to sleep.

The next morning I rose and tried to be quiet so I wouldn't wake Cassie. "I'm awake," she said sleepily from the depths of the feathertick. "Wait for me."

It took a while, but she finally got dressed and we went down to breakfast. As we neared the breakfast-room door, we heard voices and stopped. "It's probably only Owen," she suggested.

As we opened the door I froze and heard Cassie gasp as she looked over my shoulder. Sitting calmly at the table were Lymond and three other men: Captain Amherst, Lord Debenham, and the man I knew as Francis.

"Do join us, ladies," Captain Amherst said, standing up. There was nothing for it but to try to gather our wits and join them. We sat, and I tried not to gulp my tea.

"I don't believe you've met," Lymond said pleasantly. "Allow me to introduce Lord Debenham," he gestured towards the earl, then turned to Francis, "and this is my brother, Francis Lymond."

"Your brother?" I said, almost choking on a bite of toast. "Your brother?" Cassie kicked me under the table.

Lymond laughed. "Did you think I was too much the reprobate to have any family?" He grinned at me and his eyes were a dark, warm blue as he mentioned his brother. I felt my heart break for him.

"Have we ever met?" I asked Francis after we had chatted for a while, exhausting the usual small talk.

"I don't believe so," he said smoothly. "I'm seldom in this part of the country and really haven't spent very much time in London for several years."

"Francis is with the . . . the government," Lymond said. "We rarely have the privilege of seeing him." He hit Francis lightly on the shoulder with affection. If he only knew!

The earl rose. "As delighted as I am to spend the morning with you ladies, I'm afraid we have several things to do."

As if on cue, the other three rose to join him. After the usual pleasantries, they all left together. As soon as the door shut behind them, I almost collapsed. "The poor man!" I exclaimed.

Without pausing, I told her of Francis's nocturnal visit. "Poor Mr. Lymond," she said softly, "what will he do when he discovers he's been betrayed by his own brother?"

"And his own wife," I added. "I can't believe it. I couldn't believe it when I saw it, and I still can't." I bit my lip as I thought. "Cassie, there's nothing at all we can do," I said bitterly. "Nothing."

"We could talk to Amelia."

"And send her into another decline?" I thought about it. "Perhaps after all this is over, we should say a few words to her. Delicately, of course."

Cassie nodded in agreement and stood. "I'm going to walk in the garden, Roxanne. I need the fresh air."

I reached for a muffin as she went out. "Be sure not to stray from the grounds," I reminded her.

"Holmwood's outside working with the flowers," she said, shutting the door behind her. "I'll be fine."

I finished my breakfast and went back to remind Aunt Hen that Julia and Livvy were expecting the modiste to be here by midafternoon to fit new dresses for both of them. Lymond's rent money was being put to good use. Aunt Hen, Livvy, and Julia, however, were all slugabeds this morning, so I let them sleep and wandered around our apartments for a while, trying to find something to do.

I finally let Bucephalus inside for a while to keep him from scratching at the door, and I sat down to work on Papa's manuscripts. To my horror, I discovered myself writing Lymond's name over and over on the page. It was time to do something constructive. The man was married and I had no business thinking about him or writing his name. I'm a great believer in the sanctity of marriage. I shredded the paper with Lymond's name on it and went to my room to change shoes. I whistled for Bucephalus and we went outdoors. Perhaps a morning assisting Holmwood would refresh my mind.

To my surprise, neither Holmwood nor Cassie was to be seen. I went back inside and found Amelia. She was sitting with her embroidery beside the drawing-room window and was dressed all in pale blue. The light fell in on her, and she looked like a madonna in a Renaissance painting. Merely, I reminded myself, remembering the scene with Francis, another illustration of how looks can deceive. I pasted a smile on my face and asked if she had seen Cassie. She hadn't, she assured me, and asked if I could sit and talk a few moments. I did, and there was an awkward pause.

"I know we aren't the closest of confidantes," she began, "but I do feel we know each other well enough for me to ask you this question." She paused and I smiled encouragement. I needed to get out and locate Cassie. "Do you care for Robert?" Amelia asked baldly.

My mouth fell open in astonishment. "What?"

"Do you care for Robert?" she asked again. "I realize this question may seem strange, but there are . . . there are some things perhaps you don't know."

I stood. "Amelia, I'm sure you have your reasons—probably quite good reasons—for whatever you do. I assure you that I would never entertain a *tendre* for a married man. Furthermore, I would have thought you had seen the . . ." I struggled to find a word, "the rather obvious friction Mr. Lymond and I have when we're around each other."

She smiled at me disarmingly. "Please, don't be angry. Yes, I've noticed the antagonism between the two of you, but I thought perhaps . . ." She smiled again, a very sweet smile. "Never mind, Roxanne. Robert's a wonderful person and perhaps later on you'll understand why I asked you this question. I certainly would never imply any impropriety on your part."

I could have made a comment about impropriety, but I refrained. Aunt Hen entered, and I asked if she'd seen Cassie. She hadn't, and neither had Livvy. I was beginning to worry.

I went back outside and whistled for Bue. He was busy sniffling along the garden path and merely looked up at me and woofed. This was too much. I was cross enough without having to deal with a recalcitrant dog. "Come on, Bue. Let's go to the stables."

I started across the path when Bue set up a howl that would have waked the dead. He started running frantically around in circles, pausing only long enough to run up to the edge of the house and try to dig up the boxwoods. "Bue, stop that this instant!" I yelled. He paid no attention at all to me. Instead he sat in front of a shrub and yowled.

I started over to him, complaining all the time. All at once I stopped in my tracks as something came crawling from behind the boxwood. On all fours and bloody all over, it took me a moment to realize it was Holmwood. I ran to him and pushed Bue out of the way. "Holmwood, speak to me! Are you all right?"

"Noooo," he moaned, falling to the ground. "Go away." This last was directed to Bue who kept trying to lap poor Holmwood about the face. Holmwood was one of Bue's favorite people. Holmwood sat up and rubbed his head. He was bloody, but seemed to have only one bad cut across the top of his head. "They hit me with a hoe, they did," he said. "Came up behind me and when I turned, they took the hoe and hit me."

"Cassie?" I asked as I dropped to my knees in front of him. "Holmwood, did they take Cassie with them?"

He nodded yes and I felt my whole world crumble. For a moment I couldn't even speak. "Was it Justin Denver?" I asked hollowly. Again Holmwood nodded yes, and we looked bleakly at each other.

"I've got to tell Lymond," I said, getting to my feet. I couldn't see very clearly. I couldn't even feel anything. "I've got to get Lymond."

Holmwood tried to stand. Bue came and stood very still beside him to help him. Holmwood put one hand on Bue's back and I held the other until we got him to his feet. "Come inside," I said. "I'll have Woodbury go for the doctor."

Holmwood shook his head. "They'd just do something to harm Woodbury. We might as well wait on Mr. Lymond."

"I can't do that, Holmwood. I'll lose my mind if I don't do something now. I've got to go to Brighton. Surely Lymond will be there. Nothing will happen to me if I take Ned and perhaps one of the other men. I'll be perfectly safe."

Holmwood didn't believe me and neither did Woodbury. They were for waiting on Lymond to return, but I

219

knew that could be an hour from now or a day from now. With Lymond, one never knew. They were also for telling Aunt Hen and the other girls that Cassie had been captured by a man who'd done murder. "Do you want Aunt Hen to have an attack right on the spot?" I demanded. "I'll be perfectly safe if I go to Brighton and take Ned and someone else."

"I'm going with you," Woodbury said. He looked every inch the Army veteran.

I shook my head. "No, Woodbury, you're needed here. With Holmwood injured, we need a man to watch the house." This had the intended effect.

"Then you'll have to take Ned and Wyrock with you." Woodbury was firm. "If you don't take both of them along, I'll tell Mrs. Vellory immediately. As it is, if you're gone above the time it takes to go to Brighton and back, I'll go get the magistrates."

I looked at him and saw that he and Holmwood were in complete agreement. "All right," I said, yielding. "But promise me that you'll make sure that none of the others even goes outside. That means Amelia, Aunt Hen, Julia, and Livvy." I thought a moment. "Woodbury, the modiste from Brighton is coming to fit dresses today. That should be enough to keep everyone occupied." This was a coin with two sides. "How can you make excuses for Cassie and me not being here?"

Woodbury thought a moment. "I'll think of something. I'll have refreshments and perhaps I could tell them that you've . . ." He paused and looked at me blankly. "I don't know. I'll think of something."

I nodded. "Holmwood, do I need to fetch the doctor as well?" He shook his head no, and I headed for the door. "I'm off to Brighton then."

Woodbury and Holmwood exchanged glances, and the butler followed me out the door. "I think," he said at his most formal as he followed me to the stables, "that I need to make sure you take both Wyrock and Ned. Merely trying to help."

"Merely trying to make sure I do what you've insisted I do," I said. "Don't worry, Woodbury. I may be impulsive occasionally, but I'm not stupid. I don't intend to get out alone where I might be a target myself."

We found Wyrock at the stables, and when we told him what had happened, he cursed softly to himself. "He leaves me to watch everything, and look what happens," he said. "It's all my fault."

"It's not," I said, trying to comfort him. "You couldn't watch all of us all the time. The important thing right now is to have Lymond send enough men to find Cassie before anything happens to her. We've got to hurry. Do you know where Lymond went?"

Wyrock nodded. "I think I know where to find him." He looked at me slowly. "I'd best be doing this alone. I'll have enough explaining to do about why the other Miss Sydney got took without having to explain why you're along."

"I'd have to agree," Woodbury said quickly.

I turned to them, feeling anger stamped on my face. "I'm going, with you or without you, Wyrock, and that's that." I turned and glared at Ned. "Harness a horse to the gig. Wyrock and you can ride alongside." I turned back to the men. "You're not stopping me."

Woodbury muttered something that sounded suspiciously like "Has anyone ever," but he went to help Ned. Then he returned to the house and brought out a pistol for Ned to carry. "I suppose you've got your own," he said to Wyrock.

Wyrock mounted his horse and reached in his saddlebag to get his pistol. "Primed and ready," he said, putting his pistol in his waistband.

Ned looked rather rattled as he looked at his pistol. "Ever fire one, boy?" Wyrock asked. When Ned said no,

Wyrock took a moment to show him how to fire if he needed to.

Personally, I didn't think it would come to that. Surely we could travel the short distance to Brighton without the need for firearms. Still, I said nothing—the pistols seemed to make the men feel better. "Remember, Woodbury," I said as we left, "keep everyone inside and don't say a word to anyone."

The first part of our journey was calm although we didn't go as fast as I would have wished. I kept urging the horse on, but Ned and Wyrock kept holding me back, checking behind every rock, it seemed. Finally I could stand it no longer. "We've got to hurry," I told them. "The man's murdered before and he could do it again. We've got to get Lymond to get the entire Army out here if need be."

We had just topped the rise where the church was situated when we were set upon. The villains had been hiding, of all places, in and behind the church. Justin Denver wasn't one of them, but I recognized Robin Norwood. "It's them!" I cried, slapping the horse with the reins.

The horse shied a moment, but then a pistol went off behind me and the horse began galloping down the road. I didn't even have time to turn around and see what was happening. The horse was terrified, going in a dead run down the road. I could hear hooves behind me, but couldn't take the time to look behind me to see if it was friend or foe.

"Hurry, Miss Sydney, hurry!" It was Ned, yelling at me. I glanced to the side and he was riding recklessly, waving his pistol around. "They've got Wyrock! Hurry, and I'll try to stop them!"

He gave my horse a quite unnecessary slap on its rump and dropped back, yelling and waving his pistol. My horse was totally out of control now and there was nothing I could do to slow it down or guide it. Behind me I heard two pistol shots and a yell. I didn't dare look back.

The horse was flying across the ground now. We had left the road and were dashing across the fields. I only hoped we either got to Brighton or met someone before we hit a ditch. At the rate we were going, we'd probably jump the ditch, gig and all. Behind me I could hear hooves, so close behind I could hear the heavy gasping of the horse.

Horrified, I saw a rock wall loom up in front of us. It was only about two feet high, but it looked as tall as the Great Wall of China. There was no way we were going to make it over that wall. I didn't think I could survive if the gig crashed into the rocks at the speed we were traveling. There was a thicket and a big ditch next to the wall. If I could jump and make it into the thicket, there was a chance. It was a slim one, but any chance seemed better than none.

The wall sprang up before us, and as soon as the horse began its jump, I began mine. The leap through the air felt as though it lasted forever and I watched the ground come closer and closer. I rolled to the other side of the wall and felt the jolt all through my body. I heard the grunt as the horse was stopped short by the splintering of the gig, then heard the horse begin galloping off, dragging pieces of the harness and gig behind him. I got to my feet and started to run towards the thicket.

It was no use. I had barely covered ten feet when I was swept from my feet and went tumbling onto the ground again. Rough hands jerked me to my feet and turned me around. I pushed my hair from my eyes and looked right into the face of Robin Norwood. He was smiling unpleasantly.

"Thought you'd get away, didn't you?"

I shrugged and refused to answer. He tried to jerk me around so he could pick me up and toss me on his horse, but he had evidently forgotten that I was not a small person. He grunted a moment, then glared at me. "Get up on that horse," he ordered.

"I certainly will not."

He drew back his hand and for a moment I thought he was going to slap me, but then he thought the better of it. The other men were coming up, leading Wyrock's horse. "Did you take care of him?" Norwood asked. "Hurt but not dead?"

One of the others nodded. "He'll be able to tell everything that's happened. I don't know about the boy. He took a ball in the shoulder and might die. I don't know. We just left him by the side of the road. His horse had a broken leg, so we shot it." The man looked from Norwood to me. "Are you ready?"

I closed my eyes. Poor Ned. Perhaps he was dying when his whole life should be in front of him. I felt so sad. And Wyrock . . . "Why," I asked, looking at Norwood, "are you leaving Wyrock? Why do you want him able to tell anything?"

Norwood laughed, a short, ugly sound. "The Master wants Lymond, and when Wyrock tells this tale, we know Lymond'll come looking. That's when he's ours." He pulled Wyrock's horse around. "Get on."

"I certainly will not," I said. It was the next to last thing I remembered. The last thing was the other man reining up behind me and then something very hard crashing down on my head.

When I woke up, I heard a voice I recognized. "Roxie, are you all right? Please say you're all right."

"Cassie," I said groggily, "is that you? Am I dreaming? My head hurts."

"They hit you on the head. You should have seen it, Roxanne. They brought you here tossed over a horse like a sack of potatoes. I couldn't believe it."

I gingerly felt my head, then the rest of my body. "I believe it," I said. "I'm sore all over." I looked at her. "Cassie, are you all right? They didn't hurt you, did they? Where are we?"

In spite of herself, she grinned. "A dozen questions at once, as usual, Roxie. Yes, I'm all right. I was terrified at first and I still am, but I'm all right."

I sat up and turned around. "We're in the mausoleum," I said, looking around.

We were indeed propped up against Papa's Egyptian wall, right under the frescoes. There were several men in the room and they were all armed. I counted. Robin Norwood was there along with three others. Justin Denver was sitting on a box, smiling pleasantly at me, just as though we were at tea.

"I trust your adventure hasn't harmed you," he said, offering me a handkerchief. Cassie took the handkerchief and dabbed at my head.

"Ouch," I said, touching my head. It seemed to be bleeding.

"I was forced to use more drastic measures than I had intended," Justin said. "I assure you I'm not in the habit of hitting women."

"But you will—and did—do whatever it takes for you to survive," I said bitterly as he nodded in agreement. I looked at him a moment as all the final shreds of my dreams fell into dust. "Justin, why?"

He looked at me strangely. "Why? What do you mean?"

I struggled with what I wanted to say. My head was hurting and I couldn't think clearly. "Why did you have to do this? You could have been anything you chose to be."

He laughed shortly. "A pickpocket from the gutter? No, my dear Miss Sydney, I could never be what I wanted." He smiled maliciously at me, the smile of a stranger. "So I became an actor, hardly a lucrative profession. As an actor, I could be someone else, but I preferred better living conditions. This way, I seem to have the best of all worlds." He paused and listened. "Did you bring my case, Robin?"

Robin gestured to a leather case sitting near the edge of the light. "I told Wyrock and the boy to have Lymond come alone. I don't know if we can get Debenham this trip."

"One at a time will suit me," Justin said.

I tried again. "Justin, why did you bring us here? Surely we'll only be in your way. You could be far from here by now; you have a head start on Lymond."

He nodded. "Actually, with your kind warning, I could have been in France by now. However, Robin was reluctant to leave without the fruits of his labors and I had a score to settle. I want Lymond and Debenham. They've been thorns in my side since I began this little . . . undertaking."

"What do you intend to do?" My mind was beginning to clear. Already I was working on some way to escape and warn Lymond. Already I knew it was futile.

He laughed harshly. "I intend to dispose of both Lymond and Debenham, then go get the paintings and leave for France." He paused. "I haven't decided what to do with the two of you yet."

"Why did you bring us here, then?" Cassie asked. "We're of no possible use to you."

Justin stood and looked down at us huddled on the floor. "On the contrary. I really couldn't ask for better bait. As soon as Wyrock and Ned are found and tell Lymond what's happened, he'll be here in a trice. We're ready for him."

I laughed right back at him. "He'll bring enough men to keep you in here until you starve. You won't get him."

"Ah, but I will. I left word for him to come alone. I think he'll do it — after all, I have the two of you if I need you, and I have a way out." He strolled over to where

Papa had begun a small mosaic on the floor. "Your father, Miss Sydney, was a very ingenious man who loved his toys." He turned and called to one of the men. "Turner, where did you say you put the tunnel?"

One of the men with Norwood walked over, lifted a box, and then picked up a piece of the floor. There was a black hole leading into the ground. "I don't think much of this," Turner said. "I told you it don't go nowhere."

Justin turned to him in a fury. "I told you to dig it out so we'd come out the back side of the building."

"I did, but it still don't go nowhere 'cept out back."

"That's enough," Justin said with a smile. He turned to us. "Turner helped your father build this mausoleum, and he remembered that your father had originally intended to sink some kind of shaft into the ground."

"Oh, heavens, Cassie," I said, almost crying. "Papa's pyramid. He wanted to sink a burial shaft and had me do all that research on how Egyptian tombs were built."

"We never finished it," Turner said. "Ran into rock, so we had to quit. Quite put out, the old man was. He'd wanted a whole room down there."

Robin Norwood peered down the hole. "It's enough for us to get through."

Turner nodded. "Them walls is just dirt, but I went down it a few days ago. Like I told you, it's passable."

"Leave it open," Justin said. "I want it ready if I need it." He turned to Norwood. "Robin, keep a close watch and let me know when you hear or see something. I want Lymond for myself."

The wait was interminable. We had to sit, but Justin was edgy. He prowled the floor, looking first at this, then at that. He tried to converse with me but I refused to talk to him. He squatted down and inspected the tunnel opening, then questioned Turner about its width. It seemed he didn't want to traverse the tunnel unless he had to — he might get his clothes dirty.

In the meantime, Cassie and I sat, speaking only once in a while, but touching each other. It was understood between us that we would try to get away, but that we had to go together. That made our chances for escape even slimmer, but that was the way it was. The tunnel, I thought, provided our best chance, and Cassie and I edged closer to it, moving only a few inches at a time.

Justin must have known what we were about since he looked at us once and laughed. "It's no use," he said. "I could shoot the both of you before you got three feet away." He smiled pleasantly. "Lymond and Debenham wouldn't know if you were alive or dead. They'd as soon rush the place for dead bait as for live."

I closed my eyes. I had never known someone so thoroughly evil. So much for my assessment of character. Still, there was something I had to know. "Mr. Denver," I said as formally and coldly as I could, "did you kill my father?"

"I can honestly answer no to that question," he said, still smiling, "but I'm sure you want details. I told Robin to do it. The old fool was in my way, and I planned to get rid of him and then step in and buy Bellerophon from a grieving family of females. Your brother had already agreed to sell to me, but then I discovered he didn't own it."

"Why?" It was the only word I could say.

He shrugged. "It's a perfect base of operations. Wonderful buildings with access to the sea, dozens of hiding places, and enough of a patina of eccentricity so that I could do what I wanted and everyone would think I was as insane as your father."

"Papa wasn't insane," Cassie said with heat.

Justin shrugged again and turned to speak to Robin Norwood. I looked at the two of them and vowed revenge. I didn't know how or when, but they would regret ending Papa's life.

The thought sustained me. I had never felt so helpless in my life, and I'm sure Cassie hadn't either. Neither of us knew how late it was, and the evening stretched out forever. I goaded Justin whenever I could about the fact that Lymond and Debenham weren't coming to rescue us. In my heart, I didn't believe it, but I said it anyway just to annoy him. He always smiled at me and told me just to wait — they'd be here.

Once we heard noises outside, but it was only Bucephalus. He was scratching at the wall and door, occasionally barking. I called out to him, and Justin threatened to gag me with his handkerchief if I spoke again. Bue must have heard me, however, because he kept right on scratching and barking. Robin Norwood wanted to send a man outside to shoot him, but Justin stopped him. "We want to stay quiet until Lymond and Debenham get here. The dog doesn't matter. He may even help lead them here." He smiled at Norwood. "Then you can shoot the dog."

Chapter Sixteen

We marked the passing of time by how hungry we were. Both Cassie and I were getting cramped and cold. The men didn't seem to be affected. Perhaps the time only seemed longer to us.

After a while, Justin pulled out his watch, flipped the lid, and announced, "Robin, it's time for us to change."

He sent all the men away except Robin Norwood and Turner. Even though the others hadn't been saying very much, the low hum of conversation in the background had been comforting. Now, the mausoleum was strangely quiet.

Justin waited a few minutes until he was sure everyone had gone down the cliff and into the waiting boat. Then he turned and, with a smile, picked up the little case he had shown me before. "You're going to watch an artist at work," he said. "I'm quite proud of my skill at this." He set up candles on a box, opened the case, and set up shop. In spite of myself, I was fascinated. He pulled a looking glass from it, then various bits of hair, something that looked like putty, and pots of colors. Adjusting his looking glass, he began working on his face. "It's amazing what actors can do with the right tools," he said to us, smiling as he put his hands over his eyes.

To our horror, he pulled off his eyebrows and wiped off a great deal of his face. I couldn't see him clearly, but he began rebuilding another visage. In just a very short while, Justin Denver was no more. He stood and changed his shirt, boots, and coat with Turner, and he was now an old, coarse-looking man. Robin Norwood sat and, with just a few strokes of colors and a bit of putty, he was changed as well. Justin smiled at us. "Merely bearing out my theory that all life is an illusion. Tell me truthfully, would you know me?"

I shook my head. I could have stood beside him on the Steine and wouldn't have given him a second glance. No wonder he had never been caught. Justin snapped the case shut and put it near the tunnel hole. "I suspect it won't be long now," he said conversationally. He might have been talking about the weather.

He was right. It wasn't above a half an hour before Robin Norwood, who was looking through a crack in the door, turned and announced with a smile on his face, "Here they come."

"They?" Justin moved over to the door to stand beside Robin. Turner picked up his pistols. "Debenham? I can't see from here."

"Doesn't walk like Debenham," Norwood observed. "I don't think that's who it is."

Talk was suspended when Lymond stopped midway from between the cliff edge and the mausoleum and called out. "Here I am, Denver. Come on out."

"It won't be that easy, Lymond," Justin called back. "You were supposed to come alone."

"Denver," the other man called out. "Let the women go. I'll take them back to the house. They haven't harmed you."

Cassie gasped. "That's Owen!"

"Let them go," Lymond said. "There's just the two of us—Amherst and me. You have my word on that.

231

Amherst can take the women and go, then you and I can settle this between us."

"Do you think he's alone?" Turner asked, checking his pistols again.

Justin laughed a short, harsh laugh. "Of course not. He's alone out there, but the woods are crawling with troops. Of course," he said with a smile at me, "they're going to be looking for Justin Denver and Robin Norwood, so two old laborers will be able to pass without notice." He turned back to Turner. "You'll take the boat and meet us at the rendezvous. We'll have the paintings with us."

Suddenly a chilling thought hit me. "You don't intend to let us go, do you? That's why you let us see you change disguises."

He smiled again. "You could go with me if you wish."

"Never," I said as Cassie held my hand, hard. "You won't get away with this."

"I've heard that before," he said. He started to say something else, but Turner interrupted him. "They're walkin' this way again real slow. Hands up."

Justin was all business. "Turner, get over there behind the door where they won't see you. They don't know you're here. Robin, you stand ready to take Amherst — Lymond's mine. Turner, you know what to do. If the women make a sound, shoot." He glanced at me. "Snuff that candle."

"Do it yourself," I said, hanging on to Cassie. I wasn't sure what she'd do.

Justin started across the floor, then stopped and resumed his place near the door. "Leave it," he said with a shrug. "It'll be good for them to see you." He smiled again. "One last, fond look."

Cassie leaned into me. "We've got to do something," she whispered. I squeezed her hand to show I understood. "Be ready," I whispered back. We both stood poised.

Robin started chuckling. "Lymond can't get on the flagstones because that damned dog keeps nipping at him. Want me to shoot it?"

Justin looked out the door and then threw it open, hiding Turner behind it. Cassie and I could see Captain Amherst and Lymond right in front of the door, their hands raised to show they had no weapons. Robin Norwood had a pistol aimed right at Lymond's heart. Bucephalus was between Lymond and the door, growling. As one, Cassie and I threw ourselves across the room and tackled Justin. "Bue, Bue!" I yelled as I grabbed Justin's pistol arm.

Bue whirled and leaped on Robin Norwood, knocking him backwards. His pistol went off and hit Bue. "Lymond!" I screamed as Bue fell, blood streaming from his wound. I was unable to say anything else because Justin's arm locked around my throat and I felt something cold beside my temple. "Don't move or I'll shoot her," Justin said, his voice very cold and precise. Everything came to a standstill.

Lymond and Amherst were inside, against the door. "Denver?" Lymond asked, looking at Justin's new disguise. "Is that Norwood?"

Justin laughed. "You wouldn't have known, would you?"

Lymond shook his head no, but I could see he was thinking not about Justin's disguise, but about some way to try to gain an advantage. I wanted to warn them about Turner but couldn't speak. I looked out the corner of my eye. Bue wasn't dead; he was getting to his feet, looking rather dazed. I couldn't see either Robin Norwood or Cassie.

"Let's finish this," Justin said. "We've waited long enough."

He raised his pistol and aimed it at Lymond's chest. I lowered my chin as far as I could and bit down hard on the edge of his arm. I tasted blood through the rough fabric of his clothing. He jerked and swore, then knocked my chin back up. It hurt terribly, but at least I had given Lymond some advantage. He lashed out at Justin and knocked his pistol loose. It went skittering across the floor. Then Lymond reached by me to grab Justin's hair. Most of it came off in his hand, part of the disguise.

I managed to break free just as Captain Amherst rushed by me to tackle Robin Norwood. At the same instant, Cassie and I both saw Turner come from behind the door, his pistol at the ready. Both of us tried to grab him as it went off. Cassie was closer than I, and I saw her fall. It was almost as though time stood still: I could hear the men fighting in the background, but all I could see was Cassie dropping slowly to the floor as a large red stain spread over the top of her dress.

Out of the side of my vision, I saw Turner start towards me, brandishing his pistol. There was no shot in it, so he struck out at me. I moved away, and he hit Bue instead. Bue was still groggy but felt the pain. With a growl, he buried his teeth in Turner's leg. Turner cursed and yelled, but he couldn't get Bue to release him. Finally, he hit Bue with his pistol across the head, a slashing blow that ripped the skin. When Bue yelped in pain and released his leg, Turner fell into the tunnel hole and slithered out of sight. I tried to grab at him, but his leg was all bloody and my hand slipped.

I fell to the floor beside Cassie, almost oblivious to the fighting. "Don't die, Cass," I whispered, "please don't die."

She was deathly pale. "I'm all right," she whispered. "Help them. It doesn't hurt."

I risked a look. She had taken the ball in the upper arm and, while it was bleeding profusely all over her white dress, it surely wasn't a life-threatening wound. Satisfied with that much, I looked at Amherst and Lymond. Amherst had the best of his fight with Norwood. They were rolling on the floor, wrestling over possession of the pistol. Captain Amherst finally grabbed it and knocked Norwood hard on the head. With a groan, Norwood lost consciousness and lay still. Instead of going to help Lymond, Amherst rushed over to Cassie.

Justin and Lymond were still fighting. Justin picked up the stone we sometimes used to prop the door and hit Lymond a glancing blow on the head. Lymond staggered back against the wall, dazed, as Justin ran across the floor and grabbed up the pistol that had been knocked from his hand. He looked at me briefly as though he would use me for a shield, but Bue started for him, growling, blood all over him, both his own and Turner's. Instead Justin jumped for the door, firing at Lymond at close range. The whole building was filled with the smell of the powder. Lymond staggered against the doorway as Justin ran through it. Both Amherst and I lunged for Justin, but Bue was in our way and neither of us could stop him. It seemed it took forever to get to the door.

"Damn, he's gone," Amherst said, running out onto the flagging.

I dropped to my knees beside Lymond and took his face in my hands. He was covered with blood and his eyes were closed. Holding my breath, I put my hand in front of his mouth and almost fainted with relief. He was still breathing. Bue stood there and tried to lick his face and I didn't have the strength left to push the dog away. Amherst knelt and took a look. "A head wound," he said as I searched for Lymond's handkerchief. With trembling fingers I swabbed at what seemed to be an enormous amount of blood.

"He's bleeding so," I said to Amherst.

"Head wounds always do," he said. "Do you want me to do it?"

"No, I will." I glanced at him and saw he was looking at Cassie. "See to Cass, will you? I don't think it's serious, but she's in shock."

He nodded and went over to Cassie. I kept mopping Lymond's head. His whole face was a bloody mess where he had been fighting. Most of the heavy bleeding seemed to be on the side of his head, right above his temple. I gently swabbed there, and he winced. "Dammit, that hurts," he said.

As I wiped the blood, I saw with relief that it was only a deep groove in his flesh. There seemed to be more blood than there was wound. I couldn't believe he had frightened me so much for just a wound. I had thought him injured mortally.

"Am I dead?" he asked, moaning and trying to sit up straighter. "Where's Denver?"

"He got away," I said, rocking back on my heels and looking at him. He was really the worse for the wear. "Robin Norwood's over there, unconscious. You may get some information from him when he wakes up. Turner got away, but Bue bit him."

Lymond sat up and took the handkerchief from me. He regarded Amherst and Cassie. Amherst had her sitting up now and was binding her arm. "The bullet went through, so it's a clean wound," he told us. "She'll be all right."

"Good." It was more of a grunt from Lymond than an affirmation. He leaned back and closed his eyes. "Damn, I can't believe he got away again."

"Maybe the men we had posted intercepted him," Captain Amherst said. "If not, at least we're here to fight another day."

"Small consolation," Lymond grumbled. "Get some

men and let's get Miss Sydney back home." He glanced at me. "Both of them."

"And yourself," I retorted. "You don't look overly healthy."

"I don't feel that way, either," he said wearily.

Captain Amherst made Cassie comfortable and then stood and started to take a step backwards. "Watch out," I yelled, but it was too late.

He tumbled right into the hole where the tunnel was, and we heard a sharp snap and a cry of pain. Lymond cursed and tried to get up but fell back down. "Stay here," I said, restraining him.

I ran to the tunnel hole and saw that Captain Amherst had broken his leg. Relaying the news to Lymond, he said, "We'll hurt him more trying to move him. Owen, try to endure it. Roxanne can run for help." He pointed out where his nearest men were positioned. "Run, Roxanne," he said. "Hand me that pistol Owen had. I'll keep you covered as long as I can."

"Covered?" I paused in the doorway.

"Denver might still be out there somewhere. He has a pistol and wouldn't hesitate to use it. Keep as low as you can and don't run in a straight line. I think he's gone, but with a criminal mind like the Master's, who knows?"

I went outside and the last thing I heard from the mausoleum was Cassie talking softly to Amherst, trying to comfort him. I called softly to Bue, but he wasn't in any shape to come either. He tried, coming out onto the flagging, but he had been shot in the chest and had lost a tremendous amount of blood. "I'll keep him with me," Lymond said. He reached out and touched Bue, and the dog crawled over beside him.

"Don't worry," I said to Lymond, "I can do it."

I crouched and started running as fast as I could in a zigzag pattern, expecting every moment to either run right into Justin Denver or to be hit by a bullet. The apprehension was terrible, and every noise was cause for alarm. When I finally reached the ditch where Lymond said his men were, I didn't even see it. One of the men stood and, in the instant before I saw it wasn't Justin, I thought I was going to be killed. It was Francis. I almost fainted with relief when I saw he was with a group of the Dragoons.

"Hurry," I gasped, out of breath and trembling all over, both from the exertion and the strain. "Lymond and Captain Amherst and my sister are all hurt."

"Denver?" a man came up and asked. It was Debenham, dressed in dark clothes and carrying a pistol.

I shook my head. "Escaped. Robin Norwood's in there, though. He was unconscious, but I don't know if anyone can restrain him if he comes to. Everyone's hurt."

Debenham began issuing orders. Francis hadn't waited—he and some men were already on their way. Debenham sent more men out on the double. I started to walk behind them, but Debenham stopped me. "Do you want to take a carriage to Bellerophon? I have one at my disposal back here."

I shook my head. "No, they'll need it. Send it to the mausoleum." I started to walk again, but my legs didn't want to work. "I've got to go."

"I understand," he said. "Let me help you." He had me lifted onto his horse and we rode to the mausoleum. We didn't speak—I was too tired, and I suspected that he was preoccupied.

When we got to the tomb, Francis was cradling Lymond while the other men were lifting Amherst very carefully. Amherst was trying to be brave, but I could see that he was in agony. Cassie was biting her lip to keep from crying out.

Debenham was in charge at the mausoleum as well. In just a short while, everyone had been carried to Bellerophon and the surgeons sent for. The sentries had reported seeing an old laborer lurking around Jervyne House, but he had run away when they attempted to question him. The house was heavily guarded now, and Debenham and Lymond both thought that Justin had joined Turner and was on his way to France.

"At least I think he is," Lymond said. He was in bed, propped up against the pillows, looking very pale. "The man is known for doing the unexpected. I wouldn't put it past him to disguise himself as a surgeon and invade the house."

Horrified, I ran to take a close look at the surgeon, but Debenham had already vetted him. He, too, knew how unpredictable Justin could be.

I went to find Amelia, but didn't see her anywhere. I went up to my old rooms and knocked softly on the door. Francis opened the door and, behind him, I could see Amelia standing there, her hair and clothing disheveled. She and Francis had obviously not been discussing the weather.

"I thought you'd want to know that Lymond's going to be all right," I said, trying to cover my confusion. I couldn't believe they were meeting while her husband lay wounded, but that seemed to be the case. "He's lost some blood, and the doctor says he'll have a crashing headache for a few days, but he'll be fine."

Francis smiled and nodded at me. "I thought as much, but I'm relieved to hear the doctor says so as well. Tell him I'll be in to see him shortly."

He smiled at me and I backed slightly away. In a trice, the door was closed and I was speeding down the hall, torn between anger and confusion. I barged into Lymond's room, not worrying about the proprieties. I stopped short when I saw he was asleep, breathing quietly, a vial of laudanum and an empty glass of water on the table beside his bed. Even in sleep, he looked wearied beyond redemption. I tiptoed out, worried now that someone might see me, but the hall was empty.

Captain Amherst had a bad break in his lower leg, but the surgeon said that with rest and care, it would heal properly. Since he was already at Bellerophon and in bed, the surgeon advised against moving him for a week or so. Amherst, aside from being in a great deal of pain, was not happy with this situation.

Cassie, too, was all right. The ball had passed right through her left arm. She had lost a great deal of blood but would recover nicely. I wanted to talk to her about Amelia and Francis, but now was not the time. I kissed her briefly and asked if I could get her anything. She sleepily said no, that Livvy was going to sit with her, and drifted off to sleep. I gave Livvy strict instructions to come get me if Cassie needed me, and I left.

In a room off the kitchen, Ned rested comfortably and was being tended to by his aunt, Mrs. Beckford. The ball he had taken in his shoulder during our hellish race to Brighton had been removed, and his wound was not as serious as originally thought. The surgeon, however, wanted him to convalesce for the next fortnight. When I looked in on him, he was wolfing down a piece of bread covered with strawberry jam. I deduced he would be just fine.

I was truly worried about Bue, however. Brave as he had been, he had lost a tremendous amount of blood. I had made Holmwood carry him inside where I could watch after him. After all, I felt we owed him our lives. Holmwood and I made him a bed beside mine, and then Holmwood removed the bullet and applied some salve to his wound. I treated him by giving him some bits of sirloin and petting him. He seemed in better shape than I did.

I seemed to be the only one who wasn't getting treatment and sympathy. Treatment I didn't need; sympathy I did. I felt beaten and bruised all over. Over and over again I kept analyzing my reaction when I thought Lymond had been killed, and I also kept reminding myself that he was married, even though his wife seemed to have a strange relationship with Francis. Surely Lymond had to know. No man could be that obtuse. That brought up another facet: if he knew, then he condoned it. I didn't know what to think.

I used my exhaustion as an excuse to slip away and lock myself in my room. There, with only Bucephalus and my thoughts to keep me company, I intended to think through some things.

I wasn't overly successful. The only thing I determined after much thought was that I had some questions to ask Lymond, and then, no matter what the answers, I was going to do my best to get rid of our boarders.

Enough was enough.

Chapter Seventeen

The next day brought a stream of visitors, everyone from Lord Debenham to the local magistrate. I was kept busy tending to Captain Amherst and Cassie, so I caught only bits and pieces of it. It did seem that the Master or Justin Denver or whatever his new name was, had eluded the net. He was nowhere to be seen and the Dragoons had a heavy guard around Jervyne House in hopes he would return. The trouble was that no one knew in what guise he might appear. He could be anyone from an old lady to a young boy to the village imbecile. Given his artistry with putty, hair, and pots of colors, he could assume any disguise. Debenham wasn't taking any chances — he had the locals on hand and was questioning anyone who wasn't known by them. Still there was nothing.

"He seems to have vanished from the face of the earth," I heard him tell Lymond as they sat and drank tea. I didn't get to hear the rest as I had come in to get Captain Amherst's tea and then left.

Francis was in and out. He was in and out of Amelia's room as well, but no one seemed to notice except me, and I certainly wasn't going to say anything. At least not now.

It was late, about eleven o'clock, before I felt I could go to bed. I went down the hall towards the stairs slowly, tired to the bone. I noticed Lymond's door was closed and assumed he was in bed.

I paused at the foot of the steps and decided I needed something to keep me going. I started to get some tea, but somehow that just didn't seem to be what I needed. I went into the drawing room where it was quiet. There was a branch of candles burning and Lymond was sitting there, his coat off, his cravat untied, and his feet propped up. I stopped.

"Do come in," he said with a smile. "I could use some congenial company. I've had people in all day, but those were hardly congenial visits. Do join me." He gestured towards a chair and I sat down. Lymond was drinking a glass of something that looked like whiskey. I got up, went to Papa's cabinet, and got down the brandy decanter. I didn't usually drink spirits, but today certainly hadn't been a usual day.

I poured myself a small amount and sipped it. The warmth made me feel better immediately. "Pour one for me if you don't mind," Lymond said. I hesitated and then did, carrying it to him and sitting back down. We sat without speaking.

"You're quite a remarkable woman, Roxanne," Lymond said, his voice quiet in the stillness. "I've never known anyone like you."

"Oh?" I wasn't sure what to say. He didn't follow his remark, and there was silence again. I was beginning to revive and there was no time like the present. "Lymond," I said, putting down my glass, "we have to talk."

He smiled and put his glass down. "Yes, we do. We've needed to talk for a while." His smile was warm, as were his blue eyes. They were almost indigo in the candlelight.

I shook myself before the spell took effect. "Lymond," I began, "I hardly know how to ask or say this, but I need to know . . ." I started again. "Lymond, I've never thought you were what you claimed to be, but now . . ."

He laughed and sat up. To my surprise, he reached over and took my hand in his. I tried to jerk it away, but he held on to it. "I'm not married, if that's bothering you."

I felt my eyes go as wide as Cassie's. "Then Amelia and you . . . Amelia is your . . ."

He laughed. "She's my brother's wife and, no, there's been nothing improper going on. Francis knew she was here and he approved."

"Lymond, I will not countenance—" I began, but he stopped me.

"Just let me tell you what I need to, Roxanne," he said, "then you can make up your mind."

"All right." I pulled my hand away resolutely; I wanted to be able to listen objectively. As it was too confusing to look into those eyes while he talked, I concentrated on a point over his shoulder. "Go ahead. I'm listening."

It seemed Lymond was the youngest brother of Charles Sebastian, the earl of Rywicke, who had taken the Sebastian name when he came into the title. Lymond had been in India with the Army for many years and came back only last year. He was working with military intelligence, so when Debenham wanted an unknown to help trap the thief known as the Master, Lymond was tapped. He had almost captured the thief in the Midlands the season before, but the Master had escaped. They had, however, captured one of his confederates who had tipped them that Brighton would be the next place the Master would make his base of operations. The original plan had been for Lymond to come to Brighton and pose as an eligible young man, but then Lymond's brother Francis came to him. Francis had to be away for a while—he didn't know if it would be several weeks or months, and wanted his wife to stay with his family. She didn't want to stay in London with Lord Rywicke because she was still grieving over the daughter she and

Francis had had. She had always loved Robert like a brother and wanted to stay with him.

When Lymond told Debenham he couldn't come to Brighton because he needed to stay with Amelia while Francis was away, Debenham decided that Lymond could come to Brighton and Amelia could come as well. She would pose as Lymond's wife. Francis had his doubts about this, but Amelia felt it might be a good diversion for her. In truth, Lymond said, it had helped her because our family had been so good to her and had distracted her from her grief.

"I see," I said slowly. "Didn't she have any other family?"

Lymond shook his head. "No, she was an orphan. Shortly after she and Francis were married, her only surviving relative — an aunt with whom she lived — died. It was a question of her staying with Charles and his family or coming here, and it was her own decision not to stay with Charles. Since no one knew her, she was ideal for the 'wife' of Robert Lymond. We thought as well that some time by the sea would do her good." He paused. "Our whole family is indebted to yours. Nothing could have pleased us more than the way all of you took care of Amelia."

"I suppose she's glad to be reunited with Francis."

Lymond grinned. "You've noticed."

I nodded, thought about telling him about Francis's earlier visit, then changed my mind. "You've never been married, then?" I asked.

"Never, although I do admit to a close call or two."

I didn't laugh and Lymond grew serious as well. "It may be painful for you, Roxanne, but I need to ask you about your time in the mausoleum yesterday."

I felt myself blush. "Nothing happened there, I assure you."

"I didn't mean that. I need to know if the man we know

245

as Justin Denver said anything, anything at all, that would help us capture him or would help us learn something about him. We've *got* to find him."

"He killed my father," I said bitterly. "He didn't actually do it, but he told Robin Norwood to do it. He told me so."

"Why?" Lymond's voice was gentle, persuasive.

I repeated what Justin had said about making Brighton his base of operations, his plans for buying Bellerophon, and his bragging about his accomplishments. I told him everything I could remember.

"That's all?" Lymond asked, again gently, as I finished. I felt like crying all over again.

I nodded. We sat in silence for a moment as my sadness was supplanted by anger. "Lymond, I was so furious at him. You should have seen him! He was so cool, so sure of himself. He was positive he was going to escape. Even when he was changing his disguise, he knew he would get away. 'They won't be looking for a common laborer,' he said. You should have seen him, Lymond: he transformed himself in just a few moments."

Lymond leaned over, excited, and grabbed my hands again. "You saw him — you actually saw him when he wasn't disguised?"

"Yes." I was surprised by his reaction. "He took off his eyebrows and part of his face. Then he put on gray hair and some bushy eyebrows that were gray and a putty nose that was crooked."

Lymond shook his head. "No, I mean before. You saw him when he had wiped his face so he could start over. Do you realize, Roxanne, that you and Cassie are the only ones who have seen him like that. You two are the only people we know who *really* know what he looks like. Wait until I tell Debenham!"

The next day, I had to tell my story to Debenham and then Cassie was brought from her room to confirm my story. Cassie offered to sketch the man we saw, and I thought Lymond and Debenham would go into transports. Cassie was quite a good artist, even with one hand.

Debenham and Lymond talked further about locating the paintings, and Cassie excused herself to go read to Captain Amherst. I made a note to ask Lymond about him later. Right now, I wanted to listen to the conversation.

"They're not here," Lymond said, "so Jervyne House is the only logical place. Unless," he added, "he's already taken them out of the country."

"He hasn't," I said. "Or at least he hadn't when we were in the mausoleum. He kept telling Norwood and us that he was going to get the paintings before he left. He wanted to . . ." I hesitated, "to settle things with the two of you first."

"To kill us," Lymond said brutally. "Roxanne, think. Did he say anything that would lead us to the paintings?"

I shook my head. "No, but I got the impression they were close by. I thought they were probably at Jervyne House."

"Let's go take another look," Debenham said to Lymond. "We might have overlooked something."

Lymond got up slowly and carefully as though he were bruised all over. Once standing, he seemed to be all right. As he and Debenham walked towards the door, I stopped them. "Let me go. I might be able to help you."

"I don't think so," Debenham said.

"Perhaps she should," Lymond said. "Miss Sydney is quite remarkable, although a rather weak judge of character." This last he said with something of a smirk. I wanted to smack him.

Cassie appeared in the doorway. "Perhaps both of us should go," she suggested. "We've been in and out of Jervyne House for years. We would certainly know if something had been changed."

"Are you up to it, Cass?" I asked, glancing at her arm in its sling. She looked fine and didn't seem to be having any pain, but she was running the risk of jostling her arm and starting the bleeding again.

"I'll be fine," she said.

Nothing would do Aunt Hen but to go along with us. I suspected she wanted to relate the day's events to Mrs. Bocock. I told her nothing would happen, but Aunt Hen always thought the dramatic would occur.

Jervyne House looked sleepy in the sun. Without the buzz of the carpenters there, it was quiet. The house still smelled of new wood and paint. Cassie and I went all through it, looking at every room. In spite of the work, very little had actually been changed. The rooms had been redone and looked much better, except for the dining room. That hideous paper was still on the walls.

"Nothing," Lymond said in disgust as we met at the front again.

"It has to be here somewhere," Cassie said. "I know he didn't take it with him."

I rolled my eyes. "If I were a painting, where would I hide? If I were a carpenter, where would I hide a painting?" A thought hit me. "Come on!" I yelled, grabbing Cassie by her good hand and dragging her behind me. "Come on, Lymond, I've got an idea!"

I dashed into the dining room, took one look at the heavy, ribbed paper and knew I had to be right. Searching around, I found a corner and started to pull. The paper pulled away easily, much too easily, and there was a painting, carefully wrapped in oiled paper, then in brown, glued between the wall and the paper.

"That's one of mine," Debenham said, running to stand in front of it as we pulled the wrappings off. "I'd wager they're all here. This is a good-sized room."

He went out, calling for men to come pull the wallpaper down. We stood around and watched them remove most of it. They were careful, making sure they didn't damage any of the paintings. By the time we left, we were sure most of the stolen paintings were there. Debenham was ecstatic, and Aunt Hen was beside herself with joy. At last she had actually been in the thick of things. She could lord it over Mrs. Bocock for years.

Cassie, Aunt Hen, and I rode back together in the carriage while Lymond followed behind. We had gone no more than a few yards before I almost wished I had stayed at Jervyne House. My deduction, which would have been obvious to anyone who considered the problem a short while, had convinced Aunt Hen that I simply hadn't given the proper thought to the problem foremost in her mind: where was the Treasure of Agamemnon?

"Now Roxanne, as soon as we get home, I want you to think about it," she said, patting my arm. "If you just get in the right mood and put your mind to it, I'm sure it will come to you. A dark room, some tea, perhaps some music . . ." Her voice trailed off.

I looked at Cassie for help, but she was looking out the window, her face averted. I suspected she was trying not to laugh. I looked back at Aunt Hen and started to tell her there was no treasure, but saw from the look on her face that it would be no use at all. "All right, Aunt Hen, all right. Give me some time to collect my wits and I'll help you search for the Treasure."

She shook her head vigorously. "We won't need to search. All we need to do is wait until you think of the answer." She smiled beatifically. "Just think, Roxanne — all our problems solved. All that lovely money to spend." She patted my arm again. "I'll let you rest for now, dear, but just when can you begin thinking?"

"Give me a few weeks," I muttered as Cassie made stifled sounds. She was actually laughing. "I need time . . ." I groped for a reason. "I need time to . . . to recuperate." At this, Cassie laughed right out loud. I glared at her.

"Of course, dear," Aunt Hen said, giving Cassie a puzzled look as she spoke to me. "But perhaps a few days would do as well."

"A few weeks at least," I said, putting my hand to my head. "I need time." Surely in a few weeks I would be able to think of something to convince her that searching for the Treasure was a forlorn cause. I risked a glance at her — at least my answer had fobbed her off for a while. She was soothing Cassie now. Cassie was trying to hide her laughter under the pretence of a coughing fit.

I would, I realized, need to keep Aunt Hen happy and make some gesture of searching for the Treasure. Perhaps I could even get Lymond to continue his search. That would make Aunt Hen happy — anything Lymond did made Aunt Hen happy — and it was certainly better than doing it myself.

Back at Bellerophon, we were surprised to walk in and find Captain Amherst sitting in the drawing room, his leg carefully propped on a chair. "I made them bring me down," he said. "I couldn't bear being shut away from everything. Did you discover anything?"

"We found the paintings," Cassie said, dashing over to him. "Owen, you shouldn't be up. You'll injure your leg."

"Nonsense. I took a ball in Spain and it wasn't any worse than this. I'll be up and about. I've already sent for crutches." He looked up at her. "Sit beside me a while."

Cassie obliged and Lymond and I also sat while Aunt Hen hovered around. "Guess what?" she announced to Lymond and the Captain, "Roxanne's going to find the Treasure for us."

They both looked at me in surprise. "Roxanne's going to think about it," Cassie explained.

Aunt Hen smiled again. "Given the right conditions and I'm sure she'll be able to pinpoint the exact location." She patted my shoulder. "Don't exert yourself, Roxanne. Would you like some tea, dear?" Before I could answer, she was headed towards the door. "I wish I could stay, but I simply must apprise my friends of these developments." In a flash, she was on her way to arrange a visit with Mrs. Bocock, the Treasure taking secondary place to plans for a visit, a pot of tea, and some heady gossip. The four of us could have run off to Gretna Green and she wouldn't have noticed for days. As it was, we sat in complete silence for several minutes after she left us.

"Go ahead and laugh," I said to Lymond. "Cassie's already done her share."

Lymond looked at me gravely. "I place my faith squarely in your amazing thought processes." The corner of his mouth quivered.

"Be serious, Lymond."

He laughed. "I'm always perfectly serious. Right now, a serious topic needs to be discussed." He glanced at Captain Amherst, stood, and held out his hand to me. Instead of speaking to me, he spoke to Captain Amherst. "Owen, you might as well do it and get it over with."

"It's the worst battle I've ever fought," Captain Amherst said with a sigh.

Lymond laughed and took me by the arm. "Would you like to take a turn around the grounds, Miss Sydney?"

I started to say no but was so startled I stood up. Before I knew what was happening, Lymond had propelled me towards the door. As we were about to leave, he turned. "This is all I can do for you, friend. The rest is up to you." He pulled the door shut behind us.

"What," I demanded, "was that all about?"

Lymond shook his head. "For a remarkable woman, Miss Sydney, you are often quite obtuse." He kept his hand on my arm and walked towards the outside door. I was obliged to walk beside him. "Surely you've noticed that Owen is madly in love with your sister."

I stopped dead in my tracks and Lymond almost toppled over. "He isn't at all suitable," I said. "Lymond, we

251

must go back in there and keep him from making a fool out of himself. I know Cassie was attracted to him, but I've talked to her about it. She knows he isn't suitable, and she's to go to London and make an advantageous match. We've saved the money for it."

He raised an eyebrow. "And you think Owen isn't suitable?"

"Of course he isn't! You yourself said that he wouldn't marry or couldn't marry or some such. Cassie certainly doesn't need to throw herself away on a captain. I own he's mannerly, he seems well bred, but Cassie—" I stopped, thinking of how Cassie looked when she spoke of him. "She tried to save him at the mausoleum," I said, stricken. "She cares about him more than she told me."

"I think perhaps she does," Lymond said. "Would you like to take a turn around the grounds now?"

"No." I turned and looked at the closed door. "Why did you say he wouldn't marry? I don't know anything about him. Cassie doesn't know anything about him."

"You never forget, do you?" Lymond said with a laugh, turning me back around and propelling me through the door. Outside I could see Livvy and Julia walking, coaxing Bucephalus into some exercise. In spite of all my plans, I wasn't ready to see our family scattered. "I've said that about Owen for years," Lymond said, standing with me and watching the girls. It was a pretty sight. "We were in India together and were close friends. I always teased Owen about being married to the Army. That's why I've always said he'd never marry a woman— he was already married to an institution. It does seem," he said, grinning at me, "that I made a slight error on that score."

I nodded agreement, but before I could ask anything else, Lymond continued: "I know you've been worried about the girls, and Livvy told me about your scheme to take Cassie to London and put her on the Marriage

Mart. However, she could certainly do worse than Owen. Do you want to know more about him?"

"Of course. But you knew you didn't have to ask."

He laughed, then winced as the muscles in his swollen face hurt. "All right. We were, as I said, in India together. He left to go to the Peninsula. When I came back to England, I heard he had returned from Spain to discover that his uncle had left him a very handsome legacy. Owen Amherst would be a fine catch, if you're worried about that."

"I'm not, really." It was true. While I never wanted Cassie to marry a pauper, I wasn't that concerned about money. What I really wanted was for her to be content. "It'll take someone special to make her happy."

"Owen is special, and he's also very much in love with her." Lymond looked down at me and started to say something else, then thought the better of it. He smiled. "Shall we go back inside and see how events have evolved? If he's been refused, Owen will probably need my support."

We went back without a word. I was trying to sort my feelings. We both paused in front of the door and looked at each other. Lymond's blue eyes, for the very first time, looked doubtful. He took a deep breath and pushed the door open.

He needn't have worried. "Cassie!" I exclaimed, "Whatever are you thinking!" She was sitting on Captain Amherst's good leg, and appeared to be kissing him. He didn't seem to be in any pain at this juncture.

She looked up at us, her face glowing. "Roxanne, Owen has offered for me and I've accepted! Isn't it wonderful!"

I heard a strangled noise behind me. I turned around to face Aunt Hen. "Cassandra, Cassandra," was all she could manage. Mrs. Bocock would *never* hear about this episode.

Cassie got up and floated around behind Captain

Amherst. "We're going to get married, Aunt Hen. By a special license, just as soon as Owen can walk on his crutches."

Lymond caught Aunt Hen before she crashed to the ground. After we got her to a sofa, I sent Woodbury for feathers to burn and for her vinaigrette.

"You'll all be in London for the wedding, of course," Lymond said, looking down at Aunt Hen.

"It does appear that way." I felt giddy but didn't want to laugh. It didn't seem suitable somehow.

Lymond looked at me just as Woodbury returned. "Could I call on you then?"

I was so surprised that I felt my mouth drop open. "I . . . I suppose so," I stammered.

Lymond rolled his eyes as Woodbury knelt to wave burnt feathers under Aunt Hen's nose. "I had hoped for a little more enthusiasm, Miss Sydney."

Before I could answer, Livvy and Julia came in the door, and Bucephalus, hobbling along, made as much of a dash for Lymond as he could, knocking him right onto Aunt Hen. Woodbury, feathers and vinaigrette in hand, went crashing to the floor. Aunt Hen sat up and we followed her gaze while Lymond picked himself up, quietly muttering to himself and trying not to use profanity. Cassie and Captain Amherst were kissing again, oblivious to the lot of us.

"A disgrace, that's what it is," Aunt Hen said, falling back onto the sofa again. "George would die."

Livvy and Julia looked from each one of us to the other, their eyes wide.

I broke into hysterical laughter. It seemed the only appropriate response.

**LOOK FOR THE NEXT
*MISS SYDNEY REGENCY MYSTERY,
THE SECRET SCROLL,*
COMING FROM ZEBRA BOOKS
IN OCTOBER 1993!**

And be sure to ask your bookseller about
these other Dawn Aldridge Poore titles:

MISS FORTUNE'S FOLLY

Spurning the fashionable nonsense of the *ton,* Felicia
was a country miss with a mind of her own. She quite
preferred the business of helping her architect uncle
with his dream building project, until she encouraged
the delightful pleasure of the head builder, Major Adam
Temple. The level-headed Felicia had never before lost
her composure, but the major was so . . . so *masculine!*
Yet his effect on her senses was the least of her worries
when trouble on the project forced Felicia into a com-
promising position with the son of the earl who'd em-
ployed them. Still, Felicia's only real pleasure was doing
business with Adam.

BATH BRAMBLE

Callie Stone was resolved to become an *artiste* rather than a wife. She was quite content with her productive life painting portraits in Bath, except for the problem of her carousing younger brother. Bereaved of parents, Callie had only the family's legal guardian to turn to — though Callie wondered if the irresponsible James Williford would be much help with discipline! But when Jamie did arrive, Callie was thunderstruck. This childhood friend cut a dashing figure and seemed to have eyes for her! Her head dictated prudence, but her heart seemed to have a mind of its own!